ESCAPE

Past Sins

David J Antocci

ISBN-13: 978-0615987347

ISBN-10: 0615987346

Books by David J Antocci

ESCAPE, A New Life

ESCAPE, Past Sins

ESCAPE, Dead End

CONTENTS

Acknowledgements

My thanks first and foremost to my wife, Lisa. Always supportive and encouraging, she became one of my beta readers for this novel and provided invaluable feedback. To my beta readers, Nicole and Lindsay – thank you for providing such great and insightful feedback, and taking time out of your busy lives to help out an old friend.

A big thanks to my proofreaders, Cindy Fogarty, and Mark "Kaz" Kazazean. I offer you my sincere thanks and gratitude for donating your time and expertise to clean up the final manuscript.

Also, a massive thanks to my editor, John Briggs of Albany Editing. His insight into storytelling was extremely valuable in helping to make this a more solid story than it was before it went through his hands. Also, his seemingly infinite patience with my near non-existent grammar skills is always appreciated.

Finally, a HUGE thanks to you, the reader! Your encouragement and support through my first novel gave me the ability to move forward and tackle this project. You are more important to me than you can imagine! Thank you for reading my books and spreading the word to your friends! – Dave

David J Antocci

...

1

ABBY CROUCHED LOW in the underbrush. The fading echo of gunshots still rang in her ears. Her loose brunette curls were soaked with sweat and matted to the sides of her face. Her drenched tank top clung to her small frame.

He was out there.

She couldn't remember exactly how long it had been, but it felt like Bryce had been hunting her for days. She had hardly slept in that time. She stayed low, remaining still and quiet. Even breathing seemed like too much noise.

He was close. She could sense it.

Abby gripped her knife tightly, ready for action. The sound of a mosquito buzzing by her ear caused her to instinctively swat at the unseen assailant, which also knocked aside a branch. Forty feet away Bryce turned in her direction, swinging his gun out in front of him. He couldn't see her, but she was looking directly at his face.

She could see his ice blue eyes glowing with hatred. Sweat poured from his short-cropped blond hair as he took a few steps toward her, his limp from their last meeting obvious. Abby had torn nearly every tendon and muscle he had above his knee when she plunged her knife into his leg nearly a year ago. Bryce had kidnapped her to take her out to sea and murder her, until she turned the tables on him with some help from Eric. Now she regretted that she didn't just finish the job and kill him on the boat when she had the chance.

After taking a few steps, he stopped again to listen. He stood there facing squarely in her direction. He was tall, and had a broad chest that made a perfect target. She silently wished she had better knife-throwing skills. She had a clear shot, but wasn't about to disarm herself and take the chance that the knife would sail wide of her target and land in the trees behind him.

That gave her an idea, though. What if something else went crashing through the trees behind him, distracting him and giving her a chance to make a move? Without taking her eyes off Bryce, she felt around the forest floor until her hand lay upon a rock just a bit smaller than her clenched fist.

She had to aim carefully. She wanted to throw it wide to his right and high enough that he didn't see it sailing by his head. With any luck, it would fly over him silently and crash into the trees behind him. He would turn around to see what it was, providing her the opportunity to pounce on him from behind.

Abby lay still, waiting for the right moment. Bryce was scanning the trees in her direction. She couldn't risk throwing it when he was looking in her area. He would see movement, and she would be found.

She wished she knew how many shots he had left.

When he had been chasing her ten minutes ago, she had the thought that she was supposed to count the shots so she would know how many he had left. She was certain she saw this in a movie at some point. She counted five, and then realized she had no idea how many shots he actually had to begin with, so she gave up. *How many bullets are in a clip?* Abby had no idea, and realized she would simply wait for the clicking sound of an empty chamber.

Hopefully that would come sooner than later.

She palmed the rock in her hand as he scanned past her location. With his eyes diverted, she took a deep breath. *Now or never*, she thought. She cocked her arm back and launched the rock through the air. It sailed directly over his head and cleared the initial trees beyond him. It crashed through several large palm branches before slamming into the thick trunk of a tree with a thud, ricocheting off and crashing through several more branches before coming to rest on the forest floor.

Bryce whipped around toward the commotion, gun up and firing away, hoping to hit Abby. He was completely unaware as she sprang from the undergrowth forty feet behind him and raced through the trees straight toward him, the sounds of her movement masked by his gunfire.

They both heard the *click click click* of the empty magazine at the same time, the sudden silence revealing Abby hurtling through the trees and coming up fast behind him, knife in hand. Bryce glanced over his shoulder to see her coming. He slammed a fresh cartridge into his gun and loaded one in the chamber as he spun to bring it eye level.

He didn't move fast enough.

Abby pounced as he turned. He managed to fire off two harmless shots into the air. Although they had gone off inches from her head, neither the danger nor the concussive sound of the gunfire fazed her. She twisted the gun from his grip and sprang up with it pointed at his head. Lightening fast, he slapped it out of her hand as though she were a child, and they both watched it land in a small stream ten feet to Abby's right.

Empty handed, she reached down to retrieve her knife from its sheath, only to find it gone. Her thoughts were unclear, and she couldn't remember losing it. She swore that she had sheathed it just before grabbing the gun, but the fact was that it was gone.

Bryce smiled as they stood staring at each other. Each soaked with sweat from the tropical heat, and their lungs working overtime to suck in enough air. Separated by no more than an arm's length, Abby felt a primal fear in the pit of her stomach. Though her memory was missing, she knew that she had been in a situation much like this one before. The close proximity to this madman was setting off alarm bells in her head that drowned out all other thought.

Bryce sized her up. She was small, just over five feet, but strong and fast. She was beautiful, her gorgeous amber eyes still holding an innocence, though the scars on her arms and dirt smears on her face made her look tough and rugged.

Abby stared back at him. He towered over her at a

sound six feet, his confident chest puffed out. He was a man who commanded what he wanted and was used to things going his way. He didn't just look tough, he was tough. A professional killer when he had to be.

She was faced with a choice — stand and fight, unarmed and overmatched, or run. Her mind said run, her heart said fight, and her feet refused to cooperate with either. It was as though she were cemented in place. As she saw his large right fist swing through the air toward her face, she swiftly ducked forward and under it, and took off at a sprint through the trees, running alongside the stream.

Abby had spent countless hours traversing the terrain on this island. She did not think Bryce had even half a chance of keeping pace with her, never mind catching her. However, as she glanced over her shoulder, she saw him gaining on her with what she could only describe as superhuman speed. Her mind couldn't process how he was able to move so fast.

She tried to pour on the speed, but he came up fast and tackled her. Abby hit the ground first, cushioning Bryce's fall with her small frame and losing the air in her lungs. She laid on the ground, defenseless, his massive frame pinning her down.

She frantically scanned the tree line in search of Eric. *Where are you?* Just a short while ago he had been by her side, and then disappeared without warning or explanation. *I need you now, where are you?* Her eyes probed the forest, finding nothing but vegetation and boulders. Eric was nowhere to be found.

Without a word, Bryce grabbed a fistful of her hair and lifted her off the ground. Her legs kicked wildly as he dragged her toward the stream. Panic and terror set in as he plunged her face under the water. Legs flailing, she reached behind her head and clawed at his hands with her fingernails. She was already out of breath and couldn't hold it much longer. As she swung out with her fist, hoping to connect with any part of him, he shoved her head even further under the water. She contorted and twisted her body, but could not contend with his strength.

She could not find the surface.

Her heart pounded out of her chest as she filled with horror. Her eyes opened wide as her burning lungs gave way and sucked in what would be her final breath.

*   *   *

Abby shot up in bed, every bit as panic-stricken and soaked with sweat as she had been in her dream. She managed to stifle her scream as she remembered where she was. Her breath came in short gasps as she wiped her wet forehead with the back of her hand and eased back against the headboard to collect herself.

The bright moonlight filtered through the large French doors at the far end of the bedroom, glittering off the ocean. She looked over and saw Eric sleeping peacefully. He did not sleep much, usually only four or five hours, but when he did, not even an air raid siren could wake him.

Good thing, Abby thought. As the time passed and her last encounter with Bryce on the boat off the coast of

Robert's island got further and further away, her night terrors became worse. She and Eric had been living in their self-imposed exile for the better part of a year with no sign of Bryce. Yet, she had trouble getting past that.

Abby swung her feet over the side of the bed and stood. She peeled off her soaked tank top and tossed it in the hamper. In what had become a semi-nightly ritual, she poured herself a glass of water and sat on the wicker chair on the side of the bed while she waited for her damp skin – and the damp sheets – to dry before she would put on a new shirt and crawl under the covers again.

She envied the peace Eric seemed to have found in their new life. Abby knew that she was living in paradise, but was constantly haunted by the demons in her dreams. The nightmares were not always about Bryce, though often they were. She remembered the crazed look and sheer hatred in his eyes when he was bringing her out to sea to kill her. Had Eric not jumped onto the boat at the last second as they pulled from the dock, she might not have been able to fight her way out on her own.

Aside from her terrors about Bryce, she often dreamt about the island where she had fought for her life day after day, before winding up in paradise. On *Trial Island*, she had to rely on her instincts to survive. She was a fighter, a winner, and had bested every other person who had been on the island. She had taken down Tom, the madman who had tried to kill them, and all of his followers. When she closed her eyes, she could still see her knife flying through the air, and the blood spraying into the trees after it sliced open his neck.

7

Eric was also a winner, and a survivor, but he regularly reminded her that he wouldn't be alive if she hadn't plucked him out of the water when they were caught in the vortex of swirling water in that cave. Their redheaded friend, Emily, hadn't been so lucky, leaving Abby and Eric as the only contestants to not only escape the island, but to survive it.

Abby also dreamed of her family. Her parents, who had been killed by a drunk driver toward the end of her college career... *What would they think of my life now?* And she often thought of her sister, Sarah, who she had a falling out with shortly after their parents passed away. It all seemed like yesterday and, in fact, in her mind, these scars were only a couple of years old.

She had to continually remind herself that she was missing ten years of memories. A key point of being on *Trial Island* was that none of the contestants knew why they were there or even that they were on a television show. They all had their memories wiped clean, dating back as far as the announcement of the show, erasing years from their lives. In Abby's case, that was ten years.

After escaping *Trial Island*, she chose not to have her memory restored. For the most part, she trusted the letter that she had written herself instructing her not to have her memories unlocked; that she was safer that way. But she did have moments of regret, especially when it came to how things had been left with her sister. She longed to know what had happened with her. *Did we ever make up? Is she still alive somewhere?*

During one attempt on her life on the island, she

managed to climb out of a pit in which she had been trapped, only to be smashed on the back of the head with a large rock. Ever since then, she had fuzzy dreams about her previous life. It was evident that they were hidden memories trying to surface, but she knew better than to give in. She was safest here, away from everyone and beyond the reach of the psychopath she had married. She also knew that anyone she left behind was safest without her in the picture.

Abby leaned forward to feel the sheets. Still damp. She looked out the window to see the sky was beginning to lighten. The sun would be up soon. There would be no getting back to sleep at this point. She finished her water, pulled on a pair of yoga pants and a sports bra, gave Eric a kiss on the cheek and whispered, "I love you," before heading out the door.

As soon as her feet hit the sand, she was at peace. Running cleared her head. As she ran barefoot along the firm packed sand close to the water, she let her worries and fears slip away. This was her paradise. This island was where she was safe. The white sand went for miles, and she had run every inch of it at some point.

When she ran, she saw things with a clarity that let her work through her problems. She thought of her dreams, or more appropriately, her nightmares. In reality, Bryce would never catch her. She had been in the best shape of her life when she woke up on *Trial Island* nearly a year ago and had not let herself slip one bit. She had gained a little weight, and therefore her womanly figure, but was as strong and as fit as she had ever been.

9

Abby quickly got past the man who terrorized her dreams and thought about the man she was living her dreams with now. They lived a very simple life on a very simple island. The local population consisted of a few thousand people, and the necessities of life – food, clothing, and shelter – were taken care of. Beyond that, there was not much, and she and Eric loved it that way.

She didn't know what her married life had been like with Bryce, but was sure that life with Eric was substantially better. They never spoke of marriage because they didn't need to. Their lives were forever intertwined after what they had gone through. When they spoke of the future, it was a future to be spent together. *Maybe someday*, Abby would allow herself to dream. She knew it was cliché, but something inside her longed to be married to the man she loved. She wanted to proclaim to the world that they were together, forever. But for now, they were still getting used to their new life. That, and Abby was technically still a married woman.

Absent the distraction of telephones, TV, and other media, they spent extra time enjoying their meals, talking, walking, and enjoying their surroundings. When the sun went down, they would read by candlelight, build a fire on the beach, or find other more intimate ways to distract themselves before falling asleep in each others' arms. The next morning would be the same beautiful day, and they'd do it all over again.

Having turned around a couple miles out, she could see their villa coming up in the distance. It was small and perfect. Set right at the edge of the sand, the side facing the beach had a small deck and French doors that opened into their bedroom. Really, the entire structure was, in fact, just one open room. A small, three-step staircase to the right of their bed led to their slightly elevated kitchen and dining area. Behind that were the bathroom and closets.

From this distance, the pale yellow stucco exterior and thatched roof really made it blend in with the beach and the trees. It was their little piece of paradise. After parting ways with Robert, they had floated and bounced around the islands for some time before finding this one. The people were friendly, and, if nothing else, it was remote.

They lived on the beach about a mile from the main village. Village may have been a generous term. They were able to find most of what they needed there, though with only a dozen huts, an open market, a church, a school, and a bar surrounding a town square, there wasn't much to it. Most of the community lived on farms outside of the village, though there were a few fishing shacks dotting the waters close to town as well.

While Abby and Eric were both multimillionaires as a result of having won *Trial Island*, they arrived on this island with a limited amount of local currency. Money was not a big thing on this island, though. Everyone pitched in, and for the most part, bartered for what they needed. Abby and Eric needed a home, and the many local farmers were always in need of strong backs to help with the work. After weeks of toiling on the farms to help with the harvest, the farmers and their families got together to help Abby and Eric raise their four walls and the roof to go over it.

Abby was amazed at how quickly it went up. She knew Eric had spent many years working construction before they met, but she was impressed with his skills. Eric reminded her that anything was possible when folks pulled together, particularly if there are no building codes, no electricity, and only the most rudimentary of plumbing systems. It was where they called home, and as Abby slowed to a walk for the last hundred yards or so, she smiled at the thought that she would call this place home for the rest of her life.

Eric was still lying in bed when she walked in. Lying there asleep, his amber hair mussed and his face unshaven, it reminded her of how he was when she first got a good look at him. She had pulled him from the water in the middle of the night after waking up on *Trial Island*, but didn't get a good look at him until morning. He was a classic good old boy from Texas, dimples and all. The manual labor he put in kept his chest and arms strong, and his deep tan gave away the time he liked to spend on the beach.

He barely stirred as she kissed him, but he did smile, revealing his dimples. Abby smiled back and stroked his hair, much shorter than it had been on *Trial Island*, but she liked it just fine. She gave him another kiss, and then padded into the bathroom to shower. When she walked out of the shower in only a towel, he was standing in the kitchen drinking tea and admiring the view. If his smile didn't tell her what was on his mind, his not so subtle tugging on her towel did.

His hands ran down her body as they kissed, and she pushed him away. "Don't get yourself all worked up, I'm going to the market."

He smiled. "You don't have five minutes to spare?"

She gave him a quick kiss before heading to the closet, "You're such a romantic."

The closet was more of a small room where they kept all of their clothes rather than an actual closet. It was six feet by eight feet, and could be a very small bedroom if it had to be. Right now, though, it only housed a couple of racks with their clothes hanging up and a large dresser and mirror.

She called to him in the kitchen, "Do you want to come with me this morning? Ben was asking about you the other day." She was referring to the first friend they had made upon arriving to this island. A young boy named Ben, or at least that's what they called him. He was exceedingly sweet, and was probably the best English speaker they had encountered here.

"Not today. I'm going to head out for a swim."

Abby came to the door of the closet and gave him a disapproving look.

"What?" he said with an innocent smile, doing his best to diffuse her glare.

"You know I don't like you doing that alone."

He walked over to give her a kiss. "I'll be fine. I

13

always am, right?"

She rolled her eyes. "Right. Until you're not. Need I remind you, that I had to pull you out of the water to save your ass more than once on *Trial Island*?"

"That's right, and I'm never going to let myself get into a situation where you have to do that again. That's why I do this. I'll be fine, OK?"

He smiled and kissed her again, leaving her to get dressed while he went out to their small deck on the beach to watch the waves. While she was getting dressed, Abby looked at her knife hanging off the side of the mirror. She took it out of its sheath and turned it over in her hand before sliding it back in. After brushing her now shoulder-length, dirty blonde hair and pulling it back into a short ponytail, she donned a baseball cap, a yellow tank top, pulled on her shorts and walked back into the kitchen. The knife slowly rocked in its sheath, still hanging off of the mirror.

She never wore it anymore. She attracted enough attention being the lone white woman on the island and didn't feel the need to attract any more by walking around with seven inches of steel strapped to her thigh. Every time she walked away from it, though, a little part of her mind tugged at her, wondering if today would be the day she would regret leaving it behind.

2

ERIC, VERY COMFORTABLE in only his boxers, leaned against the railing of the deck and watched Abby's cute little backside as she walked down the beach and off into the trees to head toward the town center, turning to wave just before she was out of sight. He finished his tea and stretched his arms high in the air to flex and stretch his back.

Looking at the white sand and crystal clear blue water in front of him, he thought about how his new life was infinitely better than his old one. This, of course, was by and large due to having Abby in his life. Had he not had the good fortune of waking up on that island with her a year ago, his life would certainly be in a very different place right now.

Even if he had been on the show and won without her, he likely would have simply returned to Texas and spent the next few years squandering his winnings, living extravagantly and supporting his buddies, shortly finding himself back to swinging a hammer to pay the rent by the time he was forty. This was better. Much better.

He also knew that the likelihood of him winning

15

without Abby would have been much slimmer. She had dragged him from the water more than once to save his ass. Living on a small island, surrounded by the beautiful blue ocean… he thought about that constantly. It was this thought that brought him to his self-imposed task this morning. As he tossed on his swim trunks and headed toward the water, he wondered if he deserved all he had in life. This was a question he struggled with often. Maybe he did, maybe he didn't, but he certainly intended to continue enjoying this life while he had it.

Having nearly drowned several times on *Trial Island,* Eric made it his mission in life to become as strong a swimmer as possible. Almost every day, he swam along the shoreline for at least thirty minutes, often longer. He wasn't exactly sure how far that was in distance, but it was a rigorous workout. He pushed himself hard. Never again did he intend to find himself in a situation where Abby needed to save him from the fury of the deep blue sea.

Once a week, he pushed himself to his absolute limit. Today was that day. Instead of swimming parallel to the shore, he planned to swim straight out from shore, to the point of exhaustion. Only then would he turn around and swim back. It wasn't the smartest plan, but the waters were mostly calm on this side of the island, and it forced him to push himself to the breaking point. He had to; otherwise he feared someday he would be dead.

As he dove into the warm shallow water and began his journey out to sea, he thought about Abby. He felt as though he had everything he had because of her, and he loved her unconditionally. In his mind, he would trade everything he had for her, because without her, he had nothing. He pondered the improbable and wondered if, should it come to it, whether he really would trade his life for hers. Hopefully, he would never have to find out.

A familiar ache in his upper back got his attention. It was his body's way of telling him he didn't have much time left before his muscles started to wear out. He stole a glance at his watch between strokes. Nearly thirty minutes into his workout. Not bad, considering he had to turn around to swim back at some point, but he could do better. As the ache intensified, he figured he had another seven to nine minutes before his arms would simply refuse to cooperate, and he would have to float and stretch awhile before heading back.

Doubling down on his determination, he began to stroke faster. Between the splashing, the adrenaline, the pain, and his ears being intermittently underwater, he never heard the approaching speedboat. With the sun rising over the island behind him, its rays were still low in the sky, effectively blinding the pilot of the boat, who had no reason to watch out for swimmers nearly a mile from shore. He also had no reason to ease back on the throttle until he was much closer to his destination.

His face underwater, four strong strokes, head cocked to the right for a quick breath, and repeat. Eric continued like this, unaware that he was on a collision course with a three hundred and seventy-five horsepower missile darting through the water. He finally heard the low roar of the engine when it was only thirty yards away. He stopped and righted himself to look up and was immediately seized by panic. There was absolutely nothing he could do to avoid the boat rocketing toward him.

Eric floated motionless, watching his end approach as if in slow motion, staring at the pilot of the boat who seemed to have no idea what was about to happen. At the last possible second, the boat mere yards away, he heard a shout and saw another man launch himself at the wheel of the boat as it veered sharply to his right. The engine screamed as the boat momentarily caught air, sailing over a swell as the high-speed propellers came out of the water.

The engine immediately died as the pilot cut the power, the sounds of the boat replaced by two men yelling.

He heard one of the men shout, "What the hell was that?"

The other man unintelligibly shouted something back and started gesturing wildly around while looking for something in the water.

Eric made himself low in the water as he watched the two men from twenty yards away. Two white faces. Not unheard of in these parts, but not terribly common either. He listened as they argued. The passenger who grabbed the wheel insisted that he had seen someone in the water.

"You're insane," the pilot countered. "Do you have any idea how far out we are?"

"Maybe you hit him?"

He laughed. "Maybe I hit him? I think we would have heard something if that happened. Look around – there's no one here!'"

As the pilot gestured around the boat, Eric slipped underwater and swam up to the hull at the front of the boat before surfacing. He was curious about their business here, but wasn't about to reveal himself. In the open water he could be visible, but hiding practically under the boat he was completely hidden. It wasn't that he was suspicious of them, but he had a recognizable face, and he and Abby enjoyed their anonymity. The last thing he wanted was to get recognized by two guys from a big city and have their island hideout splashed across the tabloids. Their current life would be ruined.

Eventually, the engine started and the boat pulled away. As it did, Eric dove under the water and stayed there for as long as he could, waiting for the engine noise to die out. He surfaced a minute later, facing the direction of the boat. The passenger who had saved his life by grabbing the wheel and veering off – a beefy man with a big beard and shaggy, curly hair pulled back in a crude ponytail – was still looking around from a football field away. The man did a double-take as Eric slipped back under the water.

3

ABBY AND ERIC lay in bed, their bodies covered by thin silk sheets. The ocean breeze gently drifted through the French doors that opened onto the beach and the water in the distance. Her eyes were closed, though she was not asleep. She was simply as relaxed and as comfortable as she had ever imagined she could be. Her head lay on his bare chest, his right hand stroking her hair. Their afternoon nap had become an almost daily routine, though Abby rarely slept.

Her nights were often interrupted by haunting images from her past, however during her afternoons lying in the gentle sun, safe in Eric's arms, she found more rest than she ever did at night. But just as Abby felt herself finally drifting off, she felt Eric sit up a bit.

"No, I'm not ready," she whispered without opening her eyes. "Just a few more minutes."

Eric tapped her on the shoulder, and she opened her eyes.

Standing at the end of their bed was Ben, his pin-straight black hair a mess, his dark skin soaked with sweat, and his black eyes panicked. He was scared and out of breath. He held up a piece of paper with their photos on it. "A man in the village, a white man," he said in English, "he is looking for you."

The words had barely escaped his mouth before Abby and Eric sprang into action. It was an unspoken fear that they lived with every day. Though they hadn't discussed it in months, they had each gone through their actions a thousand times in their heads. Abby wrapped the bed sheet around herself and took off for the changing room, Ben's curious eyes following her.

Eric quickly pulled on his shorts and leaned down in front of the boy to speak. "It's OK, Ben," Eric said, trying to calm their frightened friend.

Ben looked at him wide-eyed. "Does this mean you are leaving?"

Eric was caught off-guard. "What are you talking about?"

Ben shook his head. "I overheard you speaking to my father when we were building your house. You told him you might not be here forever. You said if someone ever came looking for you, you might have to go. Is this he?"

Eric remembered the conversation well. He trusted Jay, Ben's father. They were about the same age, and Jay and his family had welcomed Eric and Abby with open arms. They were nearing the end of construction on the house and were enjoying a beer together around the beach fire late one night after a particularly grueling day of work.

Jay, as he was known to do, began waxing on about

the future and how their families would be great friends for generations. Eric smiled and confided that he and Abby were somewhat on the run. "We never did anything wrong. We didn't break the law or anything like that, but there are men after us," he told Jay. Of course, Jay was gravely concerned about this. To ease his mind, Eric assured him they were safe on this island and would likely never have to leave. Eric thought Ben had been sleeping on Jay's lap during the conversation, but apparently not.

Looking into young Ben's eyes now, Eric could see how much he and Abby meant to his family. He decided to be honest with him. "I don't know. What did this man look like?"

Ben thought hard. "He is very tall. He's dark, but not like me. He is a white man. He is just very tan."

Eric thought about it, but that didn't really help. Every white man is tall to a twelve-year-old boy in the South Pacific. "Do you remember anything else?"

"He had curly hair, dark brown," Ben said, proud to have remembered something more.

Eric sighed. It wasn't Bryce, or at least doesn't sound like him. "Did you talk to him or tell him where we are?"

Ben vigorously shook his head no.

Eric thought another beat. "Did anyone?"

"I don't know. My father sent me running to warn you. I saw him walking up to the man to talk to him when I left."

Abby quickly reappeared. In barely a minute, she had fully dressed, strapped on her knife, stuffed her feet into her hiking boots, slung a small satchel across her shoulders and jogged back from the room tossing Eric an identical satchel. "Let's go."

Ben's eyes went wide and were drawn to the large leather sheath on her right thigh. He asked, "Miss Abby, what's that for?"

Abby followed his eyes, then looked back at him. "Just in case, Ben, just in case."

Eric quickly finished getting dressed and stuffed the small satchel into one of the large pockets of his cargo shorts. In less than four minutes they were running out the door with Ben in tow. Their world had been flipped upside down.

Abby led the charge to the beach and through the forest toward the village center, while Eric continued to quiz Ben along the way.

Eric fired questions at him as they sped along. "Where did he come from? When did he get here? Was there anyone with him?"

Ben was upset that he didn't know the answers to any of his questions.

The route from their beach to the village was a fairly straight shot. It was about a mile all told. The first quarter was a footpath that had been beaten into the jungle floor by Abby and Eric's many trips back and forth from their villa. After that, it met up with an exceedingly narrow dirt road that curved through the trees until it reached the village. While this route had been a lovely twenty-minute saunter through the forest for Abby that morning, it would take her barely seven minutes running at a breakneck pace to reach her destination.

Abby left Eric and Ben in the dust as she followed the dirt road, staying very close to the edge so she could duck into the trees at a moment's notice should she have to. Fortunately, the trip was uneventful. Questions about who this man was and what he was looking for churned through her mind. It was obvious that whoever he was, he was working for Bryce. She had always worried this might happen, but they were so careful not to leave a trail – and were in such a remote place – she kept telling herself it was impossible. *Apparently the impossible has become possible after all,* she thought.

She arrived on the outskirts of the village, but didn't dare step from the cover of the trees without knowing what was out there. The dirt road continued from the forest and ran through the center of the village. From ten feet back in the trees, safely under cover, she surveyed the village in front of her.

After the dirt road left the trees, it continued across a small grassy open area for fifty feet or so before it met the first building. A small wooden structure with a thatched roof stood on the right side of the road, which Abby was convinced only continued to stand out of habit. It had been abandoned and in disrepair for many years before Eric and Abby had come along.

Just past that was one of the more popular buildings in the village – the bar. It was a large wooden building with a thatched roof. There was no door; the front of the building was just open. There were a handful of mismatched tables, and the bar and barstools were behind them. There was a small twenty-inch color television on a shelf on the far wall above the bar, though it was rarely on. On a cloudless day, with the wind blowing in the right direction, and a little bit of luck, it was able to get fuzzy reception on one channel.

Next to the bar was an even larger building, the largest on the island. It was the church which was also used as a function area for any large gathering, such as weddings and village meetings.

Across the street from the church was a very large open-air market that ran the length of the street until the road curved and disappeared from view. Everything was sold at this market. There was a section of tables in the area across the street from the bar where an ancient wiry man and his equally ancient but chubby wife sold coffee, tea, and homemade pastries. Next to that were many carts where merchants hocked dry goods. Beyond that were rows upon rows of fresh produce. In the center of these rows was a very neat and small hut where Ben's father, Jay, oversaw his goods.

Behind the open-air market there were many boat docks and the boat master's building. Many sorry looking sailboats populated the harbor, with several dozen or so decent powerboats mixed in amongst them. There was nothing but open blue sea beyond that.

It was later in the afternoon, and while the market was not bustling, there were many people walking around. The locals were easy enough to pick out and for the most part they seemed to be simply going about their daily business. Abby couldn't put her eyes on anyone who didn't look like they belonged and couldn't find anything out of the ordinary going on. She scanned the area impatiently for a full five minutes before Eric, and the exhausted Ben, caught up. Eric was sweating and eager to continue moving. Ben, however, was bent at the waist, panting, and staring at the ground.

Abby felt bad and rubbed his back. "Are you OK, buddy?"

Without looking up, he nodded his head yes.

Abby squatted down next to him so they would be at the same level. "Ben, I need you to look up and tell me if you see him."

He nodded his head again as he stood, looking skyward and taking a few deep breaths, before his eyes settled straight ahead and scanned the crowd. Abby and Eric also searched the area, but saw no one.

"I don't see him," Ben said.

Eric's eyes drifted toward the water and the docks, looking for the boat he had seen that morning. He had not mentioned the incident to Abby. She hated his swimming habits enough as it was – he didn't need to give her any more reasons to hate his swimming. The long dock next to the boat master's building housed ten powerboats, but there was one he hadn't seen before, or at least he didn't think he had. It could have been the boat from this morning. He made a mental note to check it out if he got the chance.

The village was just a bit too far away for them to get a good read on everyone there. Ben had said that, as he left, his father was going to talk to the man. Given this, Abby figured that perhaps they were together somewhere, though Jay was not to be seen at his normal post in the middle of the produce market.

Ben piped up, very excited, "There! There he is!" He was pointing in the distance. "On the far side of the market. See?"

Abby and Eric stood, their eyes following his arm. There they saw Ben's father and the stranger facing them as they walked toward the market. They watched as the pair stopped and spoke with a couple of people along the way. While Jay acted as an interpreter, the man showed a set of papers to anyone who would look. Each person walked away, shaking his or her head.

Eric spoke first. "What do you think?"

"He's got to be one of Bryce's guys," Abby said. "Who else could it be?"

"I wonder how many others he has with him," Eric thought out loud.

Abby turned to Ben. "Have you seen anyone else with him?"

27

"No. He walked up from the docks and into the market alone."

Eric had pretty much settled on the fact that this was the man on the boat with whom he had the near-disaster this morning. It was too much of a coincidence. He also knew that there had been two men on the boat, at least.

Abby thought through the scenario. "There have to be more men. He wouldn't be here alone."

"I don't know what Jay is doing," Eric said, "but it's only a matter of time before this guy finds someone who tells him where to find us. I'd rather control the situation and confront him on our terms."

"We can't just walk out there, Eric. Who knows how many guys are with him."

"I don't see anyone else out there, but there could be another guy or two." Eric thought a moment, trying to convince Abby to take action without telling her there was definitely another guy. "If they came on one of those boats," he said, gesturing toward the dock by the boat master's building, "there can only be a couple at best. We can handle that if it's on our terms, right?"

Abby knew they had to confront this man, or men, in a situation they controlled. They were going to meet up eventually, that much was obvious. So they might as well arrange it to happen the way they wanted it to.

"Here's what we do," Abby said. "Ben, we'll need your help. Can we count on you?" He enthusiastically nodded his head. "Wait here and give us a five-minute head start, then walk up to the village. Tell the man that you know where to find us and lead him back to our house. Can you do that?"

"You want me to lead him to you? That is crazy. Why would you want that?"

"Trust me, it will be OK. Try to make sure he comes alone. If there are two of us and one of him, we can talk to him and get more information. Does that make sense?"

Ben thought about that. "I suppose yes. How do I make sure he comes alone?"

Eric spoke up. "Tell him he has to hurry. If he doesn't follow you right away, if he says he wants to get his friend or something, just start running to the forest. He'll have no choice. He will either have to follow you, or lose you. My guess is he's going to follow you."

Ben was taking it all in and nodding away like a bobblehead. "Yes. Yes, I can do that."

Abby hadn't entirely worked out the plan of attack back at the villa, but she knew that whatever happened, it would not be for Ben's young eyes to see. It would certainly be a side of their lives he did not need to experience. She looked at him and put her hands on his shoulders. "Ben, when you get to the beach, show him where our house is and send him to us, but don't come into the house with him. Understand?" She watched his face as he nodded and gave him a smile and quick peck on the cheek. "You got this, right, Ben?"

Had it not been for his darker complexion, she would have seen him blushing. "I do," he smiled and turned to leave.

Eric called from behind, "Hey, tiger, give us a head start, OK? Wait here five minutes."

Ben stopped. "Sorry, I forgot." He was clearly nervous.

"That's OK," Abby said. "I know you can do this. We'll try again, alright?"

"Five minutes," Ben stated, then smiled. "All set. Go ahead."

Abby and Eric turned and jogged down the road back toward the beach. Eric turned to Abby, "He'll be OK, right?"

Abby gave an unconvincing, "Absolutely."

"He's fine," Eric assured her. "He's fine. He's a smart kid."

4

AN HOUR EARLIER, Jay had seen the tall man
walking around the market with a stack of papers, trying to
speak to the locals. At this time of day, the customers at
the market consisted primarily of older women picking up
items to make dinner. It was crowded enough, but the
man obviously was having no luck finding anyone who
spoke English. Not many on the island did.

The man showed his papers to a group of three
women who were picking through some vegetables. Two
of them ignored him, but the other took a second look at
the paper and rattled off something in her native tongue
and gestured absentmindedly over her shoulder in the
general direction of the jungle. The man was clearly
frustrated.

Always inquisitive, Ben walked by the man, who
handed him one of the papers. Ben stopped dead in his
tracks, staring at the paper. Jay observed this from his
post in the middle of the market. His son looked panicked
and angry. Jay could not hear what the man said to his
son, nor could he hear his son's reply.

Jay called to Ben across the market. When Ben looked
up and saw him, he went to him at a half jog, holding out
the paper. Jay took it from his hand and felt the same

panic that his son had moments ago.

He looked at Ben. "What did you say to this man?"

"Nothing," Ben said, shaking his head. "Well, nothing he could understand. I didn't speak English."

Jay allowed himself a smile before addressing his son in their native tongue, "Good job, son," He held up the paper, "I know you do not know what this means, but it is very important that we tell Abby and Eric right away".

"What should we do?" Ben asked.

Jay folded the paper and handed it back to Ben. "I'm going to speak with this man before anyone else does. Can you go to them and tell them of this?"

Ben nodded his head. "Yes, I can. I will run to them."

"Good, but wait until you get into the trees to run. We do not know who this man is, but I know that it is important that we do not lead him to them. Do you understand?"

"I do."

"Alright, go then." Jay watched as Ben walked back down the dirt road, past the man and toward the trees beyond the village.

The man was looking at Jay. Jay caught his eye and immediately offered a smile and called to him with a wave, "Hello, friend!"

The tall man smiled, revealing a perfect set of teeth

that gleamed bright white against his tanned complexion, a very rare sight in this part of the world. "Someone who speaks English! Hello, friend, indeed!"

Jay met him with a handshake, "It seems that you're looking for someone?" Jay looked up at the man because he had no choice. The man was tall, and not just compared to the island residents. Eric was certainly the tallest man most of the islanders had seen, standing just over six feet, but this man was an inch or two taller than him.

"I am sir, actually looking for two people." The man handed Jay a paper with black-and-white photos of Abby and Eric.

Jay looked at the page, feigning complete confusion. "What brings you here to look for them?"

"Well, we think they are on one of these islands out here. We've been searching... well, my boss has been searching, for a very long time."

Jay laughed. "You *think* they are on one of these islands? My friend, do you know how many islands there are out here?"

The man smiled. "Yes, sir, I do, and at this point it feels like I've been to most of them. Do you recognize these people?"

"I do not," Jay said without hesitation. "Let me help you, though. Not many people here are familiar with your language."

The man smiled. "I'd certainly appreciate that, sir. Can I give you something for your trouble?"

Jay smiled at the man, "Why don't we see if I'm actually able to help you first?"

"Fair enough." He held out his hand. "I'm JJ. Pleased to meet you."

Jay looked at him and laughed. "JJ?"

"Most people call me that, yes. Why, is that funny?"

The men shook hands. "My name is Jay."

Both men shared a laugh at this revelation.

"So tell me, JJ, are you thirsty? There is a bar across the street here. I can introduce you to some people and see if any of them have seen the ones you are looking for."

JJ clapped his new friend on the shoulder, "That's awfully kind of you, sir. Thank you."

The two men crossed the street and walked into the open front of the bar. It was not crowded at this time of day. There were a dozen or so men, mostly young, single men enjoying a beer after a long day's work. Jay knew a few of them, but not all.

He held up his hands to say hello to everyone. When he had their attention, he spoke to them in their native tongue. After explaining that JJ was looking for two people, he explained that he was going to walk around the room to have them look at a picture of Abby and Eric. Jay held up a copy of the poster to show them. He went on to tell them that for the safety of his friends, he would appreciate it if all of them could – either by shaking their heads or stating it if they spoke English – confirm for this man that they have never seen Abby or Eric.

There were nods around the room. Jay smiled and turned to JJ. "I explained to them to look at your photographs and tell us if they know your people, yes?"

"Yes, that's great. Thank you."

JJ proceeded to walk around the room, handing out the flyers with the pictures of Abby and Eric, but was met by unanimous headshakes, negative grunts, and even a few, "No, I not see them."

JJ asked, "Would you mind helping me out by asking some other folks around?"

Jay smiled. "Anything for my new friend."

With that, they set out around the market, replaying the scene from the bar over and over again, up and down the street.

*   *   *

After waiting close to ten minutes, just to be sure enough time had passed, Ben slowly and nonchalantly walked up the dirt road toward the village. He saw his father walking up and down the street with the mysterious man who had come for Abby and Eric. Ben was incredibly fond of Eric, and had nothing short of a schoolboy crush on Ms. Abby. He was still swooning from the kiss on his cheek when he remembered what he was actually tasked with doing.

He was filled with anger toward this unknown man whose mere presence threatened to take Abby and Eric from him. He picked up his pace as he approached the marketplace and quickly crossed the open area between the trees and the first building. Looking ahead, he saw his father walking with the tall man. The two were speaking as if they were friends. This confused Ben, but no matter, he had his instructions.

The closer he got, however, the more nervous he became. Should he tell his father about the plan? How could he? Was this the right thing to do? He trusted his father. He was a very good man and always did the right thing. Ben rarely made a decision without speaking to him, let alone taking action like this without consulting him. But he also trusted Abby and Eric. They had become an extension of his family.

Ben was conflicted, and as the gap between them got shorter and shorter, he slowed down, trying to work out exactly what he would say. His father glanced at him and shook his head, trying to communicate for Ben to go away, but Ben continued on course. Finally, the man took notice. He remembered Ben taking one of the papers from him and called out, "Young man!"

Jay turned to him, "This is my son. I can assure you that he knows nothing." He then spoke to Ben in their native tongue, *"Son, tell this man you do not know our friends, yes?"*

Ben replied in the same tongue, *"They want him to find them father. They instructed me to lead him to their home. Is that the right thing?"*

Jay thought about it.

JJ asked, "What did he say?"

Jay waved him off and responded to his son, *"If that is what they wish, they must have a purpose, but I am concerned about your involvement."*

"I will just lead him to the beach and show him their home, then I will leave. Those were their instructions."

"So be it," Jay sighed and turned to JJ. "My son, he says he knows something. Go on, son."

Ben swallowed hard, but could not speak.

JJ crouched slightly to make himself eye level with the boy. "It is very important that I find these people. Have you seen them before?"

Ben managed to squeak out a "Yes."

JJ smiled at the revelation, "Where? Are they on the island?"

"I know where they live," Ben said. With that, he took off running toward the trees.

JJ began trotting behind the young man, and then turned to Jay over his shoulder, "Thank you, my friend, thank you!"

5

BACK AT THEIR HOME, Eric and Abby debated how best to set and spring their trap. With no neighbors as far as the eye could see, they didn't worry about anyone seeing what happened. However, they still wanted to get the man inside their home first. With limited exits, it would reduce his option to run.

As they entered through the French doors, Eric trotted up the steps from the bedroom to the kitchen area. "We need to get him in the house and away from the door, up here," he said. He was standing in the center of the house. The main exit was through the French doors and out to the small deck. There was a second exit at the back of the house in the changing room. They never used it, and a freestanding rack with Abby's clothes hanging from it currently obscured the door. No one would ever know it was there.

"I'll be the bait," Abby said. "It's me he's after anyway, so that makes it easy, right?"

Eric stared into her eyes. He didn't want to, but he had to agree. Abby was the lure alright, the one they had traveled halfway around the world to catch. He told himself that she had nothing to worry about; that it was still two on one, and he would be right here. They could easily take the man down. But the thought of intentionally putting her in danger, even for a few moments, didn't sit well with him.

"Don't worry," she said. "I can take care of myself. Plus, you're here. We'll be fine."

"I know you can take care of yourself. Hell, the whole world knows you can take care of yourself. That's what I'm worried about."

"Why?"

"Because this guy – no, all his guys – know that you can take care of yourself. He's going to come in here and go after you hard, and he's probably going to have a gun."

She smiled and said in a sing-song voice, "Well, we'll just have to take that away from him first thing, now won't we?"

"Abby, take this seriously."

"I am. I'll be back there," she gestured over her shoulder, "and you'll be over there. I figure you should be on the far side of the house when he gets here so he doesn't see you. Maybe even behind the shed, in case he circles the house first. At least that's what I'd do if I were him."

"So he'll come in here, come up to get to you, and I'll come from behind. Sounds simple enough, but how do we make sure he doesn't see me?"

"Trust me, I'll make sure he doesn't take his eyes off me." She smiled so demurely that Eric didn't want to take his eyes off her either.

"What do you have planned?"

"Nothing you need to worry about." She looked at her watch, "We've got five minutes or so before Ben gets him back here. Maybe longer, but I don't want to take any chances." She gave him a long kiss. "Don't worry. We'll take care of this, OK?"

Eric nodded. "I'll grab some ties from the shed. When I come in, I'm going to come up from behind, wrap my arms around him, and wrestle him to the ground. I'll have the ties in my back pocket. As soon as I get him down, tie up his feet, then we'll get his hands together, got it?"

Abby scratched his nose with the fingernail of her pinky. "It's so sexy when you talk tough. I like a man who takes charge."

Eric rolled his eyes and gave her another kiss.

"OK, save some for later. Go!"

He smiled as he ran out the French doors. Moments later, Abby heard him rustling through the shed as she kicked off her socks and shoes in the corner, and then ducked into the bathroom. She turned on the sink and dunked her head under the running water to soak her hair. Grabbing a towel off the shelf she patted it down to keep it from dripping too much. Next, she slid her arms out of her tank top and tucked the straps down on her sides, leaving her shoulders bare, before wrapping the towel around herself.

Looking in the full-length mirror, she very convincingly appeared to have just gotten out of the shower. Her hair and shoulders were wet, and the large towel hung down far enough, given her small stature, that it concealed both her shorts and the knife strapped to her leg. She smiled at herself in the mirror. In her experience, men did not take their eyes off a woman in towel. They were always hoping for the same thing.

She stood in the bathroom, waiting, and thinking. She may have been cute and jokey with Eric a few minutes ago, but she took this threat very seriously. She could not believe that they had been found. Abby thought for sure they would live in secrecy for many years to come, if not the rest of their years. Yet, not even a full year later she stood waiting for one of her husband's lackeys to walk through the door. Fortunately, it appeared that there was only one here, though she wouldn't be surprised if there were two or three. Still, Abby and Eric could handle two or three of them. She didn't intend to let this one leave the house once he got there, and vowed the others would meet a similar fate.

As she thought about their simple way of life and their isolation from the outside world, Abby had a sudden revelation that made her heart rate increase. Even if there's only one guy, he most certainly has a phone. How long before more showed up? It could be hours, or several days at most. Either way, they wouldn't stay around here. Abby mentally ticked off locations throughout the world where she would like to live. She wouldn't mind settling down someplace where people spoke English, which would certainly make life a little easier. Of course, that would increase the risk they would be recognized. Maybe an isolated, English-speaking area, if they could find one.

Abby was dreaming of a little village that she imagined would be somewhere in the English countryside when she heard a man's voice on the beach.

"This the place?"

"Yes," she heard Ben say, as they got closer. "Right up there."

She heard footsteps, too many, coming up the small staircase that led from the beach onto the deck and through the open French doors. There must be more than one. *Damn it.* She quickly told herself to relax. The two of them could handle whatever creeps Bryce sent her way. She was thankful that she had instructed young Ben not to come into the house so that he wouldn't see this side of them.

Abby swallowed and put on her best actress face before opening the door and walking out of the bathroom. She had intended to feign surprise upon seeing the men standing in the kitchen of her home, but she didn't need to.

Ben gasped and shouted, "Miss Abby!"

She jumped and gasped herself, not expecting to see Ben standing there, "Ben!" She was about to reprimand him with *I told you not to come in the house!*, but caught herself and just yelled, "What are you doing in here?" She held onto the top of her towel and looked at the other man. "And who are you?"

Ben stood and stared, eyes wide open. Only a few seconds went by, but he managed to take in every visible inch of Abby. Her wet hair dripped onto her bare shoulders, the water droplets slowly sliding down her soft chest before disappearing into the towel that hid... *oh my*, Ben thought, as his imagination ran wild. As he looked back up to Miss Abby's beautiful amber eyes, he saw they were filled with anger.

"Ben!" she scolded. "Turn around!"

"Sorry, Miss Abby," he said as he turned, stealing once last glance over his shoulder. "Sorry."

"I'm very sorry, too," the man said. He began to turn around, as well. "I'll turn until you get..."

"No!" Abby nearly shouted, worried because she didn't know how close Eric was to coming in the door. "Tell me who you are!"

The man stopped and turned back toward her. He was reluctant to look at her, and instead stared down at her feet, which Abby found odd.

"My name is JJ."

She saw Eric coming in through the French doors behind JJ. Eric was surprised to see Ben, too. He jerked his thumb over his shoulder, motioning for Ben to make his way out the door. He did not want him here either. The kid was bound to get hurt.

Abby told herself, *keep him engaged.* "What are you doing in my house?"

As Ben made his way out the door and down the stairs, the sound of his feet made JJ's ears perk up. He began to turn just as Eric was upon him.

It's now or never, Eric thought. He leapt onto JJ's back, wrapping his arms around his chest in an attempt to throw him to the ground. The attempt did not go well. With lightning-fast reflexes, JJ bent at the waist and pitched forward, rolled his right shoulder, and flipped Eric up and over onto his back before either of them had a chance to process what was happening.

Eric let out a yelp when he hit the ground.

JJ was still looking down at Eric when Abby lost the towel and produced her blade inches from his face. Though her hand was steady, her voice trembled slightly. "How many of you are there?"

JJ held up his hands, never taking his eyes off the tip of the knife pointing at his face from Abby's low vantage point. "Whoa, Abby. Relax."

With anger in her voice she spit the words, "I will not relax!" She had built a beautiful new life and this man was

44

here to end it. She was scared. She was angry with herself for letting this happen. However most of all, she was pissed off and ready to fight. She allowed herself to quickly glance at the floor, "Eric, are you OK?"

In a flash, JJ's large left hand enveloped her right, and a split second later came away with the knife. "Abby, get a hold of yourself for a second."

His soft tone almost sounded caring, though she did not have much time to think about that. Eric regained his composure on the ground and made a move. He kicked out with his leg, catching the back of JJ's knee and sweeping his legs out from under him. As JJ fell onto his back, his hands flew up. Abby took the opportunity to kick his knife hand full force, sending the knife flying toward the bedroom.

Eric got to his feet and immediately jumped on top of JJ, trying to pin his arms to the ground. Abby watched in shock as JJ effortlessly flung Eric to the side and onto his back, pinning him to the ground. JJ shouted, "Stop it! I don't want to hurt you!"

Abby jumped on his back, wrapping her arms around his neck and squeezing as she did. JJ thrashed back and forth trying to shake her off. He stood up, letting go of Eric, and gripped Abby's forearms with his strong hands. Abby was strong, but he was stronger, and he pried her arms from around his neck just as Eric stood and threw a right hook looking to connect with his jaw.

Still gripping Abby's arms and holding her on his back as though she were a child, JJ sidestepped Eric's punch, causing him to catch nothing but air. Eric had put everything he had into the punch and momentarily went off-balance. JJ lunged forward, crashing into Eric and using his left leg to sweep Eric's feet from under him, sending him to the ground face down.

With Abby still thrashing on his back, JJ fell onto Eric and landed with a thud. He tossed Abby backwards and, in one motion, grabbed one of the ties sticking out of Eric's back pocket and wrapped up his wrists. He spun as Abby got to her feet and leapt at him again. Fortunately for him, she was still knifeless, but came at him full force with everything she had. He stood with one foot on Eric's back to hold him down and grabbed Abby's wrists. Twisting her and kicking her feet out from under her, he tossed her down on top of Eric so she landed face up and on top of his back.

Struggling to catch his breath, JJ held her wrists tightly to her chest as she kicked and screamed, unable to get up. He shouted back at her to stop, but the more he tried to get her under control, the harder she fought.

Ben had been standing by the tree line debating with himself about what to do. Hearing the all-out brawl, followed by Abby's screaming, he swallowed his fear and ran back down the beach and into the villa. "Miss Abby!" he yelled upon seeing her and Eric pinned to the ground on top of each other.

"Ben!" Abby shouted. "Get out of here!"

Ben stood staring for a moment, clearly nervous, but trying to put on a brave face.

JJ seized the momentary silence to thunder, "Abby, Eric, I am not here to hurt you. Please, just stop and let me talk."

A tear streamed down Abby's cheek, despite her best efforts to hold it in. With her eyes closed, she said, "Please, don't hurt the boy. Ben, leave." She shuddered and opened her eyes to look at the intruder, "Whoever you are, I don't know what he's paying you, but I've got money. I'll give you everything, every penny I have. Just please leave. Leave and pretend you never saw us."

Eric spoke up, "Me, too. We'll give you everything. Just walk away, that's all."

JJ shook his head, "You guys really don't want to be found?"

"Please," Abby said. "I'll give you whatever you want."

JJ looked into her eyes. She was just as beautiful as he had seen on TV, and just about as deadly, too. He wasn't surprised they didn't want to be found. He had been searching these islands for months without so much as a hint that they were out here. The thought had never occurred to him that his target would attack him over it. "Abby, you don't have to pay me a thing. I'll walk away and pretend I never saw you. If I let go of your wrists, do not move. Understand? I don't want to hurt you." He paused and tried to read her face. "Can I trust you?"

Abby shook her head *yes*.

Slowly, JJ released his grip and stood, backing up a step, still breathing hard.

Abby didn't move a muscle, but spoke softly, "I don't understand. You'll just walk away? You don't want anything in return?"

JJ shook his head, "No, I'm taken care of Abby. You don't want anyone to know where you are, that's fine by me. I'm just here to deliver a message."

Abby slowly rolled off Eric and sat up to look at JJ, "Bryce just wants you to deliver a message?"

JJ cocked his head to the side and looked confused. "Bryce? No. Robert sent me."

Abby's eyes lit up, and she exchanged a curious glance with Eric before looking back at the tall stranger. "Robert sent you?"

"Yes," JJ said. "Bryce Haydenson is dead."

6

ABBY FELT AS THOUGH her brain had just been smacked into wall and couldn't process the information. "What? What did you say?"

JJ was still standing over Abby and Eric, catching his breath. "Bryce is dead. He has been for a few months now. Robert wanted you to know, so I've been scouring these islands for months trying to find you."

Abby and Eric looked at each other, unsure how to react.

Eric spoke up first. "Mind getting me untied?"

JJ laughed, almost embarrassed, "Oh, yeah, sorry about that." He knelt down next to Eric, produced a blade and freed his hands even more quickly than he had tied them. "No hard feelings, right?"

Eric shook his head. "Don't worry about it."

They both turned to Abby who sat still on the floor, quietly trying to process what she had just heard. Her brain was in overdrive. Emotionally, she was conflicted. *Bryce is dead.* She knew this was a good thing, a very good thing. She had been in hiding because she feared he would kill her, and while she couldn't explain it, part of her was sad. Or perhaps part of her felt that she was supposed to be sad. *This man was my husband... is it OK to be happy about his death?*

As she sat in a daze, staring into space, Eric knelt next to her. "Abby, you OK?"

She looked at him, though her eyes did not connect with his. She almost seemed to look through him, yet she tried to reassure him. "Yeah, yes... I'm fine." Looking at JJ, she asked, "How? How did it happen?"

"Massive shootout with the FBI. A bunch of mob guys got it that day."

Abby searched his face and suddenly had a thought. "Robert sent you?"

"Yes, ma'am."

"How do I know you're telling me the truth?"

JJ let out a small laugh. "He knew that would be the first thing you asked. Hold on." He took a small phone from his pocket and with a few flicks of his thumb dialed a number and held the device to his ear. After a few moments, his eyes lit up. "Yep. No, not good news, great news." He paused, listening. "Yes, I found them. It didn't go exactly as I anticipated, but we're all OK." He listened silently for a moment, then laughed. "Absolutely, yes, that's the first thing she asked. Hold on." He held the phone out and handed it to Abby, who took it and held it to her ear.

"Hello?"

Robert's big, jovial, British voice boomed through the phone. "Abby, my dear!"

"How did you find me?"

"I had a hunch you would be out there somewhere."

"Is it true?"

"Yes, Abby, it's true. I wish I could have told you straight away. I knew you would want to know, but it took months to track you down!"

"Who is this guy you sent?"

"JJ? He's the best. He's a good man. So when am I going to see you?"

Abby was quiet for a moment.

"Abby?"

"Yes, sorry. I'm... I'm just a little overwhelmed. So... he's dead?"

"As a doornail. It was all over the news. It was not just Bryce; it was a huge sting that went bad. A bunch of these mafia guys wound up dead. Can you believe their families are suing the government? What a country. Anyhow, I had my people keeping an eye on him for news anyway, but this was impossible to miss. I saw his face on the evening news myself before my assistant even had a chance to call me. You've got your life back, Abby!"

She managed a meek, "Yes, I guess I do."

Had she been face to face with him, she would have seen him furrow his brow. "I thought you would be elated."

"It's all happening so fast. An hour ago I was living in complete secrecy, and now… this."

"I see."

"Robert, I really appreciate you tracking us down, I do. I just need to wrap my head around this, that's all."

"I understand. I'm so happy to hear your voice again. I understand this is a huge thing for you, but please promise that we will see each other again soon. That would be so wonderful."

"It would, Robert, it really would."

"Take care, my dear. JJ will see to the details, yes?"

"You, too, Robert, and thank you again."

She handed the phone back to JJ.

Abby finally allowed the thought to sink in. *Bryce was killed in a gunfight with the F.B.I.* She heard the words, processed the words, but somehow had trouble *feeling* the words. She was supposed to be thrilled. She should be dancing. So why wasn't she feeling that joy? *I've got my life back*, she told herself.

Just as quickly, a little voice in the back of her head told her why she was feeling how she was – *Do you want your life back?* She stood and walked through the open door where Ben was standing and onto the pristine beach where she stood on the white sand watching the small waves crash at the waterline.

Eric walked onto the porch. "Abby, you OK?"

She stood, not turning around, watching the water, "Yeah, just give me a few minutes."

Eric nodded his head and went back into the villa, putting his arm around Ben and bringing him inside.

Ben quietly asked, "Is Miss Abby OK?"

"She'll be fine. She just got hit hard with some pretty big news. Sometimes women need to think things through a little more than us guys."

Ben nodded thoughtfully. "Who is Bryce?"

Eric chuckled, "There's an awful lot about us that you don't know Ben. An awful lot."

Back on the beach, Abby walked down to the surf. She had spent so much time these past eleven months or so trying to force herself not to think about Bryce, not to question whether leaving him alive was the right thing, that she found it nearly impossible to will her mind to actually think *about* him.

She was thrilled – at least she told herself she was – though she didn't feel it. She was free. She could have her life back. But there was that little voice again – *Do you want your life back?* Having shed the baggage of the past ten

53

years, she thought about the new life she had built with Eric. It was a simple life, yet far more fulfilling than anything she had remembered before.

No, she didn't want her life back. Not her old life anyway. She didn't want to know what kind of person she must have been to get together with someone like Bryce. She was a new person now, so why revisit her past?

So Bryce is dead. That has no impact on me; no bearing on the life I lead. He has already taken so much from me, an entire decade, that I will not allow him to take anything more. He will not take another moment from me. I am free, I live free, and I'm here with Eric because I want to be. I am not in hiding anymore, but rather choosing to live a quiet life.

Abby smiled as she surveyed the endless sea in front of her. *I'M FREE!* She let this realization wash over her. She couldn't stop smiling. As she turned and trotted back toward the villa, Ben came out. She took him in her arms and gave him a big hug. "I love you, Ben, you know that? And I love being here. This news changes nothing, so don't you worry, OK?"

Ben was confused, but unable to look at Miss Abby and not smile. His brown cheeks beamed as he smiled back. "OK Miss Abby."

She smiled warmly. "Good. Now you go tell your dad we're alright, OK?"

"Yes, Miss Abby."

She watched him walk off toward the trees before she

bounded up the stairs and into the villa. Eric and JJ were sitting around the island in the kitchen talking over two glasses of water.

Eric stood when he saw her walk in. "You alright?"

She jumped onto him, wrapping her legs around his waist. "I'm great!" She planted a big kiss on his lips before jumping down and turning to JJ. "And you, thank you!" She gave him a big hug and kissed him on the cheek. "Seriously, I can't tell you what a relief!"

JJ and Eric exchanged a hesitant look as Abby turned her attention back to Eric and wrapped her arms around him. "This doesn't change a thing, Eric. I love our life here; we won't change a thing except we don't have to worry anymore. No more looking over our shoulders; no more wondering if Bryce is out there looking for us. We're free!"

Eric managed to smile, but Abby could tell something was bothering him.

"What?" She turned to look at JJ, "What is it?"

JJ said nothing.

She looked back to Eric. "What's the problem?"

Eric sighed. "Well, there's just a little more to the story."

"What is it?"

Eric stood with his arm around Abby and looked at JJ.

"Tell her what you told me."

JJ nodded and indicated the chairs. "Let's have a seat." He sipped his water before he continued. "Eric says you've both been pretty isolated since the show, right?"

"Right." Abby looked to Eric for reassurance, and he nodded his head in agreement.

"Well, after the show ended, the media went a little nuts that you guys just disappeared. I mean, you were the biggest thing on television, huge celebrities, and then you just vanished. The news hounds dug, but Robert keeps his people close, and frankly not many folks had any clue what happened anyway. That was what, about ten or eleven months ago, toward the end of last summer?"

"Yes," Abby answered.

"You were lucky. Robert buried the story and put a gag order on anyone from the top down. No one was allow to speak about the show. They had to go on hiatus anyway, seeing as though they were without a cast. The election coverage kicked into high gear after a few weeks, the new fall season started on TV, and the news cycle went on. After a few weeks, you were forgotten about."

"That's good, right?"

JJ laughed. "It was. In fact, it was better than good for you. It was great! Until Bryce started a shootout with the FBI. No one had ever heard of him before, and suddenly he was the biggest crime story in years. So the reporters started digging." He watched Abby for reaction, but she gave up none, as if she were an observer more than an actor in this story. When he thought about it, that actually was the case.

He went on. "It didn't take a couple of days before it hit the news that you were Mrs. Haydenson. There was nothing Robert could do, it was out there, and the hunt for you has been in the news all summer. There are a million theories out there that Bryce had you killed, that you're on the run from him, in witness protection, et cetera. I'm not the only one who's looking for you. All the big news outlets have guys out here looking for an exclusive. One of us would find you eventually."

Abby had so many thoughts swirling through her head. *Does the FBI want me for something? My life is over, again! Where am I supposed to hide now?* But a very simple question, one that the man in front of her could actually answer, came to the forefront. "So who are you exactly?"

"I've known Robert for a long time. I do a lot of work for him back on the East Coast. He keeps me on retainer. I mostly do background checks on his business partners. I'm an investigator, and I do mostly specialist work like that for a few big clients. In my former life, I was a bounty hunter. I still find people occasionally, and that's what Robert hired me to do in this case."

"So who else is out here looking for me? The authorities? The FBI?"

JJ shook his head no. "Not that I've caught wind of yet.

"How is it that you're the one to find me?"

"A little bit of luck, but I also had a head start. Robert picked up the phone the minute the news hit that Bryce was dead and had me on a plane within a few hours. I've been out here combing the islands for months now. I knew I'd find you in a small, quiet place, out of the way, so that narrowed my search. I've been to somewhere in the neighborhood of one hundred and eighteen of these quiet, out-of-the-way places."

Eric let out a whistle.

"Well," Abby said, "I'm glad it was you and not one of the others. I'm not about to put my face out there. Bryce gone or not, I love my life here, and I'm not giving that up."

JJ nodded his head. "There are some other things; things that Robert didn't share with me and insisted he tell you on his own. I don't know how long you need to get your stuff together, but I can take you to him whenever you're ready. I've been out here for a long time, and I'm itching to get back, but I can stick around a day or so if you need it."

Abby stood and scoffed, "This is unreal." She stood at the counter, looking out through the doors again. With a shaky voice, she declared, "I'm not ready. And I don't know when I'll be ready. If I'll ever be ready." She turned to face JJ. "Thank you for finding me, for delivering the message, but your job is done. I'm not leaving here."

Eric spoke, "Abby, this is a lot to handle. Let's sleep

on it."

She shot back, "No!" Closing her eyes, she breathed for a moment before speaking. "There's nothing to sleep on. I'm not leaving."

JJ spoke up. "There's going to be others, Abby. Probably not tomorrow, or even next week, but you've got a few months at best. I hate to be the bearer of bad news, but one way or another, your secret hideaway is going to be the lead story very soon."

He produced a card from his pocket and tried to hand it to her, but she simply folded her arms and said, "No thank you."

He sighed and left it on the counter, looking back and forth from her to Eric. "When you change your mind, there's my info."

"I'm not going to change my mind," Abby said.

"That's your decision. I'll let Robert know." He looked to Eric. "I'm going to leave you two alone. Talk to her. You can sit here and just wait for it all to end one day, but I'd think you want to do it on your terms." JJ turned and trotted out the door to leave.

Eric followed him out the door, leaving Abby on her own.

"Hey," he called ahead to JJ.

"Yeah?"

"I was out for a swim this morning and saw a couple guys. Did you come here with another guy on a boat today?"

JJ gave him a funny look. "Everyone here came on a boat, brother. Seriously, though, if she changes her mind, call me. It's impossible to find your way around these islands without a guide."

Eric nodded. "Will do." He turned to go back to the villa and saw Abby walking down the beach away from him. He started to walk after her, but then slowed and stopped. She wanted to be alone, or she would have come to him. He decided to give her some space.

The two of them could certainly go on hiding, and frankly, he wouldn't mind that one bit. Given the media circus that was certainly awaiting their return, he had no desire to give up their simple quiet life. But they couldn't continue to live it here. The best thing to do would be to find a new place where they could disappear permanently. Someplace they could live their simple, quiet life together, undisturbed. But he knew that until she came to that decision on her own, she'd fight it. He figured he would let her sort things out. For now, the sun was getting low and his stomach was getting hungry. He decided to make a small dinner and put some aside for Abby. No doubt she would be hungry when she got back.

He stood on the steps of their deck, watching her walk farther and farther away. He wondered how many more of these beautiful sunsets they would be able to enjoy on their beach. Despite her insistence that they weren't leaving, he knew it wouldn't be many.

7

ABBY RETURNED several hours later. Eric had set up a fire on the beach, but it had burned down to just embers. Walking through the open doors and into the villa, she found him asleep, sitting up in an armchair, with a book on his chest. She didn't understand how he fell asleep reading, but she often found him like that, whether he was reading late at night or in the middle of the day.

She removed the book from his chest and set it on the table next to the candle he had been reading by. He woke up briefly, and after kissing him on the forehead, she told him to get in bed, which he did on autopilot. She chuckled a little under her breath as she put the covers over him. She knew he wouldn't remember this in the morning.

Abby poured herself a glass of water from the tall steel water purifier, similar to the one they had seen in Robert's cave the night they had first met him. Looking down onto the counter, she spotted the card that their guest had left.

It was just his name printed in simple block lettering: **JJ ANDREWS**. On the back was a number in the 617 area code, which she was not familiar with. Handwritten under that was another number that began with (011)63, followed by more numbers than made sense for a phone number. Maybe it was a code for something. She didn't want to know. Knowing full well it was unrealistic, she just wanted to pretend that today never happened.

Holding the card in her hand, she stared at it while she thought about her decision. He found her. No one else had—yet. She knew she didn't want her old life back. When she had escaped from *Trial Island* and read the letter she had written to herself, it was obvious that the old Abby knew that she should not go back to her old life. After her brief run in with Bryce, she absolutely did not care to find out how she wound up with someone like him.

She walked out through the open doors and squatted next to the glowing embers. Holding the card between her fingers, she gave it one last look before flinging it onto the dying fire. She watched as the laminate on the card warped and curled a bit as the edges turned brown. A moment later it burst into flames, and within a few seconds was nothing more than a wisp of an ember that floated up from the fire and drifted off toward the sea.

Abby watched as it disappeared from view. Thinking about the letter she had written to herself, one line stuck out – *There are lives that depend on your ignorance*. She didn't know whose life, or if that still applied with Bryce out of the picture. She hadn't been that specific in her letter. She did know that she was very happy and content not knowing what she had left behind, and did not see the benefit of getting her memory back.

Walking into the villa, she closed the French doors behind her, stripped off her shorts, and climbed into bed next to Eric. *Today did not happen*, she thought to herself. *I wish I could forget that, too.*

*   *   *

Eric waited as several days went by. Morning jogs, walks through the forest, trips to the market, afternoon naps and the regular evening socialization. Abby was carrying on with her routine as normal, and Eric followed suit, only he was watching, and waiting.

The first day he wondered at what point she would bring up JJ. Eric had run into him at the market that day, and he had asked about her.

"How's she doing?"

His genuine concern struck Eric. This man who had tracked them down – or really tracked Abby down – didn't know them. But the look in his eyes, the crinkle of his brow, and the tone of his voice said that he was truly worried.

"I think she's OK," Eric said. "She went for a long walk last night and seems to be thinking things through. This has got to be a real trip for her, you know?"

"Yeah," JJ conceded. "I can't imagine what's going on in her head right now." He paused, looking from the market to the boatyard and the blue ocean beyond.

"Don't worry, Robert has taken care of me. Your secret here is safe, alright? But seriously, someone else is going to find you soon. I'm sure of that, and when they do…" He spun his finger around in the air, indicating everything around them, "…this place is going to turn into a circus."

Eric laughed a bit. "We're in the middle of nowhere. I don't see that happening."

"You're underestimating two things, my friend. How big your story, well, Abby's story, is back home. It went away for a while, but since it hit the news that she's a mob wife on top of everything else, you can't turn anywhere without hearing about the story or seeing her face. Second, the media will go great distances for a good story." He looked around, "This place isn't going to know what hit it."

"I appreciate the concern, but I'm sure Abby will come to her senses eventually. Hell, if she doesn't want to go back home, I'm totally fine with that. We'll just go and hide someplace else."

JJ looked at him hard, "You at least have to get her to talk to Robert, OK? It's important. He'll convince her."

The second day, Eric figured she was still thinking and didn't want to talk about it. She hadn't brought up the subject, and he figured that meant he shouldn't either. One thing he knew about Abby – if she set her mind to something, that was it. She had to bring up the topic before he tried to help her along.

By the third day, he began to worry if she was giving

their situation any thought at all. This was a major point in her life. It was a defining moment. He loved their life here, too, but if he were in her shoes, he'd be looking for a way out. She didn't need to make a snap decision, but she needed to decide something.

That same day, he found himself helping out in the market in the afternoon. Jay wanted to rearrange some of the heavier produce stands and needed his help. The sun was hot, and it had been a long afternoon, but they got it done before the evening rush.

JJ came by just as they were finishing up and asked Eric, "Got a minute?"

"Sure thing, boss," Eric said with a smile.

They took up residence at a corner table in the barroom, where JJ bought them a couple of American beers.

"Has she talked to Robert yet?"

Eric shook his head.

Of course, JJ already knew the answer. He had spoken to Robert just an hour ago. "Listen, Eric, if you think it would help for me to talk to her again, I will. But otherwise, I can't really stick around here too much longer. Robert is a great man and pays me very well, but I've spent the last few months exclusively searching for you guys. I've got other clients, and frankly, if I don't get back east soon, I'm not going to have much of a business to go back to. You've got my info and Robert's, and he knows where you are, too. Unless I'm escorting you back to him soon, I'm going to take off."

Eric thought about it. "I get it. She's stubborn. Honestly, I wouldn't hold my breath. I think she'll come around eventually, but you might be waiting a long time."

Silence hung in the air for a few moments while they thought about that. "So," Eric wondered aloud, "what else is going on back home, besides us?"

They spent the next hour, and a couple more beers, talking sports, politics, and those things men talk about. They laughed like old friends. As the place started filling up with young men giving up work for the day, they decided to move on.

"Listen, Eric, you seem like a good guy. Try to talk some sense into her, OK?"

"I will, I will."

"I'm heading out tomorrow, alright? It's going to take me a few days to cross all these damn time zones to get back to my own bed and catch up on my own life. I gave you one of my cards, right?"

"Yes, sir."

"If she changes her mind, give me a call. The other number on there is Robert's office in London. It's his private line. Who knows where in the world he'll be, but his assistant will get you through to him. Seriously, have Abby call him, OK?"

Eric reached out and shook his hand. "She will."

"Alright. It was great to meet you. If you're ever in Boston, look me up."

Eric walked past the end of the village, into the trees, and down the dirt road toward their villa. He wondered, *With Bryce out of the picture, what is she so afraid of?* He decided the only way to find out would be to ask her.

*   *   *

Abby had been going through her usual routine over the past three days, but her mind was elsewhere. *Did I make the right decision? Of course you did*, she would tell herself. She could not go back. She was scared to find out who she was. Granted, it led to this life, but even she had to admit that was about to drastically change.

As she walked along the beach, her thoughts drifted to her sister. If she did go back, Sarah would be the first person she contacted. Of course, not knowing what transpired over the past ten years or so, she had to remind herself that maybe that wouldn't be the case in reality. They were typical sisters. They had their arguments, but they always made up and had each other's back. Until that last time.

Sarah was so mad at her. Losing their parents was tough on both of them, but especially for Abby. Sarah was a few years older and had always assumed a maternal role over Abby, especially in the months after their parents passed away. Abby was in college at the time, and when her grades began slipping, Sarah got on her. It was the fall

67

semester of her senior year, and Sarah said that she should take the rest of the semester off and start up again in the spring.

"So what if you're there an extra semester, or even an extra year?" she asked.

Abby didn't see it the same way. Yes, she was struggling, but where would she go? She couldn't go back home to stay at her parent's house. It was big and empty and would not do the least bit to help her through her mourning. And she wasn't about to move in with her sister. Abby felt that if she left school, she might not come back, and didn't want to take that chance.

She was lost, sad, and unsure of her future when she met Rick. He had personality, money, and weed. She first started smoking with a friend after going back to school right after her parents' funeral. She had never done it before, but she immediately became a regular user. Her problems disappeared when she was high, and she liked that.

Rick came into town shortly thereafter. He was a supplier, not a dealer. She met him at a party and was immediately drawn to him. One thing led to another, and they became an item. She passed all of her classes that semester out of pity from her professors. The poor girl had lost her parents, so, of course, she was having a tough time. In the spring, as she started spending more time with Rick, the wheels came off. She attended class less and less and never saw her friends anymore. She was becoming a different person.

Sarah was constantly telling her she had to get rid of him; that he was bringing her down. "Mom and Dad are rolling in their graves," she would repeatedly say. When Abby couldn't graduate because she failed one of her last classes, Sarah lost it. They had a screaming match over the phone that ended with Sarah saying, "I don't even know you anymore! You are not Abby. Whoever you are, lose my number until my sister comes back!"

Abby hung up. She was furious at her sister for telling her how to live her life. She was furious at her parents for leaving her. And she was furious at God for taking them from her.

The next day, driving over to Rick's apartment, she got stuck in traffic in front of the college. She didn't realize why until she found herself driving past the quad where a tent was set up and the graduation ceremony was about to begin. There were thousands of students in her graduating class, preparing to receive their diploma and be unleashed onto the world.

And where was she going? To see her boyfriend and smoke up.

That was her wake-up call. She pulled the car over and called Rick, telling him she couldn't come by. The next day, she enrolled in the make-up course being held over the summer intercession. She tried calling her sister over the following weeks, but her calls when straight to voicemail and were never returned. Finally, she stopped leaving messages and soon thereafter, stopped calling at all.

Her class was only five weeks and would be done by

the beginning of July. She would return home after that and confront her sister directly. She would show her that she'd put her life back on track, and that it was time to move forward.

The last week before she was to go home, Rick showed up at her apartment. He wanted to make up. He wanted to repent for whatever he'd done and wasn't taking no for an answer. He was charming, and he wound up spending the night.

He was still there when she got home the next afternoon from class. She kicked him out, but only after telling him that she couldn't be with him anymore; that he wasn't good for her. He left, saying that he would see her around, but the days went by with no sign of Rick.

Abby finished her class and got her diploma. She still couldn't get through to her sister, so she decided to ride out her lease until the end of the month before packing up and heading home. She spent most of the next few weeks at the beach, in between hunting for a job. At the end of the month, as she was packing up, Rick showed up again. This time he didn't leave, and they spent the rest of the summer together.

Abby knew she had to get her life in order and he couldn't be part of that, but there was something about him that kept drawing her back in. Maybe it was his looks, maybe his money, or maybe the slight air of danger he brought to her life. More than likely, it was all three.

Outside their villa, Abby kicked the sand in frustration. As hard as she had tried over the past year, she had no specific memories of the past ten years, and how the changes in her life had worked out. That bothered her to no end. She did know that life had not been good to her, but lacked any details.

Do I really want to go back and re-live what happened?

Her instinct said no. She had a good life now and felt that she shouldn't mess with it. Still, something tugged at her mind as she tried to go to sleep at night. It was an unquenched curiosity. *What was so important to forget that I had my own memory erased? Who am I trying to protect? Me, or someone else?* She fell asleep thinking about this, and those thoughts haunted her dreams all night.

8

THEY WERE BOTH a little sleep deprived. Eric usually slept like a rock, but Abby's tossing and turning all night kept him awake. When Abby tiptoed out of the bathroom early in the morning, Eric was already making his morning tea.

He looked at her. "What are you so afraid of?"

She rubbed her eyes, asking, "What are you talking about?"

"You know exactly what I'm talking about, so stop pretending that our lives are not going to change. We have to address this."

She walked away shaking her head. "I don't know what you're saying, Eric."

Eric prided himself on his even temperament, but he was in no mood to be even-tempered today. He yelled at her back, "Abby, stop it! Whether you like it or not, we've got to make some changes. This has happened, and we have to talk about it!"

She walked down the steps and plopped down on their unmade bed, staring out at the pounding surf. She tried to wipe the tears from her eyes, but they wouldn't stop coming.

Eric sat down next to her and handed her a tissue, "Hey, sorry I yelled, but we've got to talk about this."

"I just…" She was trying to compose herself before she spoke, but couldn't.

"It's OK to cry, you know. You are human, I think… right?" He smiled with a comforting twinkle in his eye.

Abby cracked a slight smile back. After drying her eyes, she gestured out the doors with her hands. "All this. It's so beautiful. I don't want to give up what we have. I love our little world."

"So we'll change our geography and build a new world together. We can do that, you know. We did it once and can do it again. We don't have to go back to our old lives."

"What if we can't? What if we have to go back?"

He shook his head. "No one is making us."

Abby was quiet for a long time before she spoke. "I'm afraid."

"Of what?"

"Of what I've got locked up here." She tapped her temple with her finger. "I'm thinking of getting my memory back, but I'm scared. And you should be, too."

He put an arm around her and thought a minute before he said, "He's gone. He's gone for good, and you've got nothing to be scared of anymore."

"I'm not scared of him, Eric. I'm scared of losing you. What if there's something in my past you can't handle? What if I'm not someone who you can be with? What if I'm not someone *I* can be with?"

"I love you, Abby, and there's nothing about your past that can change that."

Abby gazed into his eyes. "I keep playing all these scenarios in my mind. What if there's someone else? What if that's who I'm protecting?" He smiled back at her, a little dumbstruck, not sure what to say. "Whatever I left behind was important enough to give up my entire life. Why would I do that? Why would I forbid myself to know what's in my past?"

"Abby, whatever it is, it's in the past. It's been over a year since you walked away from that life, and you haven't gone back. I'm sure if you left someone behind, they've moved on."

"I don't know. I get this feeling in my stomach that says I can't hide forever. In my letter, I was obviously scared for my own life, but for others, too. The part that says *'lives depend on your ignorance'* keeps sticking with me." She was thoughtful for a moment, and then spoke without taking her eyes from the ocean. "What if whatever I left behind was so important that I would never be able to keep myself from returning if I knew about it?"

Eric sighed. "Then there's only one way to find out. You can't torture yourself about this for the rest of your life."

"But…"

"But nothing." He hugged her tightly and laid her down on the bed. "I love you, and that means I love everything that comes with you. We'll deal with whatever you've got locked up in there, together."

She closed her eyes. Why did JJ have to find them? Why did Bryce have to die? *Damn it*, life would have been easier if he was still out there. She cursed herself for the thought. He was a piece of shit who deserved to die. She regretted that she didn't end him when she had the chance. That would have avoided this whole mess.

"Abby," Eric said.

She lay still with her eyes closed. She knew that when she opened them, this life was over.

"Abby?" Eric said again.

She prayed that everything would work out and opened her eyes. "OK."

"OK?"

She smiled, "Yes."

"Good. I don't want to rush you, but JJ said he's heading out today. Let's catch him before he leaves so we don't have to wait for him to come back." Eric knew he was rushing her, but he did not want to give Abby the opportunity to change her mind.

They got dressed, donned their satchels and headed down the path to the village hand in hand.

*   *   *

"Left? As in gone?" Abby asked the man who ran the boat yard.

Jay translated and the two men went back and forth for a couple of rounds. Jay turned to Abby and Eric. "He says he left last night. He needed some supplies we don't have here, so he went over to Kam," Jay said, indicating the island in the distance that was the more populated twin of their island.

Eric was visibly frustrated. "He said he was heading out this morning."

"He went over last night," Jay said, "Right around sunset. It is three hours to get over there, so he may still be there."

Eric sighed. "Well, at least he's not far." He looked at Jay. "I'm going to run back to the house. I've got his number. Can you find a phone for us while I do that? Hopefully we catch him before he heads out."

"Yes, my neighbor has a telephone. I'll make sure it is working."

As the two men began to go in separate directions, Abby spoke up. "Um…"

"I'll be right back," Eric said. "Unless you think you can get there and back faster."

"Well, I can, we both know that."

"Then go!" Eric urged her to hurry, knowing she was right.

Abby shook her head. "No."

Eric raised an eyebrow, worried that she'd changed her mind. "Why?"

"Where's that card with JJ's information?" Abby asked.

Eric knew he had left it on the counter, but hadn't seen it in a few days. "I don't know."

"Well, I do. I got rid of it."

"You what?"

"I was really upset. I'm sorry."

Eric kissed her on the forehead and smiled. "It's OK. We haven't emptied the trash in days; I'll dig it out. I'll be back, OK?"

He got two steps before Abby spoke again. "You can't."

He turned. "I can't what?"

"You can't dig it out of the trash." She paused, staring at him with a guilty look, "I burned it."

Eric deflated. "Damn it."

Abby spoke. "We'll just go after him. He just left last night, and it's what, eight in the morning? He's probably still there."

"It takes three hours to get over there Abby. Will he still be there when we get there?"

"Well, every minute we sit here debating is lost time. Let's go!"

Eric's mind was trying to process the timing of everything. He'd been to Kam a few times with Jay to pick up supplies when they were building the villa. There was only one major harbor, and that's where JJ would be going. Abby was right. Every minute spent debating was a minute they lost catching up to him. Eric looked at Jay and indicated the boat master. "Ask him what he's got that will get us over there."

The man who ran the boatyard had a few loaners that he would rent out for a day or two when someone needed to make a quick trip, but none were in great condition. He offered them the best available, a twenty-seven footer with a small cabin big enough for a bed and a two-person kitchen table. It was easily thirty years old. It was fiberglass and the once gleaming-white hull was a dullish brown now. The vinyl seats built into the deck were ripped, sewn back together, or patched with duct tape. The entire boat had a musty smell that came with the better part of three decades in the water, but it started, and the boat master guaranteed it would run without a problem.

He usually rented it for twenty dollars a day, American, for these type of trips. Eric opened his satchel and peeled off two one hundred dollar bills and stuffed them into the man's palm. "Just in case." He and Abby had both carried the satchels with them everywhere they went for the past several months. Their "go bags," as they referred to them, were small enough that Eric could usually stuff his into his cargo shorts pocket yet contained everything they needed to walk away and not look back if they had to.

Within twenty minutes, the boat was gassed up and pulling from the dock. Ben came running down to the boatyard to the end of the dock where Jay stood watching the boat head towards the sea. "Where are they going?"

Jay put an arm around his son, "They're going to find the man who came for them."

"Are they coming back?"

"I don't know, Ben. I hope so."

Ben called out, "Miss Abby!"

Abby turned to see the young boy standing at the end of the dock next to his father. She smiled and waved. "We'll be back!" She blew him a kiss, then turned back to Eric.

The second they left the mouth of the boatyard, Eric

called out, "Hold on!" as he throttled the engine forward which made the front of the boat pitch up. As it leveled off, he eased the throttle all the way forward, and sent the aging propeller on the back of the boat spinning full speed and thrusting them toward the island in the distance.

The wind whipped through Abby's hair as the aging hull crashed through the waves. She looked back one more time to see Ben standing at the end of the dock watching them. *We'll be back soon. Don't worry, Ben*, she thought to herself, unsure exactly whom she was trying to convince.

9

SEVERAL DAYS LATER, after stopping at four ports on three different islands looking for JJ, Abby was sure that Ben must have branded her a liar by now. They had missed JJ by a matter of a few hours on Kam. As they initially debated whether to try and catch him, he had left Kam before they ever pulled out of port to go there. When they arrived to find him gone, they put their heads together with that harbormaster and made an educated guess as to where he would head next.

They had actually guessed correctly, but wound up at a harbor on the wrong side of the island. When they got to the right harbor they found out that they had missed him by half a day. There was no doubt as to where he would be heading next. There was a highly populated island to the north where he would certainly make a stop to gas up before making the long trek to the big island to catch the only international flight out of the area. He was either headed there or back to Robert's island. Either way, he would be going north.

They spent the night rocking in the boat parked safely in harbor. It was too dangerous for unseasoned boaters like themselves to make the trip to the next island overnight, and it was so late in the day that it didn't make sense to go out for a couple of hours, then drop anchor for the night. They left at daybreak, and by early afternoon pulled into port at their destination.

Eric recognized the island as soon as they landed. They had sunk Robert's boat off this very coast about ten months ago and had begun the second half of their journey to find their new home. Their boat was running rough and needed some work, but Eric was certain he could find their way back to Robert's island from here.

"Let's see if we can find JJ first. It would be a heck of a lot easier with a guide," Abby said.

"I've got to figure out what's going on with the engine anyway. You go ahead and see what you can find. I'll talk to the harbormaster to see if there's someone here who can take a look at her for us." In reality, Eric didn't need someone who knew their way around a boat. He was nearly certain it was the air filter, which was a quick fix he could do himself. What he really wanted was to find a chart and see if he could plot his way back to Robert's island on his own if he needed to.

Abby grabbed her go bag, which contained a respectable amount of money, a fake passport and other identification, a travel kit with a small comb, toothbrush and toothpaste, a few tampons, and an extra pair of underwear. While it was anything and everything she needed to go on the run, she had been on her second pair of underwear for a couple of days now. Although she had scrubbed her clothes a few days ago, she was beginning to wonder at what point they would get up and walk away on their own.

"I'm going to look for a couple of new things to wear. I'll find something for you, too, unless you want to do some shopping on your own," she said with a devilish grin.

Eric raised his eyebrow and gave her a look that said, *Really?* He hated shopping. "Anything you pick will be fine, I'm sure."

Abby gave him a quick kiss before heading off to find a market, leaving him to take care of the boat.

It took him all of five minutes to remove a panel and take out the air filter to find that it was undeniably filthy. *No wonder the engine has been running so rough; the thing is choking for air.* He wasn't holding out hope that he would find a new one for this thirty-some-odd-year old beast of an engine. But with a vacuum and ten minutes, he could get it good enough. He had performed the same operation on his pickup truck back in Texas more times than he could count. What he really wanted were some charts of the waters around here.

He went up to the boathouse and introduced himself to an elderly local man with deep brown skin and wiry white hair who appeared to be, if not running the place, at least keeping an eye on things.

Holding up the filthy air filter he asked, "You don't know where I can get one of these, do you?"

The old man behind the counter shook his head no. Eric wasn't sure if that meant, "No, I don't know where you can get one of those" or "No, I don't speak English, and I have no idea what you're saying." Either way, Eric figured a vacuum would do.

As if it would help make his point, slowly and a little too loudly, he asked, "Do you have a vacuum?"

The man nodded and put down his paper to produce a small vacuum with a handheld attachment from behind his desk.

Eric thanked him and stepped outside. After banging the dust off the filter then methodically cleaning it, he returned the vacuum and thanked the man who just nodded, barely looking up from his newspaper.

"Do you have any maps?" Eric asked. The man looked at him a little confused. "Maps? Charts?" Eric waved his hands in the air miming what he thought was a universal sign for map. He was met with only disappointment. He looked around frustrated, until his eyes settled on a world map on the wall. Walking over to it, he patted it with his open palm, "This. Do you have one of these, for the islands?" Eric waved his hands some more, hoping to make his point.

The man produced a heavily folded paper from his top drawer and stated more than asked, "You're American? Ten dollar."

"Alright!" Eric was thrilled. "Now we're in business." He knew he was overpaying. More than overpaying, he was getting ripped off royally, but he didn't care.

It took him a few minutes to figure out where he was on the map. Once he did, he let out a whistle at the multitude of small green blobs that dotted the blue of the ocean.

Looking up at the man he asked, "Do you know where *Trial Island* is?"

The man just shook his head no, then returned to his paper.

Well, it was worth a shot, Eric thought. "Thank you again," he said, waving the map and the freshly cleaned air filter as he left. Returning to the boat, he quickly reinstalled the air filter and turned over the engine. It rumbled for a moment, and then settled into a deep purr like a lion getting its chin rubbed.

That problem solved, Eric cut the engine and spread out his map on the deck of the boat. After he figured out their location for the second time, he marked it with a pencil so he wouldn't have trouble finding it again. Then he stared. He stared for a very long time, as if waiting for the map to speak to him and tell him which way to go to find Robert. "Damn, there's a lot of those things," he said to himself, looking at the many islands charted on the map.

Staring off into space, thinking about the way he came last time he and Abby went through here, he found himself staring at a familiar boat. The name was QUEST II. He mulled this over, preoccupied with figuring out how to find their way back to Robert's island. Finally, it dawned him. *Isn't that the boat that almost hit me?*

Eric stood to peer over the side and get a closer look

at the boat that was parked in a slip about twenty yards away. "Sonofabitch, I think that's the one. I'll be damned."

His next thought was that maybe it was JJ's boat. He sat on his deck with the chart laid out in front of him, but he was watching QUEST II and waiting for some sign of life. If it's JJ, then problem solved. He didn't have to figure out where he was going.

He arranged himself so he could study the chart, but kept the dock in the corner of his eye so that he would surely notice anyone coming or going. Staring at the chart, he willed himself to retrace the steps he had taken ten months ago; the last time they had found their way to this island.

It had taken them three days to get here, and they had traveled in a southeasterly direction the entire time. That much he remembered. They made two stops on the way here, both at dusk, for gas and food. Doing some rudimentary math, he tried to figure out approximately how far they could travel in a day. Finding islands that fit within that pattern, he ultimately settled on two islands far to the north that must be Trial Island and Robert's island. The fact that they were tiny and unnamed on this chart only strengthened his opinion.

Eric finally looked up from the chart and gave a little fist pump, before he noticed that there was a man on the boat that he had been trying to watch. The man, in fact, was watching him, but quickly turned away when Eric looked up. It was not JJ. He was tall like JJ, and even had the curly hair, but it was not JJ. The man on the boat was a big guy, not out of shape, but just large and broad, whereas JJ was built like a swimmer. His curly hair was longer, and he had a full beard. "Oh, well," Eric said to himself. He was sure he knew where they were going anyway, and was very excited to share the news with Abby.

* * *

Much like the island they had called home until a few days ago, the market on this island was right near the harbor. This harbor was much larger and busier, and therefore the same could be said about the market. This was the most populous place they had visited since going into their self-imposed exile, but Abby was comfortably sure that with her long brunette curls now dyed dirty blonde, straightened, and tied up in a bandana, and her right leg bared of its hunting knife, she would not be recognizable.

As had become habit over their past few stops, she asked a few men working the gas lines at the edge of the boatyard if anyone meeting JJ's description had passed through in the past day or so. As usual, the men were less than helpful, and she walked away unsure if they had understood the question, though she was reasonably sure they were watching her backside as she strolled down the dock and exited to the market.

Assuming that JJ would have the same needs as they did, she made her necessary rounds through the market to pick up some food and water, all the while asking the various vendors if they had seen the tall, curly haired American. None of them had. Given how many times she had done this, she no longer became frustrated – she just smiled and moved on.

She came close with a vendor at a produce stand. "Yes, yes, I have seen this man," he said.

Abby lit up. "When? Today?"

"Yes, yes, today I see him. Very tall, bushy curly hair." The man used his hands to indicate around his cheeks, "Big beard. American, not clean," he said, shaking his head.

Abby sighed. Another strikeout.

The man went on. "He seem in a hurry. Probably trying to race the storm."

Abby gave him a puzzled look.

"Big storm coming," the man said. "He said he leaves before the storm. I tell him no, no, no." He threw his hands down, exasperated. "American no listen to me. He will see. Bad storm." He turned, shaking his head.

After purchasing some fresh vegetables and fish that she would cook with some rice back on the boat, she wandered further into the market to find the clothing vendors. She bypassed the ones selling local garb and visited the carts that featured baskets and shelves overflowing with American brands manufactured here. Not wanting to travel too heavy, she picked out a pair of shorts and a few pair of underwear for each of them, as well as another tank top for herself and a couple shirts for Eric.

Walking by a rack of sundresses, she stopped to admire one in the front. It was a pattern she has seen a million times, but was apparently still in style. There were large shapes of tropical flowers on a white background. The flowers were a beautiful orange, the color of cantaloupe, and the front was low cut and trimmed with a simple lace that also trimmed the bottom of the dress. She held it up in front of herself in a full-length mirror.

It was fun, flirty, and wasn't practical in the least. Eric would like it, though, so why not give him something nice to look at? She smiled at the thought.

The woman manning the cart noticed her and walked over, standing behind her. "The color is beautiful with your hair," she said.

Abby pushed her sunglasses on top of her head so she could see the colors better. The woman was right. Her shoulder-length blonde locks and the cantaloupe looked great together. She smiled at the woman. "How much?"

She asked, "American?"

"I can pay dollars, yes."

The woman smiled and said in her accented English, "You look familiar. How long you been here?"

Abby lowered her sunglasses back over her eyes and smiled uncomfortably. "Just passing through. How much?"

The woman looked over everything Abby had in her arms, then seemed to take in what Abby was wearing – a less-than-impressive shorts and tank top combo that she had been wearing for a week straight now. Abby was obviously American, but didn't give the appearance of having much money on hand. "Eighteen," the woman said, indicating everything Abby had in her arms.

Abby returned to the boat to find a rather excited Eric. He flashed her a smile. "I know where we're going!"

"You do?"

"Yep, come here." He still had the chart spread out.

He put his arm around her and pulled her close. Abby smiled. He smelled freshly clean, like he had just gotten out of the shower. She loved being close to him.

"Look," he said, indicating a large island. "This is where we are right now." His finger traced up and to the right, "and this is where we are going." He indicated two very small islands. "The one on the right, that's where Robert is; the one just to the left is Trial Island. I'm sure of it."

Abby nodded. "How long to get there?"

"I figure about three days. We'll stop each day, like we did on the way here."

Abby thought about it. "You're sure?"

"I'm pretty sure."

"How do you know?"

"Honestly, it's just my best guess. I figure it was three

days to get here from there, and I know we were heading southeast to wind up here, so I just did the math and started looking."

Abby looked over the chart. "But there are so many," she said, indicating all the green dots.

"What have we got to lose?"

Abby thought about it. She desperately wanted to find their way back to Robert, but didn't want to keep wasting time by island hopping. She silently cursed herself for disposing of JJ's contact information, but no amount of beating herself up would change what she had done.

Eric could see that she was hesitant. "How about this?" he said. "We're still stopping a few times between here and there. If nothing else, we're getting closer. Plus we know JJ must be heading in the same direction. We'll keep asking around for him, but we can ask around about *Trial Island,* too. People must have heard of it and know where it is, right?"

"Eric, if we start asking about the island, people are going to recognize us. We're not on our little island off the grid anymore."

"You're right," he said, then had a second thought as he tucked her hair behind her ear. "Actually, babe, I don't know if they'd recognize you." He stood back to take her in and nodded his head. "You're blonde now, and you put on a couple of pounds. And with those sunglasses, someone would have to be a pretty big fan to pick up on it."

"Put on a couple of pounds?"

Eric sighed. Of course that was all she heard. "I mean you look normal now. You were super skinny on the show after eating so little for all that time. Too skinny, like one of those waif supermodels that are built like little boys." He pulled her close. "Now you look like a real woman." He kissed her. "An irresistibly beautiful woman."

"OK," she said, "you're off the hook for now, but watch it." She smiled and kissed him again. "I got you a present." She reached into the bag and pulled out the underwear, shorts, and T-shirt. As Eric was in the cabin changing, Abby added, "I got you something else, too. You'll see it later."

Eric popped out of the cabin in his new clothes. It was midday, and he was eager to get moving, "How about I see it over a romantic dinner at sea?"

Abby shook her head. "I meant to tell you – I heard there's a big storm coming. We should probably sit tight until it passes."

Eric looked around at the sky. Aside from a few puffs of white, it was clear blue as far as he could see. "Where did you hear this?"

"A guy in the market told me."

"You see anything going on out there?"

Abby looked around and conceded, "No, but he was pretty insistent."

Eric looked up again, "We must be able to see for thirty miles out there, and I don't see a thing. If we head out now, we can go until dark, then drop anchor around one of these islands out here." He indicated a small group of islands an inch or so away from their current location on the map. "I'm seeing a candle-lit dinner at sea in our future. If you're lucky, maybe we'll even rock the boat afterwards." He winked at her.

"If *I'm* lucky?" she laughed. Looking up at the sky one more time, she said, "You're right. I assume the boat is ready to go?"

"Yep. It was the air filter. It was filthy, but now it's squeaky clean and ready for action."

"Well, wait are we waiting for?"

After getting everything in order, Eric fired up the engine and eased from the slip. As they drove toward the open sea, he took one last look at QUEST II and the bearded man standing on the deck who was having a very animated conversation on his phone.

As Eric turned back to the sea, Abby wrapped an arm around him from the side, and he put an arm around her shoulder to pull her close.

The man on QUEST II hung up the phone and turned to watch Eric ease forward on the throttle and head for open water. The man threw his phone onto his seat, ran his hands through his bushy hair, and shouted, "Damn it!"

10

THEY HAD MOTORED toward their destination for six hours when they saw a cluster of small islands in the twilight. They picked a calm spot in the water between two of them to drop anchor for the night. Abby was putting the finishing touches on dinner and brought it up to eat on the deck while they bobbed gently in the water and watched the stars.

Looking up, Abby said, "I'm going to miss this view." There were no large islands or cities of any kind for a hundred miles. The cloudless sky revealed so many stars, that it was hard to see just one. The sky was brilliantly lit with stars as far as the eye could see.

"Me, too," Eric sighed. "We'll be back, though."

"Promise?"

Eric laughed. "Absolutely."

"But you don't even know me. Not really, anyway.

There's so much about me that I don't know myself..." Her voice trailed off.

"What are you talking about 'I don't know you'? I know you plenty. We went through hell together and came out the other side to live another day. We've been living together ever since. So your memory is a little spotty – you're still you." He squeezed her tightly. "Whatever happened, happened. It's in the past. I know exactly who you are, and I love who you are today, and that includes whatever surprises come with that."

They retired to the cabin early so they could get an early start in the morning, but they didn't do any sleeping for a while.

It was not a very large boat, and so it was not a very large cabin. Coming down the steep steps from the deck of the boat, there was a small door immediately on the right that opened into the tiny bathroom. On the left were a stovetop and a few cabinets. A small, two-person table also stood on the left, with the bed at the very front of the boat. Abby and Eric lay in the bed breathing heavy and exhausted, when the wind began to pick up.

Abby felt the boat begin to rock a little more as she listened to the wind while it whistled up above through the open cabin door. She was just starting to drift off when a particularly strong gust slammed the door shut at the top of the stairs.

Abby sat up half dressed. "What was that?"

Eric didn't stir.

She crawled out of bed and, guided by the very weak nightlight, made her way to the stairs. Climbing to the top and opening the door, she stepped onto the deck and looked around. The wind whipped her hair around, and the force made her wary enough to grab onto a safety bar by the steering wheel. The boat rocked heavily despite the relatively calm waters they had chosen several hours ago.

The storm is here.

They had picked a good spot to drop anchor, but in retrospect, they should have docked somewhere. Eric, ever the romantic, thought that a candle-lit dinner at sea would be a wonderful way to spend the night. It was. However, as the boat began to pitch more steeply with each passing swell, Abby began to get a knot in her stomach that could ruin any romantic evening.

She knew from experience that this area was prone to exceptionally harsh and fast-moving storms, and when she looked up, she knew it was bad. The sky was completely black. There was not a star to be seen; not even a sliver of moonlight. They had better get moving, and fast. She knew they would not be able to navigate through a port that they were unfamiliar with, but if they could get close to land or find a cove or harbor, they would be better off than sitting out here in the open water.

Abby went to run down the stairs as a huge swell lifted the boat and pitched it hard to the right, and as it rode the side of a wave, it sent Abby airborne, past the last few stairs and crashing to the floor.

"Eric! Wake up!"

He sat up, groggy and unable to make out anything in the faint light. "What?"

"We've got to get moving. The storm is here!"

As if on cue, the cabin lit up as a flash of lightning pierced the sky above. Seconds later, the hard crash of thunder told them it wasn't far away.

Eric quickly jumped out of bed as Abby got back to her feet. Just then, another swell pitched them hard to the right again, and they both slammed into the wall. Then, just as quickly, it pitched to the left and they hit the other side of the boat. They both realized that the waves were hitting them from the side, so they were going sideways down the backside of the waves.

This had Eric slightly panicked, "We've got to be going into the swell, not sideways like that. If we get hit with one much bigger, we'll flip."

He ran up the stairs with Abby following behind. The rain had started and was being driven sideways by the high wind. It stung Eric's bare skin as it pelted his back, and he immediately regretted not tossing on a shirt. He grabbed the keys from the storage compartment. He had to get the boat moving soon before a strong enough wave hit them from the side and capsized them.

There were several keys on the ring that was attached to a large, fist-sized piece of plastic, making it awkward to handle. He fumbled with the keys, trying to find the one for the engine. With the wind whipping around him and driving the rain into his eyes, it was no easy task.

Suddenly, the boat pitched hard again. Abby fell to the deck and Eric tripped over her. Arms flailing out, he searched for anything to grab onto as he tumbled toward the edge of the boat. He fell to the deck and slammed into the short wall at the edge of the boat. His right hand smashed onto the rail, sending the keys flying over board.

"Dammit!"

Abby managed to get a hand hold on one of the safety bars and into a standing position as the boat leveled off before pitching to the right as they slid down the back of the swell. She heard Eric scream as he hit the deck, and watched as he whipped his head around, looking in all directions in the water. His back was to her, but it was clear that he was searching over the rail for something. Seeing his empty hands gripping the railing, she realized the worst.

The keys went overboard!

Another bolt of lightning tore through the sky above, and as she heard the hard crash of thunder, she saw the bright orange floater that the keys were attached to barely ten feet from the boat. Abby didn't bother to take a second to process the thought. *Now or never*, she thought, as she ran uphill on the pitched deck and jumped as far from the boat as possible into the black ocean.

Eric hadn't seen her until she was airborne. It was futile, but he screamed as she hit the water, "Abby! No!"

Abby rubbed the water from her eyes and searched frantically for the keys. She figured she must have landed close to them.

"Abby, get back here! You're going to kill yourself!"

She ignored him. It took all of her concentration to keep her bearings and search the water as the wind-driven rain pelted down around her.

"Abby! Come on!"

She screamed back at him, "Turn on the light!"

"What?"

"Turn on the light! I can't see a thing!"

Eric ran over to the steering wheel, pointed the floodlight toward Abby, and hit the switch. Nothing. He flipped the switch on and off several more times. Still nothing.

He ran back to the rail. "Get back here!"

"Just turn on the fucking light!"

"I can't turn on the light without the keys!" Eric was screaming over the sounds of the storm, "Follow my voice and swim back here before you drown!"

She wasn't going back. Not without the keys. *I'm already in the water. They've got to be here somewhere.* She feared that if she didn't find the keys, they would both drown. She swam further from the boat.

"You're going the wrong way!" Eric was yelling, unsure if she could hear him above the noise of the wind and rain pounding the ocean. "Abby, you're going the wrong way! Damn it!" He looked around for a life jacket or anything else that might float. There was nothing on the deck.

He tore open a small door to a storage compartment by the steering wheel and found a life preserver. He screamed out to the sea, "Grab onto this!" She was at least twenty feet from the boat now, and he wasn't sure he could throw the light life jacket that far.

He was pitching into the wind, and hurtled the life jacket toward Abby with everything he had. The wind took it, and blew it straight back at him and over his head, carrying it at least twenty feet in the wrong direction on the other side of the boat. He cursed and looked back over the railing, straining his eyes to find Abby as he heard her shouting.

"I've got it!"

"OK, swim back! Follow my voice!"

She slid the elastic lanyard attached to the floating key ring over her wrist as she began paddling back, following Eric's voice.

He shouted, "Good! I see you!"

She swam hard, but suddenly couldn't see or hear him anymore. She called out, "Eric?"

As another bolt of lightning lit up the sky Abby saw only a wall of water in front of her. She was on one side of the wave; the boat was on the other. She swam in the direction it should be and finally saw it as she crested the top.

"Abby!"

The water calmed a bit between the swells, and she took advantage of that, swimming as hard as she could toward Eric and the boat, quickly closing the distance now that she knew where she was.

He reached over the edge, holding fast to the railing, as Abby reached up, but the rocking and bouncing kept them from connecting. As the boat suddenly bobbed toward her and bumped her hand, Abby was struck with the very real fear that if the boat suddenly lurched in her direction, it would hit her and she would be in big trouble.

"Lower the ladder in back," she called up to him. "I'll climb up there!"

Without hesitation, Eric ran to the back of the boat and unlatched the small ladder hinged to hang over a small wooden ledge on the back of the boat next to the dormant propeller. Abby came toward the back of the boat as the ladder splashed into the water.

"Come on," Eric called, reaching out toward her with one hand, holding onto the rail with the other.

Abby reached out, and while she couldn't grasp his hand, she managed to get a hold on the bottom rung of the ladder, which was under the water. She quickly grabbed onto the top rung with her other hand and held on as the bobbing boat seemed intent on shaking her off.

She called out, "I got it!"

Eric grabbed her hand to help her up. As she got her feet situated to climb, the boat bobbed and lunged, and her feet slipped. Eric lost his grip on her wet hand, and she went straight down into the water.

Abby popped back to the surface almost instantly. "I'm OK!"

"Give me your hand!"

She reached out to grasp his hand just inches over the water as he leaned precariously over the edge to get her. Just then, the boat bobbed and lunged again, and the small wooden ledge on the back of the platform came crashing down on Abby's head and she disappeared under the water.

"Abby! Abby!" Eric stood searching for her for a few moments before finally spotting her. She surfaced about ten feet from the back of the boat. She was face up and not moving. Without a second thought, he dove off the back of the boat and swam to her in seconds. He couldn't tell if she was breathing, but he didn't have time to mess around.

Wrapping his left arm through her shoulders and over her chest, he paddled back to the boat and grabbed onto the top rung of the ladder with his free hand. Adrenaline pumping hard through his veins, he lifted Abby out of the water with one arm and set her on the wooden ledge before quickly scrambling out himself and hoisting her back over the railing to set her down on the deck.

He leaned down to her face and felt her breath on his cheek. *Thank God she's breathing,* he thought as he let out a sigh. As he went to kiss her, the boat lurched hard again, snapping him back to reality and their predicament. He slid the keys off her wrist, found the one for the engine, and fired it up.

Eric jerked the wheel to the left and powered up the throttle, sending them up and over the next swell. As they came down the back side, he got a sinking feeling in his stomach, like he was on a roller coaster, but it was better than taking the waves from the side and risk being capsized.

He looked back at Abby, who lay still on the deck behind him. There was nothing he could do at the moment. *She's just got a bump on her head; she'll be OK,* he told himself. He spent the next hour riding waves, up, then down, up, then down. He couldn't see anything in front of him, and had no idea where he was anymore in relation to the islands. He just hoped he wasn't going to hit anything.

Eventually the storm took its leave as quickly as it had come. Over the course of an hour, the wind and rain died down. Clouds were starting to clear, and there was a faint glow in the distance that indicated dawn was coming. He still couldn't see much of anything, but once the water settled from enormous swells to ordinary waves, he set the engine to neutral and crouched next to Abby.

"Hey," he said, nudging her. "You in there?" He watched her. "You scared me half to death. You're crazy, do you know that?" He bent down and kissed her. Her eyes fluttered open as she smiled.

It was a few seconds before she realized that she was lying on the deck. She was soaked, but the warm engine was rumbling just beneath her, and she was alive. "What happened?"

Eric laughed. "You lost your damned mind and nearly lost your damned life, that's what happened."

She managed a chuckle.

"We're even now," he said.

She smiled and sat up, "Where are we?"

"I'm not sure." He stood and helped her get to a seat at the back of the boat before looking around. In the faint light he spotted an island. "Not sure what that is, but I think we're going to find out. Why don't you go put on something dry while I point us in that direction?" He helped her to her feet and gave her a kiss before she walked down the stairs into the cabin.

Eric put the boat back in gear and fed some more power to the throttle as he brought the nose of the boat around and motored them toward the island in the distance.

Down in the cabin, Abby put on her shorts and one of Eric's T-shirts. It wasn't a cold day, but she certainly had a chill in her bones from being drenched. She grabbed a blanket off the bed and wrapped it around herself before heading back up to sit with Eric on the deck. She felt the boat slow significantly as she approached the stairs. *We can't be there yet, can we?*

She was halfway up the stairs when the engine choked and died, and she heard Eric shout, "Son of a bitch!"

11

"WHAT HAPPENED?"

"We ran out of gas," Eric shook his head. He had spent the past few hours in survival mode. It never occurred to him how much fuel they were burning by taking on all the waves.

Abby looked to the island in the distance, still several miles away. "I don't think we can swim it."

"We won't have to," Eric said, yanking open the door from where he had retrieved the life preserver a few hours ago. "We've got back up." He smiled as he pulled out a small three-gallon gas can from the storage cabinet. "It's not full, and God knows how long it's been here, but it's better than nothing."

After pouring the gas into the tank, he pumped the throttle a few times to prime the engine, then turned the key. The engine whined and sputtered, but would not turn over. He cursed under his breath.

"Try it again. Maybe pump some more fuel in?"

Eric pumped the throttle and again tried to turn over the engine. It made a straining sound. It was trying, but just wasn't catching. "Come on!" he yelled at the boat, pumping the throttle again and turning the key. The engine whined, like a child's wind-up toy, and finally caught. He smiled as it rumbled to life. It belched and roared and made every sound but the right one. However, it was running, and that was all that mattered at the moment.

"It sounds awful."

"It's running," he said, pointing the boat toward the island and slowly increasing speed. The boat sputtered and the engine died. He started it again, cursing under his breath, and continued on.

They traveled slowly like this, stopping and starting, taking an hour to cover the two miles to land, until the boat limped into the harbor and took up residence in the nearest empty slip.

Abby hopped out and tied them up as the engine died for the last time.

A young man came running down the docks. He appeared to be local, probably in his early twenties, but when he opened his mouth he spoke perfect English, "You guys were out there last night?"

Abby nodded her head.

"Wow. That was a very bad storm. You were lucky to

ride it through!"

Eric smiled. "You're tellin' me! Damn boat almost left us marooned out there."

"Engine problems?"

"Yeah."

"Start it up. Let me take a look."

Eric started the engine. It sputtered, but it ran. It wouldn't idle at a constant speed, and after a few minutes, it choked again. "Spent the last two miles like this," Eric said.

The man shook his head. "Probably took on some water in the engine compartment."

Eric didn't agree. "I don't think so. She was running fine until we ran out of gas. Had to use the back-up can."

"You ran out of gas in this thing?"

"We were out there fightin' the storm for hours. Had no choice."

The young man looked the boat up and down, "She's what, thirty years old at least?"

"I'd say, about that."

The man laughed. "I'm surprised you got it started again at all. When you ran out of gas, you sucked up thirty years worth of junk from the bottom of the tank and gummed up all the works inside."

Eric hadn't even thought of that.

Abby spoke up. "How about you boys play with it later? I just want to be on land for awhile, if you don't mind."

Eric agreed. "Is there someplace we can grab a bite around here?"

The man directed them to a coffee house down the street and told them to take their time. Abby and Eric quickly changed into some new clothes, and went in search of a hot cup of coffee and hopefully some type of pastry. It had been a wild night, and they were both exhausted and starving.

As they passed by the boathouse, the young man came out to stop them, "I'll take a look at the engine while you're gone, yes?"

"Sure thing, boss."

A few minutes later they settled into two chairs at a small table in the coffee house. It wasn't a fancy place, but it was warm and on dry land, so they were completely thrilled.

They sipped their coffees and picked at a couple of pastries in silence for a while before Abby spoke. "How bad do you think the boat is?"

"I don't know. The kid back there seems to know what he's talking about. Hopefully we get it running soon. I just know we're close."

"If we're so close, maybe someone around here knows something."

"Maybe."

As they finished their breakfast, Abby decided, "How about you head back and check on the boat while I ask around and see if I can find any info that will get us back to Robert. Sound good?"

"What are you going to do? Just start asking folks if they know where the island is?"

"I figured I'd start over there," she said, pointing to a long desk toward the back that housed several computers. "My computer knowledge is probably pretty outdated, but assuming the internet is still alive and well, I bet I can find out the location of the island in five minutes online."

"Alright, well, you do that, and I'll see you back at the boat in ten." Eric smiled and kissed her before he left.

*   *   *

Her search took far longer than five minutes. Abby killed the rest of the morning and the better part of the afternoon reacquainting herself with the Internet. Basic search functions really hadn't changed in the ten years she had lost. Nothing is more simple or intuitive than having a box where you type in what you're looking for and hit enter. So with nothing to improve upon, the features hadn't changed much. She did, however, become increasingly frustrated with her inability to track down any information on the location of *Trial Island*.

What did come up in the searches, though, were news stories about where Abby and Eric had gone, and more recently, several articles about Bryce and his death. She clicked through some of the articles for her own curiosity. He was a figure in organized crime, though not a well-known one until recently. She clicked past another article that featured a large picture of eight men laid out on the street, dead after the gunfight. Right at the top of the next article his photo suddenly confronted her. It was an old mug shot; it had to be. He looked much younger than the man she fought a year ago. She found herself staring at it.

Who are you? How did we meet?

On the other side of the coffee house, a tray of dishes and mugs went crashing to the floor, sending Abby up out of her chair in panic. When she realized what it was, she sat back down and slowed her breathing.

Enough of Bryce, she told herself.

She decided to change tactics and try to track down information on Robert. Specifically, how she could contact him. She was far from a computer whiz, and was unable to find anything but general contact information. Basic email contact forms for his various companies that probably received thousands of messages a day, and phone numbers that would connect her to a call center. What were the chances they would believe who she was and get her in touch with him? Probably zero. She doubted the phone numbers would even connect her with anyone who would have the slightest idea how to get a message to Robert if they did believe her.

Although she had already done so in a dozen various ways over the past couple of hours, she went back to the search page and typed in "Location of *Trial Island*?" Exasperated, she sighed, seeing nothing but a list of links she had already clicked on.

Abby sat back in her chair, defeated. A young man sitting next to her smiled at her, and she smiled back.

He asked, "You a fan?"

Abby looked confused. "A fan?"

"*Trial Island*," he pointed to her screen. "You've been pulling up pages on it since I sat down twenty minutes ago."

Abby laughed and spoke without thinking. "Try three hours!"

The young man shined a youthful smile. "Well, I guess you are a fan, then. Me, too. What are you looking for?"

Abby thought for a second. Maybe he would know, if he's a fan. "I'm trying to figure out where the island is." She watched him for a reaction.

"Good luck. There are a ton of theories on the message boards, but no one really knows. No one I've ever heard of anyway." He drummed his fingers on the table. "Why are you looking anyway? Are you going to try to crash the party?" He laughed.

"No, no, just curious, that's all. Our travel agent said it was near here, so I don't know. I thought maybe we could catch a glimpse, fly by or something. Silly, huh?"

"There's not much happening this season anyway. I mean, it's been all right, but a little boring now, don't you think? Since Abby and Eric escaped, the last few couples have sort of paled in comparison."

Abby smiled, a little uncomfortably, but thankful that they were sitting side by side so that he wasn't looking directly at her. She shut down the screen to leave. "Nice talking to you."

As she stood to leave, he looked at her and did a double take. "Hey, wait a second."

Abby froze.

The young man looked her over. "You said your travel agent, so you're on vacation?"

"Yes."

"Well, if you've got some cash to spend, go talk to Captain Frank. He knows all these islands like the back of his hand. If anyone knows where the place is, it's him. If you pay him enough, maybe he would be willing to take you by."

Abby sighed, relieved. "Thanks." She turned to walk out the door before he could stop her again, but stopped herself after only a few steps. "Where do I find this Captain…?"

"Frank. He's usually down at The Shantyman's at night. It's by the docks. I'd start there."

Abby smiled, trying not to look directly at him. "Thanks."

"Good luck." He watched as she walked out the door. He turned back to his work and mumbled under his breath, "Tourists."

* * *

Eric looked up to see Abby walking down the dock. "Hey, good lookin'. I was starting to get worried."

She jumped down into the boat. "Since when do you have to worry about me?"

She kissed him on the lips as he gave her a look that said, *Really?*

"Fair enough," she said. "You're greasy." She examined his forearms and T-shirt, both black with sludge from the engine. "How does it look down there?"

Eric turned to indicate a pair of legs sticking out of the engine compartment, "Ray here is pretty handy. You'll have to ask him."

Ray, the young man who had greeted them when they first docked, turned around upon hearing his name, "Hello!"

After reintroducing themselves, Abby spoke, "Do you think you can get it running again?"

Ray nodded his head, "It's a mess in there, but we just need to clean things out and flush the system. It'll be a little bit, but we'll get you going again."

"That's great news!" She turned to Eric, "I have good news too. I've got a lead."

"A lead?"

"A lead!"

"What are you, some kind of detective?"

She playfully punched him in the arm. As she turned and walked down the stairs, she called over her shoulder, "Don't rain on my parade. I've got to go meet someone."

Contrary to his entire life's experience with women, in the two minutes that Abby was out of view, she had stripped, changed into her sundress, put on some lipstick and ran a comb through her hair, emerging from the cabin a new woman.

Eric took in the view. The flowing sundress hugged her curves in the right places, like it was made just for her.

"Who are you going to meet?" he asked.

She had a devilish look in her eyes. "No one you need to worry about." She kissed him before climbing up to the dock.

He called after her. "Who are you going to meet?"

"Captain Frank."

Ray perked up, "Captain Frank? Bring him back with you. He still owes me money for the parts I got for him

115

last month!"

"I'll try." She smiled and walked down the dock back toward the shops.

Eric looked at Ray. "Who's this Captain Frank guy?"

Ray smiled. "He's a good guy. Just isn't real good about paying his bills, you know?"

Eric nodded.

"Why does she need to see him?" Ray asked.

Eric shook his head, unsure. "Does he know his way around these parts?"

Ray chuckled, "Absolutely. If you're looking to get somewhere, he'll know better than anyone."

"I can take a guess then." Eric watched as Abby disappeared from the end of the dock and turned into town.

*   *   *

The Shantyman's was very small and very local. It was a literal hole in the wall. Walking in, Abby saw that the bar took up most of the interior real estate, with a few tables scattered around the outside wall. She walked to the far corner of the bar where she could take a seat and still have a view of the door.

She didn't know who Captain Frank was. However, local faces populated the place for the most part, and no one she saw appeared to be a "Frank". Being the only woman – and the only white face – in the establishment, she immediately garnered her fair share of attention. A quick survey of the faces surrounding her showed they were curious more than anything else. No one seemed to recognize her.

These were working men, not tourists. Judging by the smell of the establishment, and the locale, they were mostly local fisherman and dockworkers. She wondered why she hadn't thought of this before. A local place like this, where everyone who ventures the sea comes to congregate, was the perfect place for her to dig for information. If anyone knew how to get where she wanted to go, it would be someone in here.

The barkeep, a local man with gray hair, a deep skin tone, and even deeper wrinkles, approached her. "You want drink?"

"Cranberry tonic with a lime, please." Abby said with a smile.

The man stared at her as though he didn't understand.

Abby thought a moment. *He did just ask what I want in English, right?* She repeated herself, but slower and more specifically, "Cranberry juice, tonic water, with a wedge of lime?" She asked him, more than she told him.

"We no have here." His words were sharply cut, reprimanding her like a child. "No water. You want drink, you drink. You no want drink, you go. OK?"

Deciding that apparently her order was unacceptable,

she just smiled and said, "Light beer, please."

He nodded, twisted the cap off a brown locally labeled bottle and placed it in front of her before moving on to wipe down the bar.

Abby had planned to ask if he knew anything about the island, or knew anyone who would, but she determined that the barkeep wasn't in a talking mood. He was probably never in a talking mood from what she could tell.

She examined each of the dozen or so patrons around the room. All of them were young men, around her age, or younger. No one looked the part of someone named "Captain Frank". She was sure that she had the right place, but maybe he wasn't here.

After some effort, she was able to get the barkeep's attention to ask, "Captain Frank, is he here?"

At the mention of Captain Frank, the barkeep's eyes lit up, "You here for Captain Frank?" He laughed a fast, high-pitched laugh. "You here for Captain Frank! Yes. No, he is not here." He looked at his watch. "He be here usually five, five thirty. He be here soon." He beamed a huge smile at Abby and laughed again. "You here for Captain Frank!" Shaking his head, he walked away. "Oh, he like you. Captain Frank like you very much."

Abby thought the barkeep seemed overly amused at the fact that she was looking for Captain Frank, and this gave her pause. *What exactly does that mean?* She rubbed her right thigh, feeling the knife under the thin fabric of her sundress.

She looked up at the clock behind the bar. It was a few minutes before five. She smiled and said, "I'll wait."

12

IT WAS FILTHY WORK, but Eric and Ray finally got the engine running again. They let it run for about twenty minutes with no problems, so they called it a victory and topped off the gas tank.

Eric was just finishing cleaning himself up in the cabin when he looked out the porthole and saw what was becoming a familiar sight – the hull of QUEST II pulling into the harbor. He was looking at the front of the boat so he couldn't see the name, but it was QUEST II, he was sure of it. The boat was too far away for him to get a good look at the pilot, but the longish, dark curly hair and rough beard were easily seen from this distance. "Who is this guy?" he asked himself aloud.

Eric remembered that JJ had warned him that there were other investigators out here looking for them. Was he one of them? And if so, why hadn't he confronted them yet? Eric figured he should do some confronting of his own and find out the story. Showing up three times, like this man had, was too much of a coincidence, and Eric was going to get some answers the first time the opportunity presented itself.

*   *   *

Abby was still nursing her beer twenty minutes later when a notable patron walked into the bar, or rather, stumbled in. He was older, probably mid-to-late fifties. He wore an old blue Hawaiian shirt over his thin-built, tan frame. Wavy hair that hung just below his ears appeared from under his well-worn straw cowboy hat, and he had a short, trimmed beard. The hair and the beard were probably black once upon a time, but were now a salt-and-pepper mix of gray and white.

With some effort, he found his way to an empty barstool closest to the door and plunked himself down. His head flopped forward, and he stared straight down at the bar. *Is he collecting his thoughts?* Abby wondered, unable to take her eyes off him. If nothing else, he promised to be interesting people watching.

The barkeep set a rocks glass in front of him filled with ice, gave him a heavy- handed pour from the rum bottle, and slid it forward under his face. As the intoxicating smell of rum hit the man's nose, he lifted his head and nearly shouted with a jovial voice, "Sammy! Well, aren't you a sight for sore eyes." Abby assumed he was talking to the barkeep, but the man smiled at the drink as he spoke.

The barkeep walked over to Abby and beamed, "That is Captain Frank."

Oh! Abby thought. *Well... interesting.*

She watched him for a few minutes. He stared into his drink for a long time, as if contemplating it. Finally, with a nod of approval, he took a sip and looked toward the silent television above the bar.

Well, it can't hurt to at least talk to him, right?

Abby made her way down the bar and stood behind him for a moment, unsure what to say. "Um... Captain Frank?"

Still facing the television, he slurred, "There's no such thing as a free ride, honey. It's gotta be cash, grass, or ass, no one..." As he turned around, he stopped mid sentence, "Whoa."

Abby smiled.

Captain Frank stared a moment, taking her in before apologizing. "My apologies," he said, standing up. "Captain Frank, at your service." He tipped his straw hat, which was somehow endearing and made her smile.

"Nice to meet you, Captain." She gave a little curtsey in return.

"Young ladies are always asking me for a ride to one island or another. I've never met one quite so lovely as yourself, though. If you need a ride, I'd be honored. The typical rates don't apply to you, my dear."

Abby examined his face. He was probably a decent-looking man when sober. He was older, yes. The tanned skin and wrinkles around his eyes told the tale of a great many years spent in the sun. And even through the slurring, there was a certain charm about him. Abby couldn't place it at first, but then decided it was his eyes. They were a bluish gray, like the sky before the dawn. They were the eyes of a good and trustworthy man, albeit one who has made some poor life decisions, but a good man none the less.

Still standing, she replied, "Well, Captain, it turns out I don't need a ride. But I am trying to figure out how to get somewhere, and I'm hoping you can help me out."

"Absolutely," he said, motioning for her to sit down in the chair next to him. He took his seat once Abby was seated, and gave the bartender a big smile. Looking at Abby, he asked, "So, where you trying to get to?"

Abby originally had been concerned that she might be recognized, or possibly run into one of the investigators JJ said were out here looking for her. However, none of the locals in here seemed to know who she was, and with the Captain half in the bag already, she was less than concerned about him. "Have you ever heard of the show *Trial Island*?"

Captain Frank let out a short laugh. "Seriously?"

Abby nodded.

"Of course I have," he said with a smile.

She looked around; making sure no one was listening to their conversation. "Do you know where the island is?"

The captain was curious now. "I sure do. You looking to go there?"

Abby nodded. "Yes."

Frank stood out and shouted to the barkeep, "Sammy, put this one on my tab, and this lovely lady's, too." He turned to Abby, "I'll have you there in two hours. Let's go!"

"Whoa, uh… Captain… slow down." She indicated for him to have a seat. "I'm actually looking to go to the island next to it. You said it's only two hours from here?"

"Yes, ma'am." Frank looked at his watch. "I can have you there by eight if we leave now. Just gotta put some gas in the tank." He began lumbering toward the door.

"That's very nice, Captain Frank…"

"Just call me Frank."

"Thank you, Frank. I'm A… Annie, by the way."

Abby held out her hand, which he took gingerly in his and kissed it. "Nice to meet you, Annie."

Abby almost blushed a bit. "You're very nice, Frank. I can't leave tonight, though. Would we be able to make the trip in the morning?"

Frank studied her face as he thought. "I have a charter in the morning, but I'll reschedule them. As long as you wear another beautiful dress like that one, then I say absolutely!"

Abby giggled a bit, playing along. He was being very accommodating, and Abby was sure it was because he was more interested in finding out what was under her dress than in just having a companion at sea for a few hours.

She asked, "Can I take a friend?"

"It's a tight squeeze, but if she's as cute as you, then most definitely."

Abby decided not to let him know that her friend wasn't another cute and diminutive woman, but her six-foot-something boyfriend. They could sort that out tomorrow. "Sounds wonderful. I can't believe we're so close. I figured it would be further away." Abby pulled out a map that she had printed off the computer back at the coffee house. "Can you show me where it is?"

Frank took the map and set it down on the bar, trying to get his bearings. He pointed at an island, "This is where we are now." As his finger traced the map, it came to a stop at two islands several inches to the northeast. "That's where you want to go."

"That looks pretty far away. It will only take a couple hours?"

"Absolutely. Stick with me. I can get you anywhere you need to be in no time flat."

Abby finished her drink. "Well, it was great meeting you, and I can't wait for tomorrow!"

He looked genuinely disappointed. "You're leaving so soon?"

"I've got to get ready for our trip," Abby winked at him playfully and gave him a kiss on the cheek for good measure. He seemed to be the type to spend most of the night drinking, and she didn't want him to forget her. She asked, "How early can we get started?"

"Nine o'clock sound reasonable?"

"Sounds great."

"Alright then, I'll meet you at the boatyard at nine tomorrow morning. Thank you again."

"No," he smiled, "thank *you*!"

Captain Frank watched Abby leave, then turned to the barkeep. "Sammy, you got any coffee back there? I gotta sober up."

*   *   *

Eric had finished cleaning up and was walking down the street just outside the harbor when he found Abby.

"Hey, I was just going to look for you."

Abby smiled and gave him a quick kiss. "Well, you found me, sailor."

"How did your meeting go?"

"Oh, not bad I suppose. I just got us a ride to the island in the morning, that's all."

"You got us a ride?"

126

"Well, if we want one. But even better, I confirmed where we're going." She pulled the letter-sized map from her satchel and unfolded it. "Look, right here." She pointed out where they were, then, as Frank had done, traced her finger up to the islands where they were going. "Captain Frank says he can have us there in a few hours tomorrow morning!"

Eric looked skeptical and took the map to examine it closer, "A few hours?"

"That's what he said."

"Abby, I think that's a lot further than a few hours. That's got to be three hundred miles away. That's either one very long day at sea, or a couple days at least."

It was Abby's turn to look skeptical. "He said just a few hours. Are you sure?"

Eric nodded, "I'm pretty sure, but let's go compare it to the chart back on the boat."

They walked around the corner of the boathouse to go back down the dock toward the boat. Just then, the bearded man from QUEST II came around the corner, and they almost ran into each other.

Abby smiled and said, "Excuse me," as she walked around the man to continue down the dock.

"Sorry," the man said as he moved to let them by. He tried to avoid eye contact, but Eric locked eyes with him.

The man nodded and continued past them.

As the man passed, Eric decided that he had enough and was going to find out what exactly was going on. If he was one of those investigators looking for them, which Eric was reasonably sure of, he probably didn't expect them to be aggressive. Well, he was about to get a little wake-up call.

Eric grabbed him by the shoulders and spun him around. "What the hell are you doing following…"

That's as far as he got with his line of questioning.

The man grabbed Eric's arm, spun it behind his back, and pushed him up against the side of the boathouse.

"Take is easy, I'm not here to…"

And that's as far as the bearded man got before his words stopped short in his throat. He felt the swift breeze of Abby's knife as it sliced through the air just a breath beneath his beard as it came to rest at his throat.

"I don't know what's going on here, but I suggest you let go of him."

The man let go of Eric, who immediately turned the tables by grabbing him and pushing his back into the wall. Eric put his elbow and forearm into his chest to hold him while Abby held her knife on him from a few feet away.

"Back to my question," Eric said. "What the hell are you doing following us?"

At that moment, a voice came from behind. "It's OK, he's with me."

13

ABBY AND ERIC both turned to see JJ standing behind them.

"This is my brother, Ace."

"Your brother? Why didn't we meet him when you found us?" Abby asked.

"He stays in the background. An insurance policy, so to speak."

Abby turned back toward the man Eric was holding against the wall. He did look like JJ. He was tall, curly hair, but also different. Where JJ was lean, like a swimmer, this man was broad, like a football player. His curly hair was much longer than JJ's, down past his ears and shaggy, with an unkempt beard. As she studied their eyes, she saw they both had the same beautiful blue eye color, and shape. They looked very different, but there was no doubt that in seeing them together, they were brothers.

The man with the beard spoke up. "It's about time."

JJ shot back, "What the hell are you doing off the boat?"

"I found them, so I was following them, because I had no idea where the hell you were!"

"How about you pick up the phone and say, 'Hey, bro, guess who I found?'"

"Yeah, because that worked out so well last time. I was standing on the boat like an asshole watching them cruise right past me while you were off dipping your wick in the local talent pool."

"Ace, there's a lady here. Mind your mouth," JJ said, indicating Abby.

She spoke up next, "Will someone please tell me what's going on?" She looked at Eric, who still had his arm across Ace's chest. "Eric, what's our problem with him?"

"I've seen him in the last three harbors we've been in. I thought he was following us."

"We are," JJ said. "Or at least we were trying to, since Ace spotted you in the last one."

"You mind?" Ace asked Eric.

"Oh, yeah, sorry," Eric said as he eased off Ace so he could stand upright.

"My brother and I work together. He saw you pulling

out of the last harbor. I couldn't get back to the boat in time. We tried following you, but we were hours behind, and with the storm coming, we had to turn around and stay put for the night. Finding you here was just our best guess."

Abby turned to Ace with a bit of a guilty look. "Sorry about that," she said, indicating his neck.

He waved her off. "Don't worry about it."

"No, but you're bleeding a little. I got a little carried away there."

Ace felt his neck. Abby's blade had given him just the tiniest cut. It was as thin and fine as a paper cut, and her blade was so sharp he never even felt it. As he wiped his hands on his pants, he made a mental note not to tangle with her in the future.

He smiled. "Really, don't worry about it. No big deal."

"Sorry anyway," Abby said before turning to JJ. "We've been chasing you since you left."

"You've been chasing us? Why not just call? I could have turned around and saved you an awful lot of trouble."

"Somebody," Eric said, staring at Abby, "trashed your card. We thought we could catch you at your first stop, but we missed you by a couple hours. Fortunately, we got pointed in the right direction. Same thing happened, though, and well, we've been playing that game for a few days now."

"Unbelievable," JJ said. He looked at Abby, "So, I assume you decided you want to go back and see Robert?"

"Absolutely," Abby said.

"Well, he sure will be happy to hear that. When I told him that we finally found you, he flew down here right away. He was pretty disappointed that you weren't coming, but said he'd stick around a few days, hoping that you'd change your mind. Looks like he was right. Good thing we found each other, you'd never make it there without us."

"Believe it or not, we actually know where we're going now. It's funny that we finally found you, but we don't need you anymore."

JJ looked skeptical. "You know where the island is?"

Abby recapped her story about meeting Captain Frank, and how he showed her the location. "He said he can have me there in a couple of hours."

Eric spoke up. "I'm not so sure about that, though. We were just going to compare her map to the charts back on the boat. Looks more like a couple of days to me."

"Let me take a look." JJ took the small map from Abby and studied it for a few moments. "Well, I've good news and bad news. Your Captain Fred…"

"Frank," Abby corrected.

"Captain Frank knows where he's going. Those are the islands all right. Bad news is there's no way that it's just a few hours. We've got another two days underway before we get there. We're returning to Robert's boatyard and have the whole thing charted out."

"Well, he said a few hours," Abby said. "He seemed pretty sure of himself."

Eric asked, "Where did you meet this guy, anyway?"

Abby hesitated a moment. "At The Shantyman's."

"The Shantyman's? Is that what it sounds like?"

"What does it sound like?"

"Like a crusty sailor's bar."

"Then it's exactly what it sounds like."

"So you met some guy in a bar that calls himself Captain Frank and you're ready to hop on a boat with him because he claims to know where he's going? Abby, I realize you want to get back and all, but that doesn't seem like a good decision."

Abby chuckled. "Eric, first off, he's harmless, and second, you'll be with me. If he had any bad intentions, I'm sure we could take care of things. Heck, if you've got our boat running, we don't even have to wait for him. We can go ourselves."

"Or come with us," JJ spoke up.

Abby thought a moment, "He was very sure of
133

himself. I'd like to at least have you meet the guy."

"I'll meet him," Eric said, "but we'll get there ourselves."

"We'll cross that bridge when we come to it," Abby said. She turned to JJ, "Would it be possible for me to talk to Robert?"

"Sure thing." He pulled out his phone and put the call through.

Abby took the phone and said to the men, "I'll meet you back at the boat, OK?"

Eric gave her a kiss on the cheek, and they left her to make her call.

After a couple of rings, Robert picked up the phone. "JJ, please tell me you've got better news than last time."

"He does!" Abby said, her smile beaming through the phone.

"Is this Abby?"

"It is!"

"Fantastic! So you changed your mind. I'm so happy. When will you be here?"

"Well, soon. I'm just not sure how soon. JJ says we're a few days away, but I met someone else who says it's no more than a few hours." She recapped her discussion with Captain Frank.

"I don't know, Abby." Robert sounded concerned. "As always, you can do what you want, but if I were you, I'd stick with JJ. He knows what he's doing."

"Well, don't worry, I'm meeting up with Frank tomorrow, and we'll decide then. I'm just so excited to see you, and to get my memory back. By this time tomorrow, I could know the answers to everything I've been questioning. I don't expect you to understand, but that's very exciting to me."

"Oh, I do understand. Trust me, I do. But about getting your memory back – it's not going to be a quick and simple procedure like Eric's was. I'll explain the details when I see you, but it's going to take much longer than Eric's."

"Well, that's another reason to get back sooner rather than later, wouldn't you say?"

"You're a smart girl. Trust your instincts, but promise me you'll be careful, alright?"

"I will."

"Bryce may be dead, but I don't know what kind of history you have with his people. I don't want to alarm you, but you need to be practical."

Abby hadn't considered that angle and was thankful for Robert's advice. "I'll be safe, I promise. I hope to see you tomorrow."

"Very good, Abby. Travel safely, and be smart."

14

IT WAS NINE on the dot, and Abby, Eric, JJ and Ace were on their boat when a sober and chipper Captain Frank came strolling down the deck. He was whistling between sips on a strong coffee from a paper up. He wore his trademark outfit, similar to what he was wearing last night – a straw cowboy hat, Hawaiian shirt, and khaki shorts. However, Abby thought he looked significantly more crisp and put together than he had at their first meeting.

Abby called out to Frank with a smile and a wave. "Captain Frank! Over here!"

He looked toward Abby through his sunglasses with a smile, which faded when he saw three men with her. Quickly putting a smile back on his face, he walked over. "Annie, good morning!" He nodded at the rest. "Gentlemen, good morning."

"Last night you said you could get me where I'm going within a couple of hours, right?"

"Absolutely!" Frank consulted his watch, "If you're ready to go, I can have you there by a little after lunch time, but we'd have to leave now. Where's your friend?"

Eric spoke up. "Captain Frank, right?"

"Yes, sir. And you are?"

"Eric. I'm the friend."

"Oh."

"Is that a problem?"

"Well, my vessel is a little on the small side, and you're a pretty big fella. Honestly, I'm not sure we can all fit."

JJ spoke up. "What kind of boat is it, exactly? That's a three hundred mile trip, and you claim you can make it in a few hours?"

Frank smiled. "Oh, she's an old girl, but she's fast. Faster than what you've got here, I can say that for certain."

Frank led them down the dock to a walkway that went around to the far side of the boathouse. As they turned the corner, tied to the dock with the sun gleaming off its windows, was Captain Frank's pontoon plane.

To Abby, it looked like every other tiny crop duster she had ever seen, but instead of wheels it had two large floats resting on the water.

"She tops out around eighty miles an hour, but with a good wind at our back, we'll get her into the nineties."

Eric looked into the windows and saw that it was

barely a two-seater. There was no way he was going to fit in there with them. "I don't like it."

Abby was a bit concerned, but optimistic. "JJ, how fast did you say you could get there?"

"Two days. Our boat tops out around thirty if we push it hard, but I wouldn't want to work the engine ten hours straight, so we were going to break it up into two days."

"Two days," Abby sighed, thinking hard. She looked at Eric. "Two days, or I can be there in time for lunch. What would you do?"

"I'd take the two days," JJ said. "No offense, Frank," he said with a friendly nod to the captain.

"None taken. I've got a daughter myself, probably just about Annie's age. I don't get to see her as much as a father should, but I sure do hope that she thinks twice about hopping in a plane with a man she just met."

Abby couldn't be sure, but it looked like Captain Frank even got a little misty at the mention of his daughter.

Frank looked toward Eric. "If it eases your mind at all, I'm well known around here. I ferry folks around all the time, so this is nothing new for me. Heck, Ray stopped me out front to ask me about a few dollars I owe him. This plane is my livelihood, and I get people where they need to go. I promise you that Annie here is safe with me. But with all due respect, if we're not going flying today, I have a charter that I cancelled so I could help her out. I'd like us to make a decision here so I can call them and maybe get them on again."

Abby was impressed with the sober Captain Frank. Last night, when he had obviously had a few, she found him charming, and harmless. This morning, sober and sentimental, she found him even more so.

Eric was taking it in and sizing up Frank. His words were genuine, but he hated the thought of letting Abby out of his sight.

Abby spoke. "Eric, Robert said..." she stopped a moment. "Frank, will you excuse us a minute?"

"Sure thing."

Ace took Frank by the shoulder, "Why don't you show me around this thing." The two went off toward the plane while Abby, Eric, and JJ walked down the dock to talk out of earshot of the pilot.

Abby continued. "Robert said that my procedure isn't going to be as simple as yours. So, I'm thinking I take a quick flight and get there today, and you ride with JJ. By the time you get there tomorrow, I could be done."

"For what it's worth," JJ said, "I don't think it's a good idea. You've waited this long. What difference is an extra couple of days going to make?"

"I guess it doesn't make a difference. I mean, when you were missing ten years of your memory, you took your time getting it back, right?"

JJ just looked at her. He understood her point, but he didn't like the idea of her going off with this guy.

"Eric, how about you?" she asked. "How long did you wait to get your memory back? You did it while I was taking a nap! And your life wasn't half as screwed up as mine."

"Abby…"

"Don't, Eric. Don't. I know that I probably sound like a silly girl right now, but I disappeared from my old life. I have no idea what kind of life I left behind. All I know is my husband was pissed off enough to track me down halfway across the world to kidnap and try to murder me. Not an hour goes by that I don't think about that. I wonder every day what happened with my family, my sister, and what else I left behind. Now that I've got a chance to get my mind back, I don't want to wait another minute longer than I have to. Is that so crazy?"

Eric and JJ looked at each other. They had nothing to say.

"Frank is harmless," Abby said, then added for good measure, "and in case you've forgotten, I can take care of myself just fine."

Eric took her face in his hands and brought her close to look into his eyes, "I love you. I nearly lost you before, and I don't want to take any chances."

Abby smiled. "You're not. I'll be fine."

He sighed, defeated. "You're stubborn, you know that,

right?"

She smiled again and kissed him. "Isn't that why you love me?"

JJ had been watching Ace inspect the sea plane with Frank in the background, and decided to walk away from the two lovers to see what his brother thought.

"Well, she looks airworthy as far as I can tell," Ace observed. He knew a thing or two about planes. He was a licensed pilot and had a small recreational plane back home.

Abby and Eric walked up, hand in hand. "You ready, Frank?" she asked.

Captain Frank looked a bit nervously from Eric to JJ to Ace, before settling back on Abby. "I'm ready if you are."

"Don't worry about them," she said. "They're just overprotective, that's all."

"There's nothing wrong with that. I hope my daughter has three big, tough, overprotective men in her life." He looked toward the men. "You boys have nothing to worry about. I've been flying for forty years, since I was a teenager, and I've come back down every single time." He smiled, trying to put the men at ease.

Eric reached out and shook his hand. "Frank, I'll trust you because she does. Just take care of her and don't make me regret it, OK?"

"I most certainly will. I guarantee when you get there tomorrow, she'll be there." With that, he opened the door and tossed a bag into the small cargo area behind the seats.

JJ pulled Abby aside for a moment as Ace put his arm around Frank's shoulders, his big frame and large arm enveloping the Captain, as if they were old friends. "Frank, I just need you to know, the three of us here are pretty fond of the young lady you're transporting."

Frank nodded nervously. "I gathered that much."

"The man who is paying me and my brother over there to look after her, he's even more fond of her than we are. You're bringing her to this man."

Frank nodded again, curious to see where this was going.

"I need you to know, Captain, if she isn't on terra firma by lunchtime today, there's going to be trouble."

Frank swallowed. "I understand. She'll be there."

"Good, because you seem like a nice guy. But I *will* kill you." Ace gave him a wink and a smile, and then smacked him on the shoulder.

There was no doubt in Frank's mind that this large man was serious. He did some calculations in his head and prayed that everything would work out as he hoped. He smiled at Ace. "Understood, and you've got nothing to worry about."

JJ handed Abby a small phone as Frank turned over

the engine and started the plane. "My satellite number is the first speed dial, and Robert's is the second. It's simple. Just hold down number one for me, or number two for Robert. If you need anything—anything at all—you call, understand?"

"Yes, sir," Abby said, mocking his seriousness, though JJ didn't break a smile.

"We'll be on the boat heading straight there. As soon as you land, call us. I know we'll be there tomorrow, but if you don't call us, we're pushing through and taking our chances—so make sure you call, OK?"

"Nothing to worry about, I'll talk to you in a few hours, OK?" Abby walked over to give Eric one last hug. Yelling over the motor, she asked with a smile, "Are you going to be OK without me?"

"I'll be fine." Eric pulled her close and gave her a long kiss. He pulled away slightly and whispered in her ear, "You've got your knife?"

She nodded. "Yes, and you know I know how to use it."

"Absolutely," Eric said. She would be fine; she can take care of herself. Heck, he wouldn't be alive if it hadn't been for Abby. He smiled at the thought that maybe he should be worried that *he* wouldn't be alright without her by his side.

The Captain hopped down. "We're ready."

Eric and Abby embraced and kissed one more time

143

before he watched her climb in and cross to the far side, followed by Frank, who strapped into the pilots seat before closing the door and offering a salute to the men standing on the dock.

JJ and Ace were already back on their boat idling the engine by the time the seaplane gained speed and took off before banking hard to the left and settling on course.

As Eric watched the plane disappear, waving to Abby, he thought, *She's right – that girl can take care of herself.*

JJ yelled from the boat, "Hey, what are you waiting for? Let's get moving!"

Eric trotted back to the boat, jumped in, and the three of them were off at full speed within minutes, following the increasingly distant plane.

"They'll be out of sight in ten minutes," Eric thought out loud.

"That's OK, we'll still keep an eye on him." Ace smiled, holding up a small glass screen that displayed a basic map and a blinking red dot that Eric assumed was Captain Frank's plane.

"How'd you do that?"

"I put a small GPS device on the plane. It's magnetic, no big deal. About the size of a quarter."

"That's smart thinking," Eric said. "You guys are prepared for anything, huh?"

"We like to be," Ace said. "That's why there's a little explosive device in there, too."

Eric's eyes lit up, "You put a bomb on Abby's plane?"

"No, there's no bomb, don't worry. It's part of the GPS device. It's a sliver of plastic explosive. We usually put them on cars as a 'just in case' when we're tracking someone. I figure it'll blow a hole in the side of the plane and force him to land if we need him to. Probably wouldn't even make them crash."

"Probably?"

"I'm almost sure." Ace gave him a devilish smile. "It's nowhere near the gas tank."

"Are you screwing with me?"

Ace laughed. "Relax, Eric, it's fine."

"Well, let's plan on *not* blowing up Abby mid-air, OK?"

"You got it." Ace looked down at the screen and nodded. "They're right on course."

15

ABBY AND FRANK had been in the air for an hour or so. Conversation was light and at a minimum. Frank didn't have a headset for his passenger, so any conversation to be had was, out of necessity, screamed over the sound of the propeller thundering through the air a few feet in front of them on the other side of the windshield. He occasionally spoke into his headset, presumably to local air traffic control or other pilots, but not to Abby.

Each time Abby saw a group of islands coming up in the distance she got excited only to be disappointed as they flew over them and on toward the horizon.

Finally Frank leaned over and shouted, "We'll be putting down in about twenty minutes, up ahead."

Abby felt butterflies in her stomach. She was excited to finally fill in the blank pages that were the past ten years of her life, but also terrified about what she would learn. Would the new Abby be horrified at the life she had led? What drove Bryce to hunt her down and try to kill her? What brought her and Bryce together in the first place? The worst thought of all seemed to make her heart stop: *Was I still in love with him? Will I be upset that he's dead?* That thought gave her a knot in her stomach.

Question after question swam through her mind. The high-pitched drone of the propeller got lower as Frank eased up a bit on the throttle, and they began their descent. Abby looked toward the coast of the island they were approaching, searching for the massive Victorian structure that served as Robert's home away from home.

Abby looked over toward Frank, who was speaking into his headset, but he wasn't speaking to her, and she couldn't make out a word he was saying.

She had only seen the coastline once, and it was from the water, but she did not remember the buildings she was seeing now. She also couldn't find Robert's grand estate, which would be hard to miss. Leaning over, she shouted to Frank, "You're sure this is the right island?"

He shot her a look and said, "Yeah, why?"

"I don't see Robert's house," she shouted.

"Don't worry... it's around the other side."

Abby thought a moment. "This is a sea plane. Why not just land on the other side? There's water, right?"

Frank was quiet a moment before he shouted back, "The winds aren't right. This will be better."

Abby conceded the point, then had another thought, "Is that who you were talking to before? Letting them know where we are landing so someone can come out to meet us?"

Frank nodded. "Yep, that's it." He smiled without

making eye contact.

Abby was consumed with both the excitement of getting her memory back, and seeing Robert again. It was a small island, and a few extra minutes to ride over to the other side of it wouldn't hurt, she thought.

She took her eyes off Robert's island in front of them and gazed out her window at the empty blue sea. It was beautiful here, and she had a hard time imagining herself leaving, but who knew how she would feel a couple of days from now when she knew more about her past.

Looking at Frank, she saw beads of sweat gathering at his temples. She didn't think it was particularly hot, but it must be stressful landing a plane. Looking past him, she found herself staring at the beautiful blue water that stretched as far as the eye could see. Her eyes settled back on the front window as they approached the island.

Abby suddenly had another thought. Checking the side windows again, she wondered, *If this is Robert's island, where's Trial Island?*

*   *   *

"They're landing!" Ace shouted.

"What?" Eric rushed over to look at the readout over his shoulder. "They're already there?"

"Nope, they're shy by almost seventy miles."

"How can you tell they're landing?"

Ace looked at him. "They're slowing down and dropping altitude like crazy."

"Could they be having engine trouble?"

"I don't think so. It looks like a controlled gradual descent. They're landing."

JJ didn't take his eyes off the water. "Where are they putting down?"

Ace studied the readout. "Small island, direct on the line from here to there. One of a million, and nothing special about it."

"How far?" JJ asked.

"About a hundred miles from where we're sitting, as the crow flies."

"Can we go any faster?" Eric asked, though he knew the answer.

JJ shook his head no. He had the throttle pegged for the past two-plus hours. Depending on the wind, they were going between thirty to thirty-five miles an hour. JJ did some quick math. Relatively speaking, they were not that far behind, but they still couldn't get there for close to three hours at best, and that was being extremely optimistic.

"Dammit!" Eric shouted to no one in particular, though he punched an innocent seat cushion as hard as he could.

JJ tossed him a small phone. "Hey! Calm down and see if you can get her on the line. Just punch in the number seven and send."

Eric did just that. He waited a few seconds before the phone began to ring. "Come on… come on…"

*   *   *

Abby had been sitting quietly for the past few minutes, pretending everything was fine, though it was apparent to her that things were far from it. She watched the beads of sweat on Frank's temples drip down the side of his face. He was clearly nervous. If they weren't at Robert's island, why was he telling her that?

They were still hundreds of yards off from the shoreline. She could see that they must be aiming for the beach in the distance. There were a few people around a large black SUV, but she couldn't even tell their size, never mind gender.

Who is waiting for us?

Her hackles were raised, and she slowly reached down her right side and slipped a hand into her satchel to wrap her fingers around the familiar grip of her knife. Had she or JJ had the foresight to put the phone on vibrate, she would have felt it buzzing as Eric anxiously sat a hundred miles away willing her to pick up. Unfortunately, the roar of the engine drowned out any sounds in the cockpit, and her mind was racing so fast that she had entirely forgotten the phone was there.

They bounced down with a splash about a football field away from the shore. Frank kept the engine on and increased the power to keep them slowly moving toward the beach.

The SUV was clearer now, though the half-dozen people were still nondescript. She couldn't tell who they were, or if they were men, women, or both. However she quickly decided this was as close as she was going to get to them for now.

In a flash, she produced the knife under the pilot's chin.

"Holy shit!" Frank's eyes went wild as he sat up straight and lifted his head trying to get away from the blade. "Abby... Abby, hey now!"

"Kill the engine, Frank."

He paused, weighing his options.

"NOW!"

He reached forward and put the engine in neutral, effectively killing the propeller. They were dead in the water, bobbing gently on the small waves. Abby saw that the people on the beach immediately took notice.

"Talk Frank, and do it fast."

"What do you want? I brought you where you wanted to go. Now, come on, Abby, put the knife down."

She laughed. "So you know who I am?"

Frank looked confused for a moment, replaying what he just said back in his mind. *Abby… shit*, he thought. *She told me her name was Annie.*

"Where are we Frank? I know this isn't Robert's island. Robert's island is right next to *Trial Island*. Can't be more than ten miles out. Problem is, there's nothing within eyesight of here."

The beach was still the better part of fifty yards away, but Abby could see that the people had walked to the waterline and were conversing with each other, trying to figure out what was going on.

Abby lifted the knife, pressing the flat side harmlessly against the bottom of his chin. "Last chance, Frank. Where. Are. We?"

"Listen, don't kill me, OK? I was just trying to make some quick money."

"How? Talk."

"There's this guy. Tough guy. Said he's an investigator; works for one of those big Hollywood shows. He came through the bar about a month ago talking to everyone in the place. Said he was looking for you, and he knew you were out on one of the islands. No one had seen you, but he left a handful of cards. Said he'd pay a ton of cash if you turn up and we call him first."

Abby thought back to what JJ said about others out here looking for her. She lowered the knife.

Frank let out a nervous sigh. He felt as though he had

been holding his breath since they started the descent. "I'm sorry. These people are paying a ton of cash, and I need it." He reached forward to engage the propeller again.

"Hey! What are you doing?"

"What?"

"I'm not talking to these people, Frank, and I'm still the one with the knife. Turn the plane around."

Frank studied her face, "Abby, you're not going to kill me. Just talk to the guy, OK? He's paying me a truckload of cash. I think they just want an exclusive interview or something. They'll probably pay you ten times what they're giving me."

"Are you serious?"

"I am."

They stared at each other as Abby thought. Maybe it was just an investigator trying to track her down for an exclusive. Maybe it was something else. Either way, she wasn't about to find out. "How much are they paying you?"

"Five grand."

Abby let out a whistle. "I'm going out on a limb here, but I think you're getting taken for a ride. How about this – you turn this plane around right now and get me where I'm supposed to be in the next hour, and I'll give you double that."

"Seriously?"

Abby held up her knife. "I don't joke around."

He looked at the folks on the beach as they bobbed up and down in the plane, and then looked back at Abby. "I've got your word?"

"You'll get your cash. Time is ticking."

"Well, hold onto your hats then!"

Reaching forward, he engaged the propeller and pushed forward on the throttle, causing the plane to lurch forward. Abby was jostled hard in her seat.

"You might want to put that big knife away, sweetie – it's gonna get bumpy for a few."

Once the plane gained enough speed, maybe fifty feet from shore, Frank cut hard to the right to turn the plane around in the water and faced them back out toward the open sea. As they turned, Abby could see men on the beach in shorts and tee shirts running and waving their arms. There was a man leading the pack, toting a clipboard, and he finally threw it down in frustration. There was a woman in a business suit with what looked to be a microphone, along with a cameraman, who just stood by watching the plane as it turned around. She giggled a bit. These guys were desperate for a story. Maybe the world hadn't changed all that much in ten years.

Well, they have some footage of a man and a woman in a seaplane landing, and then turning around... I wonder how many times that will run on a loop while they speculate if it was really me?

As the plane came around, Frank opened up the throttle, and they picked up even more speed as they bounced over the waves. The roar of the engine drowned out any other noise around, but it was music to Abby's ears. *I'll be there soon, Robert, I'll be there soon.*

*   *   *

Pulling the phone away from his ear, Eric shook his head. "Nothing."

"No connection?" JJ asked.

"No, it rang a couple dozen times. No answer." He looked to JJ, hopeful that he would have a suggestion, "What do we do now?"

Ace spoke up. "Looks like they've stopped."

JJ stood fast at the helm as their boat sped forward. "That can't be good. Hopefully it's just engine trouble or something like that. The only thing we can do is get there as fast as we can." He looked down at the gauges and took note of the oil pressure and temperature. He hadn't run the boat this fast for this long and was hoping he wasn't inviting trouble.

"What if it's not engine trouble? Ace said it was a controlled landing. I think he meant to stop there." Eric silently wondered whether Bryce still had men out here looking for them. Maybe there were others who had it out for Abby. It was impossible to say, and the speculation was driving him mad.

"It's not engine trouble," Ace said emphatically.

JJ called back over his shoulder, "What makes you so sure?"

"They're moving again."

"What?"

Ace brought the tablet over to show the others, "They landed right here, about fifty yards shy of the beach. They sat for a couple of minutes. Then they just turned around. You can see they're picking up speed."

"Are they in the air yet?" JJ asked.

"No, but they will be in about thirty seconds."

"Blow it. Blow the charge. Keep them on the ground."

"WHAT? NO!" Eric shouted.

"We keep them there. Who knows why they stopped? Did he drop her off? Pick someone up? No more games. Ace, blow the damn thing."

Eric pointed at Ace. "Don't you dare. What if they just had to... I don't know, stop for gas?"

"They weren't there long enough, and we're running out of time. Now, blow it!" JJ called.

"Don't! Fine, no gas, Maybe he just had to take a piss, and now you're going to blow them up and kill Abby!"

"Fifteen seconds," Ace said calmly.

JJ tried to match Ace's calm tone, "She'll be fine. As long as they're not airborne, she'll be fine. She might not even be on the plane anymore. We blow it, keep it in the water, and take her from there. No more detours." He stared at Eric, waiting for him to concede.

"Five seconds," Ace called out.

JJ looked to Ace. "Do it."

"No!"

"Do it, Ace!" JJ shouted.

"No!" Eric tackled Ace as he began punching in a code. Given the height and weight advantages Ace had, it was more of a collision than a tackle, but it caused him to lose his balance and fall backwards onto the bench seat at the back of the boat. The tablet sailed over the back and disappeared into the engine's wake behind them.

"Shit!" Eric hadn't intended for that to happen.

JJ looked back to see the two men looking off the back of the boat and, upon seeing that Ace's hands were empty, quickly figured out what happened. "I'll come around to pick it up."

Ace shook his head and called back, "Don't bother. It's twenty feet down by now and sinking fast." He looked at Eric. "Nice."

Eric gulped and asked, "Are they still in the air?"

"Can't say for sure," Ace said. "But you got your wish

— we didn't disable the plane, if that's what you're wondering."

Eric exhaled. He was thankful for that.

*　　*　　*

"Can I at least call to let them know what happened?" Frank asked.

"No. Get us where we are going. You can call them when we get there." Abby was in no mood to be trifled with any more. She didn't want Frank telling them where they were going either. She wanted to be greeted by Robert upon her arrival, not some Hollywood reporter looking for an exclusive and apparently willing to kidnap her to get it.

That did give her an idea, though. She shuffled things around in her satchel until she found the phone JJ had given her. She hit the speed dial and heard his voice on the other end of the line after barely a ring.

"Oh, thank God!" he said.

"What?"

"You're alright?" JJ asked.

"We had a minor problem, but I'm fine. Why?"

"We're tracking you and saw that the plane had stopped. We were a little worried."

"Tracking me? What right do you have to be tracking me? I'm not a child that needs to be looked after JJ."

"Listen, I promised Robert that we would get you there. We're just taking every precaution we can to make sure that happens. It's nothing personal."

Abby sighed, "Well, I'm fine. I appreciate your concern, but really, there's nothing to worry about here."

"Good. What happened?"

"Nothing. I'll explain it when I see you. Everything alright on your end?"

"We'll be there tonight, late, around ten or so, but yes, we're fine."

"You're not going to rest tonight?"

"Naw. Eric's excited to see you." *That's true anyway,* JJ thought.

"Well, be safe, and don't rush on my account. We're fine."

"OK then," JJ said. "I'll call ahead and let Robert know that you're still on track and will be there soon."

After they hung up, Abby sat looking out the window. *Tracking me?* She sighed. Part of her was a little insulted. *Haven't I proven that I can take care of myself?* She knew he was just doing a thorough job, though. There was no doubt Robert was paying a huge sum to make sure Abby was kept safe. It made her smile to know that he cared so deeply for her, and she gave up feeling insulted.

*   *   *

159

When the phone rang, Robert had been sitting in his garden watching the skyline like a little boy waiting for Santa on Christmas Eve. He spoke with JJ for a few minutes, hung up with a smile on his face, and flagged down one of his security men.

"Greg, where are the other guys?"

Greg checked his watch. "Just wrapping up lunch. Why, do you need something?"

Robert couldn't stop smiling, "I've got some big news. Let's join them in the kitchen, and I'll tell you all at once."

He hadn't told anyone yet. The small production team occupied several guest homes that were out of sight of the main house. Aside from the technician who would perform the procedure to unlock Abby's memories and the staff psychologist who would guide her through the confusion over the next few days, none of them needed to know of her return. They were occupied with the current season and rarely noticed anything else going on around them anyway.

He would speak with the tech and the psychologist when the time came, but seeing as how Abby was less than an hour away, Robert decided to notify his small personal security team that she was coming home. The security team for the production crew didn't need to know, nor did anyone else.

In the kitchen, the other two men were just putting away the plates from their lunch when Robert started in, telling them Abby would be there soon. "There is no need to bring in extra security. Bryce is dead, as you know."

Mike, Robert's longest-tenured guard and de facto leader of the small team spoke up, "With all due respect, sir, I think that's our call. Mr. Haydenson is no longer a factor, but when word gets out that she's here, I expect the press to descend on this place within twenty-four hours. Probably quicker."

"So, let's not let word get out, but just in case, close the gates and monitor the parameter," Robert said, attempting to mock Mike's serious tone. "There will be some news cameras out there. They can take all the video they want from outside the gates. I don't really care about that. The last time we brought in extra detail, we needed to protect Abby from a killer, and it was a fiasco. Half the guys were Bryce's men. We're not protecting her life this time, just her privacy. The last thing we need are a couple of reporters getting in here masquerading as security. I think we've learned that having back-up is more trouble than it's worth."

He looked at Greg, who had been on staff as back-up security the night Bryce tried to take Abby. He had suffered a broken nose and orbital socket that night at the hands of that lunatic. His face still didn't look right because of it. "No offense, Greg."

"None taken, sir."

"You're one of the good ones, but there were plenty of guys on that crew that weren't playing for our team," Robert continued. "Now, she'll be landing via seaplane at the beach within the hour. Greg, I'd like you to be on the beach with me to meet them. We'll pay off the pilot to keep his mouth shut, but I'd like you to give him some added incentive. Again, we're just trying to keep things quiet here. Questions?"

Greg had a bit of a nervous look when he spoke up. "Sir, I appreciate your confidence, but I think Mike is your man for the beach. We all know he's the strong arm around here." He smiled, attempting levity, but it was clear he was not interested in being part of the Abby welcoming committee.

"Oh, have more confidence in yourself Greg," Robert said. "Mike, Ted, let's lock up the gates. Greg, you're with me."

16

THIRTEEN TIME ZONES away in Chicago, Bryce stood scowling out the window at the dreary skyline overlooking Lake Michigan. It had been nearly six months since he faked his own death and had been living in relative secrecy.

He had spent several months and a small fortune trying to figure out where Abby was hiding. He had a crew of six guys scouring the islands and interrogating the locals, but they turned up nothing. Not even a hint that anyone had seen her. He spent two months himself island hopping, with no luck. Realistically, he had to admit there was just too much ground to cover and not enough men to do it. He would go broke or get his legs broken, or both, if he kept it up.

He had ignored the duties he had to his boss and to the organization, and he was warned that things were going to come to a head very soon if he didn't get his shit together and get back home. He was pissed, he was panicked, and he had to make sure she kept her mouth shut. Abby dead seemed to be the best way to go about that.

Somehow, she knew who he was and that she should avoid him. He had no idea how she possessed this information, as she was supposed to be missing the last ten years of her memory, but the fact was, she did. She would never come out of hiding as long as she knew he was out there waiting for her, trying to find her.

That's when he hatched an ingenious plan: to fake his own death. He had to make it big and spectacular. Something that would make the news, and therefore make its way back to Abby. Once she knew he was dead, he was sure she would come out of hiding. Who could give up ten years of their life like that?

He went to his boss, Mr. Rosso, with the plan. It was risky, and he needed manpower and the boss's blessing to make it work. Mr. Rosso was skeptical at first, but once Bryce explained how he would benefit, he was all for it. Like any business organization, the mob had their top performers, the top ten percent, where Bryce and a select few resided. After that, there was a solid eighty percentage of middle-of-the-road guys, making a living and loyal to the organization. It was the bottom ten percent that, like any manager, concerned Mr. Rosso the most. These were sleezeballs – guys loyal to the almighty dollar instead of the family.

Bryce's plan was to get these guys together on a job, make sure the authorities got tipped off, and then make sure they were slaughtered like lambs – including him.

Bryce recruited the guys that they wanted to get rid of, with promises of huge personal cuts above the norm, and they took the bait. The plan came together over the course of a couple weeks to make it look legit. All in all, there were eight men, plus Bryce, who would pull the job. Four more would man the getaway cars and act as lookout. There was also one more that no one but Bryce knew about, and he would be the key to making sure everything came together.

The day came. They would hit the bank at the end of the business day, when there would be the most cash. There was an empty warehouse on the same block as the bank, behind the building. That was their staging area. Getaway cars were set on all four corners of the block. Bryce would be inside the bank itself and give them the go when the time was right. The plan was set.

The FBI received an anonymous envelope twenty-four hours beforehand containing the blueprint for the heist. There were drawings of the warehouse and the rest of the block, mapping out their approach. There were also descriptions of the getaway cars and their locations, along with a roster of names. From inside the bank, at five minutes to five, Bryce called the number two man in the warehouse.

"It's time," he said, then clicked off the phone.

The plan was for the crew to exit the warehouse, come down the alley next to the bank, and enter through the front door with an immediate show of force. The crew exited the warehouse, guns drawn and made it halfway down the alley.

"FREEZE, FBI!" came a booming voice.

The men found themselves surrounded by dozens of agents clad in black and weapons hot. The men in the getaway cars were pulled from their vehicles and arrested at the same time.

From inside the bank, Bryce waited for the sound that would seal the deal. Suddenly, the crack of several gunshots rang out next to the bank, quickly followed by an eruption of gunfire. Bryce's other man, the one only he knew about, was situated in an apartment above the alley. He never showed his face – just reached out the window, blindly fired three shots down into the ally, and fled the scene like a bat out of hell.

That was all it took. The authorities took over from there and cut down all eight men in the alley within seconds. The mob already had their man in the medical examiner's office. His palms were greased, records falsified, and Bryce officially declared dead. The getaway drivers, whose lives had been spared, gave statements that Bryce had been the ringleader of the operation. One of them even speculated, "Hell, he was crazy. He probably fired the first shot."

The stories led the late-night news programs across the country, and Bryce was officially dead. He was a crazed mobster no one had heard of yesterday, but today he had started a gunfight with the authorities and was now on the cold steel of the coroner's table. It was a win for the good guys.

In reality, Bryce had walked out the front door of the

bank unscathed, got into a waiting Town Car, and disappeared for a couple months while the dust settled.

He had traded his short-cropped blond hair for a longer brown mane and grown in his beard. Mr. Rosso and the few other top guys in the organization had been in on the plan, and, in fact, the whole charade made him even more valuable. Bryce was a ghost. He did not exist. He kept a low profile, didn't associate with any of his former crew, and he waited.

Bryce had a dozen fake identities, and a dozen more if he needed them. Every one of them with no record. He had been trying to enjoy his new anonymity, but he was losing faith that Abby would ever surface. Lately, he had started to wonder if it had been all for naught.

He glanced at his phone, and it took him a moment to recognize the name on the incoming call. When he did, he immediately hoped that his dreary day was about to get a great deal better, "Greg, I haven't heard from you in weeks. You got some news, I hope?"

Bryce beamed a self-satisfied grin as Greg told him that he would have eyes on Abby within the hour.

"You done good, Greg."

"Thank you, sir. I've had plenty of time to think about the extraction, too. Getting her out of here is easy enough. I could grab her in the middle of the night and be hours away before anyone knows a thing. The problem is what to do with her after that. Do you have a plan for getting her back to the States?"

Bryce laughed. "Greg, I appreciate your eagerness, but I have a plan in place."

"That's excellent news, sir. Just tell me what I have to do."

"Keep an eye on her." Bryce said abruptly.

"Absolutely, but then what?"

"That's the best part. You don't have to do a thing. When she gets her memory back, she's going to come right back to me."

Greg was a bit dumbstruck. He obviously lacked any sort of insight into the details of the situation, but he did know that Abby had gone to extreme lengths to hide from his boss. "Um, sir, forgive me for asking what is probably a stupid question, but why would she do that?"

"The only direct flight out of the big island to the states is to Chicago, yes?"

"As far as I know, sir."

"And that is where I happen to make my home."

"But why would she come to you?"

"She won't be coming to me, Greg. She thinks I'm dead, remember? Let's just say that she left something awfully important behind. Once she gets her memory back, there is no way that she won't return. No way. You just keep me in the loop. I have a man I'm calling in a favor to. He's on the big island. You let me know when she's heading there to fly home, and I'll have him take care of things from there. You're too valuable. I don't want to blow your cover. You never know when your position may come in handy again."

Bryce was filled with glee, to the point that he was nearly giggling like a schoolboy despite the pain in his leg as he limped away from the window. Abby had damn near severed his leg on the boat, and now he was looking forward to returning the favor. The wheels were in motion. Abby's days were numbered, ticking down into the single digits. He sneered at her photo on the mantle.

This is going to be fun.

17

ROBERT WADED INTO the water as Frank cut the engine and his seaplane floated the last few yards to the beach.

"Sir!" Greg called from the beach.

Robert simply waived him off as he flung open the passenger-side door of the plane. "Abby!"

She squealed and jumped down into Robert's arms, where she squeezed him tight.

He squeezed her tighter and stroked the back of her hair like a father comforting his daughter. When they separated, Robert was clearly overcome with emotion. His huge smile couldn't hide the tears gathering in his eyes. "Let me look at you!" he said with a shaky voice as he held her at arm's length. He shook his head, trying to gather himself, and wrapped his arm around her shoulder as they walked onto the beach. "Welcome home, Abby."

She smiled. "Thanks. I'm so happy to see you!"

Captain Frank hopped down from the plane after it was secured and stood by, waiting to be spoken to. He watched Robert and Abby embrace, and saw the bond between them. That was something the cameras had never revealed on *Trial Island*.

He knew who Robert was. For that matter, most of the world knew who he was. He was a billionaire, albeit a wildly eccentric one, but anyone with that much money is very powerful. Frank also saw with his own eyes just how deeply Robert cared for Abby. He couldn't help but think of his own estranged daughter. He also couldn't help but think of what Robert might do to him for having deceived Abby and nearly delivering her to the media.

Frank had done some soul searching over the past seventy miles and already felt horribly guilty for nearly destroying Abby's life for five thousand dollars. She was right; he was getting taken for a ride. Her story was worth a heck of a lot more than that. He was ashamed to think that his life was in such a sad state that he had been willing to do that. Seeing her now, happy beyond anything to be reunited with Robert, made his shame worse.

Robert saw him standing by and reached out for a handshake. "You must be Captain Frank!"

"Guilty as charged," Frank smiled.

"I'll be honest, I was skeptical of Abby hopping on a plane with someone she didn't know, but obviously I was wrong. It's very nice to meet you."

Frank looked at the ground and kicked the sand. Robert would find out anyway. He may as well be a man and own up to it now. "Well, sir, we did run into a bit of a problem."

"Oh?"

Abby looked at the pilot. "Frank, it's OK."

"No, Abby, I was wrong." Frank told Robert about the investigator who told him to get in touch if Abby ever showed up. "I know it was wrong, but they were going to pay a ton of money if I delivered her for an interview. So, I was going to, until, uh, Abby persuaded me otherwise."

Abby smiled at Robert. "I told you I can take care of myself. Besides, Frank, I can tell you're a good guy at heart. Obviously you're in a tough spot or you wouldn't have done that. I told you I would take care of you if you got me here, and you held up your end of the bargain."

Frank shook his head. "Absolutely not. I can't. Consider this trip on the house."

Robert considered that for a moment. "So, Frank, you know who Abby is obviously. What you might not know is that it is extremely important to me that her whereabouts remain a secret. That investigator you spoke with is one of dozens combing the islands out here. Back in the States, any news outlet would kill for the story. You seem like a decent guy. Can we count on your to keep this whole thing under wraps?"

"Yes, sir," Frank said without hesitation.

Robert was still skeptical. It would take more than just his word. He had been planning to pay him off. If he didn't want the money, he would have to figure out something else. "This is a huge story, Frank. Massive. There's a lot of money out there for whoever breaks it. You're willing to give that up? For what? Honestly, I'd feel much better if we compensated you for your cooperation."

Frank thought about it. The money *would* be good. It wouldn't change his situation, though – sleeping in a dump and getting hammered every night in a bar. Yes, he needed the money, but he was wise enough to know he would blow through it in no time and be back in the same situation a few months down the road.

He had just been through a very sobering morning, made more so by thoughts of his daughter. He needed money, but more than that, he needed a change. He had a thought and chuckled under his breath.

Robert and Abby exchanged a glance. "What is it?" Abby asked.

"It's just... I guess I'm having a moment here. I make my living on this plane, flying packages and vacationers around the islands for a few bucks. I live in a room where my bed is a few feet from my sink. And this," he gestured around the beautiful grounds of Robert's estate, the huge Victorian mansion up a bit from the beach, and a dozen or so out buildings and villas in the background, "this is beautiful, and seeing the two of you together, caring about each other so much... well, I'm thinking my life is sort of shit. Maybe that's just the clarity of twelve hours without a drink, but man, what am I doing?"

Robert didn't know this man at all, but he knew

people, and he could see Frank's pain. "Well Frank, it *does* sound like you are having a moment. A little clarity is a good thing now and then, right?"

Frank nodded his head.

"Stay for a bit. Have some lunch. You seem like a decent fellow, and I appreciate that you did right by Abby. I'd like to make things right with you, and make it worth your while not to share the story." Robert called to Greg, who was standing further up the beach. "Greg, get her bags and put them in her room. We'll be in the kitchen."

Greg cleared his throat. "Yes, sir."

Abby turned to him. "Umm, I don't have any bags." She stared at Greg an extra second, thinking he looked familiar.

Robert laughed. "Well, let's go have us some lunch then."

"Sounds great!"

Back at the house, Robert instructed Greg to take the pilot out onto the patio to eat while he caught up with Abby. Captain Frank did seem like a decent fellow, but he was an extra piece of the puzzle now, and one that could throw a serious wrench in the works. Robert didn't want him knowing anymore than he already did.

Robert and Abby stood at the counter making sandwiches, and were so excited to catch up that they just ate their lunch standing right there without stopping the conversation for a moment. Between sips of iced tea,

174

Abby told Robert all about their adventure to find a new home, the fate of his boat that they sank nearly a year ago, and the paradise that they found where they built a new life.

"This area's addictive isn't it?" Robert asked. "I don't know if you remember, way back on *Trial Island* when we met, I told you that I took holiday out here and fell in love with the geography. That was absolutely true."

Abby was quiet for a moment, trying to figure out exactly what she was trying to say.

"What is it?" Robert asked.

"You've been a great friend and a great guide. Truly, I wouldn't be alive today if it wasn't for you. So I have to ask, what do you think about me getting my memory back? Is it a good idea?"

"Absolutely. As I always say, you can do what you want, but with Bryce out of the picture, I feel like you really should."

"What if there's more than Bryce? I mean, I know I was running from him, but what if there was more that I wanted to forget?"

"I've reminded you before, and I will again, you and I know each other much better than you realize. Yes, you very well could have hidden some details about your life from me. However, from what I know of you and your life, I feel that you would be positively thrilled getting your memories back. That's just my humble opinion, though."

175

Abby was nodding her head. "I told myself that you would be the last piece of the puzzle. You haven't steered me wrong yet, so let's do it!" She jumped from her seat.

Robert laughed a bit uncomfortably. "It's not quite that simple." He gestured for her to sit and then took her hands in his, leaning forward. "Eric was quick and simple, right? We did his procedure while he was waiting for you to come to dinner. Do you remember what he told you?"

She thought about it, but she couldn't remember anything that stuck out. "Not really. I mean, he said that his life hadn't really changed much. I remember that."

"Exactly. Twenty-two-year-old Eric lived in a small apartment in a questionable neighborhood with a handful of friends. He got up early every morning to work construction, and when he clocked out every night he went home, had some beers, and did it all again the next day. Thirty-two-year-old Eric was leading the same life. Same apartment, same friends, same routine."

"OK," Abby thought, "but why is this important for me?"

"Eric's procedure was simple. We just had to flip a switch. There was nothing in the memory banks, so to speak, that would be a shock to his system. You, on the other hand, have a significantly more complex history. The psychologist has determined that we cannot just 'flip a switch' for you. It would be too much for you to process all at once."

"So, what does that mean?"

"It's going to take much longer. Probably the better part of twenty-four hours. We're going to have to open the doors of your past slowly, one by one. Let your conscious mind process it a little at a time. Does that sound reasonable?"

"I suppose so. As long as we can get started right away, before I change my mind."

*   *   *

Abby stared in amazement as she walked into the bedroom of her college apartment to find the shades still drawn and Rick still sleeping in his jeans and T-shirt at three in the afternoon when she got home from her latest temp gig. *Has he been here all day?*

As aggravated as she was that he had spent the past several months freeloading in her apartment while she bounced from temp job to temp job trying to make enough to pay the rent every month, she still tip-toed around the bedroom as she changed out of her business appropriate dress and into her favorite pair of yoga pants and a tank top. She felt shallow to admit it, but his money had certainly been an attention grabber when they first met. Unfortunately it turned out that he was mostly trying to impress her. Now that they were together, he always had one excuse or another as to why he couldn't kick in for rent, or pick up the check at dinner.

She stood in the kitchen eating ice cream directly out of the half-gallon container and staring at the calendar, doing the mental math on the number of paydays she had left before the next rent check was due. It was nearing the holidays, almost the end of the year, and she had given up on reaching her sister. Rick had become a permanent fixture in her apartment, despite her best attempts to get rid of him over the summer.

He contributed nothing but weed, which she couldn't even partake in given that she was drug-tested on a regular basis through the temp agency. She had spent the past several months bouncing from position to position, trying to keep a roof over her head, and wondering exactly where her life was going.

She was stressed, and when Rick finally offered to pay for something, she said yes without a second thought.

After he stumbled into bed one night, through the haze, he said, "You work so hard, baby. Let's go to Vegas for New Year's Eve. Whaddya say?"

"Let's do it!"

She had to blow off some steam, and she had no work lined up yet for the following week. Companies were nearing the end of their fiscal year and money for temps was pretty much dried up until late February or March. Heck, maybe they would stay in Vegas for a few days. He had been living on her dime for long enough, and she certainly didn't feel badly about making him shell out for a hotel room for an extra couple of nights.

Abby and Rick arrived in Las Vegas on New Year's Eve in the late afternoon. She wore a tight, black-sequin dress for the hour-long flight. Her low cut dress displayed her healthy bust and garnered the attention of every man on the flight. Rick loved it. They were all looking at his girl, and he made sure they knew she was his girl.

With no more family, no friends, and little in the way of a support system, Abby enjoyed the attention, too.

Rick wore a black, button-down shirt and a flashy silver suit. They were going straight to meet some associates of his and weren't expecting to wait long for the party to start. She landed with two changes of clothes in her carry-on, both as skimpy as the black dress. Abby was ready to party for a couple of days. It had been months since she had cut loose. She had been on the straight and narrow, despite Rick's best efforts over the past few months. A weekend of partying wouldn't hurt. *I deserve it, damn it!*

Abby never returned to her college apartment.

She didn't leave Vegas for over a year.

Of course, Rick didn't stick around that long.

At three a.m. that night, she had been awake for nearly twenty-four hours. They were at a party in a high-rise penthouse right on the Strip with a beautiful view of the city. Rick had disappeared hours earlier, just after their midnight kiss. However, she had quickly made friends with four beautiful women. They saw her looking lonely and brought her into their little group.

Abby assumed they were the wives or girlfriends of suppliers who were much more successful than Rick. They wore designer dresses, high-end perfume, and beautiful jewelry. It was clear that they had money. A woman, especially one who has been scraping pennies together to buy instant noodles for the past year, can smell money like a bloodhound tracking an escaped convict.

Their outfits and jewels combined were worth more than Abby had made since graduation. She was instantly taken with them, and truth be told, she was a little jealous. *Why couldn't I land a high roller? How did I wind up with Rick?*

One of them saw her laying back on the plush leather couch, eyes half closed, and said, "Oh, no. No, no, no. We're going all night, girlfriend!"

She instantly produced five lines of white powder on the coffee table. The first four disappeared in quick succession, and the alpha of the group, a curvy woman in a revealing dark green dress, held out a small metal straw for Abby.

As the four women watched her, Abby thought, *Why the hell not?*

Rick was watching from a corner of the room with one of his buddies and laughed.

His friend punched him in the shoulder. "You're lettin' your girl chill with those whores?"

"Those aren't just whores, bro, that's some high-end tail over there. Those bitches pull a couple g's a night!"

"Well, Abby's better lookin' than any of them. You better not let them recruit her."

Rick laughed. "Depends. You think I'd get a cut?"

*   *   *

The ladies Abby met that night in the penthouse did not recruit her, though after getting a taste of the life they led, a lost, broke, and confused Abby, with a little nudge from Rick, figured she could make some decent money wearing a skimpy dress and serving cocktails at the right places.

Rick introduced her to a manager at his favorite casino on the Strip, and that very night she found herself bringing drinks to patrons who were savvy enough to find the hidden bar between floors at the newest and swankiest Vegas high-rise. Abby, being exceptionally young and beautiful, was instantly the most popular girl in the bar. This made for great tips, but also made her draw the ire of the other girls.

She had been serving drinks for about a month when a stocky Latino who introduced himself as Manny sat down on a cushy chair.

"I haven't seen you around here before," he said to Abby when she came over to take his order.

Abby flashed her friendliest smile. "I'm new here."

"New here, or new in town?"

"Both."

"Where are you living?"

"I'm staying with friends." In reality, she was staying in a crappy hotel room with Rick, way off the Strip.

Manny nodded, making no effort to conceal that he was undressing her with his eyes. "How much do you make a night?"

"Depends on how much a man wants to impress me."

"Come on, how much?"

"A big spender might leave a few hundred in tips," she said hesitantly, unsure where this was going.

Unimpressed, he let out a *tsk, tsk* sound and handed her his card. "You're the most beautiful girl in this place, you know that, right? I run a club up by Old Vegas. You want to make some real money, you come see me."

She laughed him off, pushing his hand away. "No thanks. I'm not interested in having sex with random guys for money."

"No, not a girl like you." Manny assessed her up and down again, "You don't have to do that. You'll rake in over a grand a night just for letting them look at you." He could tell Abby was confused, so he clarified, "Stripping."

She shook her head. "I'm not doing that either, thanks."

"Take my card anyway, and think about it. I can give you a good job and a place to stay until you get on your feet." He folded his card into her hand, wrapped in a one-hundred dollar bill.

As she watched him leave, she did think about it. *A thousand dollars a night? Just to look at me?* Abby looked at the card in her hand. She was tired of supporting Rick. The story here was the same as it was in California. She kept a roof over his head and food in the fridge, and he contributed almost nothing. A thousand dollars a night and a place to stay was certainly an inviting proposition. She figured it couldn't hurt to at least check out the place.

However, it did hurt. The place looked like a dump. It was in the general vicinity of Old Vegas, but nowhere near the action. It was in a sketchy section of what was fundamentally a sketchy city – but the promise of money drew her in.

It was good the first month or so. Then Manny told her about the expenses she had to cover. She had to tip out the bar staff that kept everyone drunk, as well as the bouncers who kept grabby customers at bay and the limo drivers who brought customers in from the Strip – mostly whatever groups of guys they found wandering the streets and talked into hopping in the limo.

Then Manny told her if she was going to continue to stay in the apartment with the other girls, she had to contribute to the rent. After everyone took their cut, she found herself with less in her pocket than she had made waiting tables, but now she was stuck.

The final part of Manny's strategy clicked into place when the other girls reintroduced Abby to the white powder that they all used to forget their current lot in life. It wasn't as good as what the high-class escorts had shared with Abby her first night in the city, but it did the trick.

She had thought about packing up and leaving, but couldn't ever put enough together for airfare. Besides, where would she go? With her parents dead, her sister estranged, and anyone who ever had been a friend in the rearview mirror, Abby had no place to run.

By her second New Year's in Vegas, Abby found herself grinding against a polished brass pole without even remembering that it had been a year ago today that she arrived in Sin City for the first time. Truth be told, she barely remembered last night, never mind last year.

Had any of her former friends or family walked in, they wouldn't have recognized her. She was too skinny, but somehow managed to keep her tits despite the twenty pounds she had lost over the past year. Fortunately, her face was still undeniably beautiful, despite its thinned-out appearance, and her amber eyes were as captivating as ever. Those couple of assets at least kept the tips coming in. Otherwise, after ten months working in this shithole, she took most of her meals through a straw up her nose and looked every bit the part.

Rick had drifted in and out of her life for a couple of months. He liked to hang out at the club occasionally, which was usually the only place that she saw him. He told Abby it was to keep an eye on her, but it seemed that he liked to keep his eyes on the other girls, too. One night Rick went back into the girl's dressing room to see Abby. She wasn't in yet, but some of the other girls were. When Abby walked in, she found him with his hands on one of the girls.

Abby flipped out and went after him, harmlessly

clubbing his chest and back with her clenched fists. Rick laughed it off, which enraged Abby even more and she began screaming at him. This got Manny's attention from out in the club, and brought him running back into the dressing room.

"What the hell is going on back here?"

Abby pointed at Rick, "This piece of shit... I walk in here, and he's got his hands all over Candy!"

Manny glared at Rick, "What the hell are you doing back here anyway? I told you before, stay outta here."

"But..." Rick started.

"But nothing," Manny rubbed his chin to compose himself. "All these girls, they work for me. If you get them pissed off, the customers aren't gonna be happy, and if the customers aren't happy, you're costing me money."

Rick was about to respond, but thought better of it and just said, "Sorry Manny."

"Don't do it again. If I catch you back here again, I'm gonna break something. You got me?"

"I got you Manny."

"Good, now get the fuck outta here."

Abby flipped Rick the finger as he sulked out the door.

When Abby took the stage, there was Rick sitting at the bar, smiling ear to ear. Abby was sick of the smug look on his face. She decided that she'd had enough of Rick, and with Manny already running hot, she thought she might be able to get rid of him for good.

She slid down off the stage onto the lap of a good-looking businessman. She knew that Rick was watching from his seat at the bar. Abby led the man by his collar into the back room with the private booths and picked one that gave her a view of Rick through the doorway. She was extra nice to the man, and gave him the private show of his life, all the while staring straight at Rick.

This pissed him off to no end, and Abby could tell he was squirming in his seat. He managed to keep his composure for a little while. Then Abby broke him. She clearly and gratuitously reached down and slipped her hand down the front of the man's pants, and mouthed the words *Fuck You* to Rick, then began kissing the man's neck.

Rick lost it. He ran from the bar and through the open curtained doorway, grabbed Abby, and threw her off the man. A fight instantly broke out, and the bouncers just as instantly descended on the scene and dragged the two men apart.

The businessman, in his clean black suit and striped button down shirt, was profusely apologized to and enjoyed the rest of the night on the club's dime. Rick, on the other hand, was dragged out the back door into the ally, where Manny's knee swiftly met his crotch. Two bouncers, one on each side, grabbed onto Rick's shoulders to keep him from falling to the ground.

As Rick was hunched over, Manny grabbed him by the collar and brought his face close, "What the hell was that in there?"

"I'm sorry Manny, it's just, she was trying to get to me and she did."

"What's your problem? Why are you hanging around here? I warned you."

"I'm sorry Manny, it's tough watching your girl with other guys, I just... I just snapped. It won't happen again."

"Your girl isn't with other guys. In this club, Abby's not your girl, she's my girl, like every other piece of ass in there." Manny thought a second, "You're right, Rick, it won't happen again." He nodded to the bouncer on the right, who grasped Rick's right arm and held it up.

Rick was confused, "What are you doing?"

While the bouncers held Rick still, Manny grasped his thumb in his meaty palm, and bent it backwards until it snapped like the stem of a banana and Rick screamed out in agony.

"I warned you!" Manny yelled in his face. "I warned you! Now get the fuck out of here, and I swear if I ever see you in my club again I'll break your fuckin' legs, you got me?"

Rick nodded as tears streamed down his face and he blubbered like a child.

"Get him outta here before the customer's hear him."

The bouncers dragged Rick down the alley and threw him onto the sidewalk, where he stumbled down the street to find an emergency room.

That was the last time that Abby or anyone else at the club saw Rick. It was also the last day that Abby had a real clear memory of.

Every day was the same shitty day as the one before. She woke up in pain, feeling that today was the day she would die. The only thing that took the pain away was the same thing that caused it. The thing she craved more than anything. It was the same thing that drove her to let strangers feel her up while she buried their faces in her chest. It was the same thing that drove her to let them do more than that when she was either exceptionally broke or exceptionally high. That white powder turned her depression around and made the world a bearable place, at least for a little while.

The owner kept her and most of the other girls at a shitbox hotel in an alley behind the club. Dirty sheets that hadn't been washed in years barely covered the mildew and fluid-stained mattresses where the girls passed out each night after huffing the bulk of their tips.

While she smiled and winked at the customers as she danced, Abby's head hurt and she was looking forward to lying down on the flat limp bag that passed for a pillow.

That's when she saw five one-hundred dollar bills laid out on the stage in front of her. Her eyes struggled to focus on the man who had laid them down. Abby commanded her eyes to look straight and focus, but it was a losing battle. Realistically, she didn't care at all what he looked like. His money was green, and that was all that mattered.

She slid off the stage and directly onto his lap, putting her arms around his neck. He reached behind her and picked up the bills, folding them neatly, and sliding them into the string of her thong. In her mind, she leaned forward to whisper something flirty and clever in his ear. In reality, she fell into him and slurred, "I'm going to fuck you so good…" That was all the eloquence she could muster.

The man smiled without having understood what she said. "Let's go someplace private."

She led him to a private booth in the back room. On the way there, he flagged down a cocktail waitress and whispered something in her ear. The waitress seemed confused.

"Really?" she asked.

"Is that a problem?"

She smacked her gum. "Well, no, but…"

"Then do it," he said, and sent her away.

Abby stood in the booth waiting for her man to follow, and when he sat down, she immediately straddled him. "Just tell me how you like it." She burped and threw up in her mouth a little. Swallowing it back down, she

189

smacked her lips and said, "Sorry," as she started to grind against him.

He smiled and firmly placed his hands on her hips, stopping her, then lifting her slightly off his lap. "Have a seat a minute." He nodded, indicating the chair next to him.

"It's your dough, pal." She collapsed into the seat.

They looked at each other for a moment. Between the dim light and the drug-fueled haze she was slowly coming out of, she couldn't make out his features. She could see he had a good build and was significantly older than her. He stood up and took off his sport coat. "Here," he said, putting it around her shoulders and covering her bare chest.

She smiled a bit uncomfortably, not sure what to think. "Um… thanks."

"What are you doing here?" he asked.

Abby laughed. "Making a living, like everyone else. This your idea of small talk?"

"You don't belong here. You're better than these other girls. Prettier, too."

"Sure thing, pal." She attempted to stand on her wobbly legs. "You want a dance or not?"

"I already paid for your time. Sit down." His voice was as firm as his grip around her hips had been. She sat as the waitress came over with two espressos and a large glass of water. The man leaned forward and said, "Excuse me," before he opened the sport coat Abby was wearing and took a packet from the inside pocket before covering her up again. He ripped open the packet and dropped two tablets into the water, which immediately began to fizz. He held it up for her. "Drink this."

She furrowed her brow. "Fuck you, pal, I'm not letting you drug me."

He raised the glass to his lips and took a swig, "It's not gonna hurt you. Besides, I paid for you. I don't have to drug you. Remember?"

Abby shrugged. *What's the worst that could happen?* Whether this guy drugged her or paid for her, she would likely wake up in the morning with no recollection of the night before, probably having fucked a random stranger and feeling like her head was a melon bursting at the seams. Deciding that his drug might at least make her standard morning better, she downed the water as he sipped his espresso. When she was done, he gestured to her espresso, which she took and began to sip.

"So, you paid me five bills on New Year's Eve because you wanted to have coffee?"

"I want to help you. I've been here before, but we've never talked."

She looked at him closely. Her focus was better. He was a good-looking man with beautiful eyes, but she had seen so many faces come and go; he was one of thousands and didn't look the least bit familiar.

191

"And how are you going to help me?" she asked.

"You can do better. What's your name?"

"Lacey." She smiled weakly.

He returned her grin. "OK, Lacey, let me be straight. I'd like you to give this up and spend some time with me. I do well for myself, and I'll take care of you."

She laughed. She'd heard it all before. Two or three times a night. So much so that it was just background noise. The men thought they should say something like that; the ones with a soul anyway. Hell, with enough drinks in them, a few of them probably even meant it. Once they get home to their wives and families, though, Abby became just another pleasurable Vegas memory.

She stood up, shot the remainder of the espresso, and slid his coat off her shoulders to reveal her perfect breasts in the dim light. "You seem like a nice enough guy, but I don't need saving. I can take care of myself just fine." She leaned over and kissed him gently on the cheek and whispered. "Thanks for the coffee."

Abby turned and walked back toward the stage. He called from behind her, "Think about it! You'll come around."

She waved over her head without turning around. Something about him struck her as different. She instantly wanted to smack herself for even having that thought. He wasn't different. None of them were.

From the stage, she watched as he stopped by the

door on the way out to speak with the club manager, Manny. Manny laughed, though the customer was not laughing. That's when Manny stopped laughing, suddenly looked angry and appeared to threaten the man. The man proceeded to take a fistful of Manny's shirt and leaned into him, saying something into his ear. As one of the bouncers closed in, he released Manny's shirt and left, without anyone laying a finger on him.

Manny turned to face the stage and saw Abby looking at him. She turned away as he turned to the bouncer and began a very animated conversation that went on until Abby left the stage

What was that all about? she wondered.

18

ABBY FOUND OUT what that conversation was about when she arrived for her shift the following afternoon and saw Manny waiting at the door for her. He pulled her to the side as soon as she walked in, and he explained that she no longer worked at the club.

She was confused, but immediately angry. Her first thought was that she needed cash and a place to stay. Without her job at the club, she had neither. "That's bullshit! What did I do?"

"You didn't *do* anything Abby. You remember your client last night?"

"I had a lot of clients last night. Did someone complain?"

"No, no one complained. The blond-haired guy, he bought you a coffee or something?"

It was coming back slowly. "Yeah, what about him?

He said something about wanting me to run away with him or something. I told him to take a hike. Did he bitch about me, 'cause I didn't do anything out of line, I swear."

"No, no. Listen, he told me last night that he didn't want you working here anymore. I laughed and told him to fuck off, but he wasn't kidding. I've never heard of the guy before, but I guess he's a big deal. There's some tough-looking dude and a chick sitting in my office waiting to take you to him."

"So what, this guy wants me fired, and that's that?"

"He's not just some guy, Abby. He's connected. There's nothing I can do."

"Well, if he's connected, then he can get me my job back." She pushed past him and threw open the door of Manny's office to face her chaperons.

The woman could tell Abby was unhappy the moment she walked in the room and did her best to calm her. "My employer just wants to speak with you. If you don't like what he has to say, then you can be on your way." She smiled, though she knew her employer didn't just 'speak' to anyone. He commanded and got what he wanted, especially from women.

"Fine," Abby sighed. "Let's just get this over with."

On the way to the meeting, they offered to stop off at Abby's poor excuse for an apartment so she could grab anything she might need.

Abby laughed. "There's nothing there I need, honey."

"My name is Elyse, not honey. My employer plans to bring you to G's tonight. Do you have a nice dress you could wear?"

Abby raised her eyebrows and used her hands to indicate the skintight, sequined, black miniskirt and tube top she had on. "This isn't good enough?"

She shook her head. "Never mind. We'll do a little shopping first."

Two hours later, Abby sat at a candlelit table for two in the back of a very exclusive restaurant wearing a short, black, designer dress that cost more than she had brought home in the last month. She was actually a bit nervous. Elyse gave her a quick bump of the white powder to help take the edge off, though her foot still tapped anxiously on the floor as she waited.

"Can you at least tell me his name?" Abby asked.

"His name is Bryce, and he is very fond of you. You don't have anything to be nervous about."

When her date arrived, she didn't recognize him at all. His handsome face and neat, cropped blond hair looked vaguely familiar from the night before, though she wouldn't have recognized him if they had passed on the street.

She had originally agreed to meet him so she could give him a piece of her mind and get back to the club before the end of her shift. *As long as I'm here, I should at least enjoy a nice meal, I guess.* Abby thought and thought, and determined that it had been years since anyone had taken her out to a nice dinner, despite the fact that she had more male companionship over the past twelve months than any self-respecting woman should see in a lifetime.

He ordered a very nice, and very expensive, bottle of red wine. It was a smooth pinot noir that easily glided over her lips and down her throat, and gave her a warm comfortable feeling. They talked and laughed. For the first time since coming to Sin City, Abby actually felt connected to someone. He asked her about where she was from, how she had found her way to Vegas, and where she was going from here?

Abby found herself half drunk, craving another bump of the white powder, and without a real answer to his question. *Where am I going from here?* It caught her by surprise. It had been so long since she had given any thought past the next score that when she honestly asked herself the question, she was terrified by the answer: *My life is going nowhere.*

Bryce interrupted her thoughts. "I don't know if you remember what I asked you about last night, but I meant it. Come stay with me, keep me company, and I'll take care of you."

Abby scoffed. "Why me? You don't know me at all."

"You're different. I knew it the second I saw you a few weeks back. I don't know what you're doing on that stage, but you don't belong there. There's more to you than that. I don't know... you looked... lost. I don't mean that as an insult. You just looked like a child that wanders off at the store and can't figure out how you got where you are." He placed his hand on hers and gave it a little squeeze. "I want to help you find your way back."

Abby looked into his blue eyes and smiled. Something inside told her that her life would never be the same again.

*   *   *

Dr. Chang Lee was a brilliant mind in the relatively new field of bio-digital engineering. He had originally worked in government research until Robert convinced him that the private sector could pay much more and offer him more opportunity to direct his own research. He had been the one who locked away ten years of Abby's memories and spent the last couple of hours going about the task of unlocking those memories. He went through the process slowly and methodically while Abby slept peacefully on her back on the bed in front of him.

The room was set up for maximum comfort, as well as sensory deprivation. The patient, for lack of a better term, lay in a delicate balance of natural sleep and medically induced anesthesia. The anesthetics brought the patient to a natural state of sleep, but administered very lightly, or not at all, depending on the state of sleep the patient was in.

As Dr. Lee unlocked her memories, the brain processed them as a dream. Before they started, he tried to explain it to Abby, who had a difficult time wrapping her mind around the process.

"So ten years of memories are going to suddenly flood

my head? Isn't that going to be confusing? I mean, that's a lot of information at once. How does that work? I mean, I'm not going to sleep for ten years and experience them all over again, right?"

"Think of it this way – what did you do yesterday?"

"What do you mean?"

"Yesterday, what did you do?"

Abby thought a moment. "Well, I had breakfast with Eric, then spent a few hours at a coffee house on the computer trying to figure out how to get here. I met Captain Frank last night at the bar, and then had dinner with Eric on the boat. That's about it."

"Alright," said Dr. Lee with a smile. "You just told me what you did yesterday. You summed up twenty-four hours in about fifteen seconds. If I asked you what you did last week, you might take a minute or two to explain it to me. If I asked you to tell me what you did last year, maybe you would sum it up in fifteen minutes or so. Your memories are the same way. You don't remember every second of every moment of every day – you remember the highlights. I'm going to unlock what we've hidden away for you, but you're not suddenly going to recall every conversation you had, every meal, or every moment. You're going to recall the important ones. Does that make sense?"

Abby thought about it. "I guess so."

"Because you're going to be asleep when the

procedure is done, those scenes are going to play out in your head like a dream. I'm sure you've had the experience of waking up from a vivid dream and asking yourself 'Was that real or a dream,' right?"

"Of course. Who hasn't?"

"Well, that's what it's going to feel like when you wake up. You will have just had a remarkable dream, so vivid you're going to say, 'That had to be real', and you'll be right – it was real. It just happened in the past."

Abby took a deep breath. "Well, what are we waiting for?"

*   *   *

Abby never returned to her apartment after dinner with Bryce that night. They left Vegas the next morning to go to Chicago, where he lived, and she never went back to the City of Sin.

Life was very exciting with Bryce. He was in the business. The syndicate, the mob, organized crime, whatever you called it. She didn't know the details of what he did, but he made boatloads of money and saw to it that she was taken care of. They went to dinners, to clubs, and he was always the main attraction at any party – and the parties were endless. She was constantly meeting new people and going to new places, and there was always an element of danger.

She found that the rush of all of the constant excitement in her life made her almost forget about drugs.

Biologically, she couldn't forget about them, but Bryce had sent her through rehab. It was rough, but she came out the other side and replaced her addiction to nose candy with an addiction to an exciting and dangerous life.

She eventually started using again, as it was impossible to avoid traveling in the circles they did, especially at parties. However, gone were the times when she would do a few rails a night and not remember one day to the next. A bump now and then socially kept her balanced just fine.

After just a few months, a Justice of the Peace married them, and Abby committed to spending her days fawning over Bryce. She was at his beck and call for whatever he wanted, whenever he wanted it. Bryce was quickly moving up in the ranks. To the outsider looking in, it seemed he had been extraordinarily fortunate to be in the right place at the right time.

She didn't know a great deal about the organizational structure of the "business," but she knew that there was one man at the top: Gaetano Rosso. She had never met him. All she knew was what she heard through Bryce or read in the papers.

Mr. Rosso, as Bryce usually referred to him, had suffered a personal tragedy not long after Bryce and Abby wed. His son, Nick, had been brutally murdered. Nick was someone whom Abby was more familiar with. She met him often, as Bryce was part of his crew.

One night, not long after they married, Bryce came home a complete mess in the middle of the night. His clothes were soaked in blood, and he was mumbling to himself. Abby had been sitting up waiting for him, as she often did, and panicked when she saw him. "Oh, my God! Are you OK?"

He looked up, almost shocked to see her, but also relieved. "Abby, I... I need help."

She grabbed a kitchen towel and soaked it to dab away the blood from his face, "Don't worry, I'll take care of you. Are you hurt?"

"No, it's more than that..."

They stared at each other a moment while she waited for him to continue.

"I... I killed him."

She was confused. "Who?"

Bryce stared down at his shaking, blood-soaked hands and whispered, "Nick".

"What?" Abby gasped.

"I had to Abby. He *knew*. He was going to ruin me, ruin us."

Abby stared in shock, unable to formulate words or ask a question. They had just had dinner with Nick and his wife, Angelina, three days ago. They shared appetizers, ate to their hearts' content, and went through four bottles of wine. It was a great night spent with friends, laughing and joking. What could have possibly happened? Finally, she spoke, "What did he know?"

"Abby, you're my wife. I need you to know I did this for us. I need you to cover for me."

"What did he know, Bryce?"

He sighed. "I've been skimming money off the top. A lot of money. He knew about it and called me out. He said he wanted to give me a chance to come clean to his old man." He looked up at her. "I can't do that. You don't get a second chance with these people. They'd let me pay them back, then kill me. That's how it works. I had to make a decision, and… I killed him."

Abby's mind was racing. Her entire life was tied to Bryce. If he went down, so would she. Morally, she was conflicted. Nick, despite his line of work, was a good man. Abby had a knot in her stomach thinking about his wife and two daughters. But if Bryce goes down, what would she do? Go back to stripping? Never. *I can't go back to that life*.

She touched her hand to his chin and lifted his head so they were looking eye to eye. Her voice shook with indecision as she spoke, but it was the only choice she had. "Tell me what I have to do."

They left all the lights off in the apartment so no one would wonder why the place was lit up at three in the morning. It was a huge apartment building with two hundred units, but it was safe to assume that anyone connected with Bryce would know which windows were his and take note that the lights were on at an odd time of night.

While Bryce scrubbed himself clean in the shower, Abby brought his clothes in a paper bag into the basement and burned them in the incinerator. They met in bed and rehearsed every detail of the evening many times over. The story was that Bryce came home around nine, they had dinner, and he was with Abby all night. They went over every excruciating detail until they both knew the story inside and out.

What really had happened was that Nick had called Bryce and asked him to meet. They were friends, and Nick trusted him, which was his first mistake. Bryce may have been a friend, but first and foremost he was a sociopath and held his own interests above everything else. They met at a bar way outside of town so no one would recognize them. Despite his position in life, Nick was there by default as the boss's son. He was still young and naïve, and thought Bryce would do the right thing. He never told anyone he was going to meet Bryce, and never brought any back-up. He didn't want to ruin Bryce's reputation; he was a friend. He just didn't count on Bryce murdering him in his car and ditching it behind an old, abandoned school building.

Mr. Rosso was furious and heartbroken. He launched an investigation when his son was found dead, and Bryce thought for sure it would lead back to him. His top guys shook down everyone in the city and got nowhere. Bryce figured Nick must have mentioned what he knew to someone, but apparently he hadn't. Mr. Rosso quickly assumed that a rival family, the Patrizios, who had been infringing on the Rosso's turf, had murdered his son. An all-out war broke out in the organized crime world in the

Midwest.

Bryce had, in fact, been in the right place at the right time. He took over Nick's crew, and over the next several months laid waste to the Patrizio family and anyone associated with them. He endeared himself to Mr. Rosso, having avenged his son and proven his loyalty. Bryce soon filled the power vacuum left by Nick's absence.

Only he and Abby knew the truth. That fact didn't scare Abby at the time. She saw herself as Bryce's only true ally. In her naivety, it never occurred to her that she had actually become his biggest liability.

Bryce went from a glorified thug, the number two man in Nick's crew, to a position of prominence and power within the organization in a matter of just a few short months. In her heart, Abby still mourned Nick, especially whenever they saw his family. However, she still enjoyed the life that Bryce's newfound position afforded them. They moved to an expensive condo that overlooked Lake Michigan and got a much nicer car. Well, Bryce got a much nicer car. Abby had no car at all.

When she asked him about getting one for her, he laughed. "What do you need a car for? I'll bring you wherever you need to go, and if I'm not around, just call one of the guys."

By one of the guys, he meant one of his associates. One of the criminals who did what he told them to do when he told them to do it.

Abby forgot about it. She told herself that Bryce just

wanted to take care of her himself. But really, he didn't just want to take care of her, he wanted to control her. She had no skills, no job, no friends, and no money. In fact without Bryce, she literally had nothing. She knew his secret, but buried it deep down inside. She made the mistake of bringing it up to him exactly once; pointing out that she could destroy him so he had better respect her. He beat her within an inch of her life, and swore that if she ever spoke of it again, even to him in private, he would end her life.

With nothing of her own, and everything to lose, she cowed to him and did her best to play the part of the perfect wife. She doubled down on submitting to his every whim and lived her life to serve him.

Abby was on his arm at every party and in his bed every night. She did anything he asked, and everything else she could think of to stay in his good graces. Their lives went on like this for the better part of a year before they hit the next road bump in their relationship.

Bryce crawled into bed and was ready to get on top of her and prove to them both what kind of man he was. She hated to say no and almost never did, but that night in bed she had to. "I'm sorry, babe. This heartburn is killing me, and I think I'm going to throw up. You definitely don't want to bounce me around tonight. I'm sorry."

He was pissed. "It's been a week now with the fucking heartburn? Take something for it."

"I did. It doesn't help."

He got out of bed and started to get dressed.

"Where are you going?"

As he walked out the bedroom door, he just said, "Out," over his shoulder.

The next morning, she woke from a sound sleep and, on a sprint, barely made it to the bathroom before she vomited.

After a week of this, she went to see a doctor.

Abby submitted to some tests, answered a battery of questions, and the doctor went over her vitals, after which he said, "Well, the good news is that you'll be feeling better soon. For a lot of women, the heartburn and vomiting let up after the first trimester. Worst case, you'll feel better in nine months. Congratulations." The doctor smiled. "I'd say your about eight weeks."

"What?"

That night Abby was over the moon with excitement. "We're going to have a baby!"

Bryce was less than thrilled. "Now's not really a good time for that. I mean, it's just not a good time." He thought a moment, then said very matter of fact, "I've got a doc that owes me. I'll make an appointment for you to get it taken care of."

"What are you talking about?"

"Abby, come on. We can't keep this thing. We'll have

a kid someday maybe, but not now."

"I don't get a say in this?"

They went back and forth for at least an hour. Bryce liked their life how it was, but his job was getting very demanding, and he needed her to be there for him, not taking care of a baby. Abby assured him that she would be a great mother and wife. "Besides, I should clean up anyway. I barely use anymore. Don't you want me to stop?"

He shook his head, "I just want you to be happy. If this is what you want, I guess we'll live with it."

She squealed with excitement and jumped up on him, wrapping her legs around him. It was one of the happiest moments of her life, and she would never forget it.

*   *   *

Abby was clean and happy, though Bryce grew distant and angry as her pregnancy went on. The last few months he spent more time in Vegas on business than he spent at home. She wondered if he really had to be there as much as he had been. He obviously hadn't been happy lately, despite her best efforts. She was sure it was work, and that once the baby came along, he would come around and love it and see that it was the right decision.

It didn't go like that at all.

Abby gave birth to a beautiful baby girl and named her Ava after her grandmother. The first few months of the newborn's life were fraught with a palpable tenseness in their household. The colicky infant was only fuel to the fire that had been smoldering for months. Abby had promised to be a great wife and mother, but the baby consumed her entire existence. She couldn't do anything right in Bryce's eyes. He wouldn't sit for the meals that she cooked, wouldn't come to bed with her, and would hardly look at the baby, let alone hold it or take care of it.

He snapped at Ava left and right, and finally one night, as the baby relentlessly cried for several hours, he lost it. "I HATE that fucking thing!"

"Bryce, don't say that!"

The veins in his temples bulged as if his head might explode, while Ava screamed furiously in her mother's arms, "We had a good thing, Abby, and this little... GOD, will you make it shut up!"

"I'll bring her in the other room. I'm sorry, I just don't know. What do you want me to do?"

"Forget it, I'll go." He stormed down the hall and into his office, slamming the door behind him.

Abby rocked and comforted the baby, but was really trying to comfort herself. Bryce was terrifying when he was angry.

That was the start of a bad night that got worse.

Hours later, with a three-month-old Ava still screaming, Abby had to put her down and lay out on the floor next to the crib just to close her eyes for a moment. While she never imagined sleep would come with a screaming child just a few feet away, having been awake for twenty hours, she was physically and mentally exhausted and passed out cold within seconds.

Her eyes forced themselves open some untold amount of time later. She was disoriented. It was the middle of the night. At least she knew that. She was awakened by the silence that her brain was not accustomed to any longer. She sighed and decided not even to relocate to her bed. That would require movement, and that simply would not do. Abby smiled as she poked her head up to do a quick check on her peaceful angel.

Terror quickly gripped her when she saw the empty crib.

Abby shot to her feet and nearly dove into the crib as she tossed a light blanket aside, though it was clear the baby was not under it. *Where is she?*

Just then, the faintest sound came through the door that led to the hall. It took a second for her brain to process what she was hearing. It was a muffled, high-pitched shriek filled with otherworldly terror. It was Ava.

Abby bolted from the baby's room and down the hall where she burst through the door into her bedroom to find Bryce with his hand clamped firmly over the baby's mouth and nose. All fourteen pounds of the infant thrashed from side to side, struggling to get free. Her mouth came free for a split second, and her little lungs released a screech that sent ice through Abby's veins.

There were no words. No thought. Abby leapt onto

Bryce's back, tearing at his face with her fingernails. He screamed and violently shook her off as she sunk her teeth into his right shoulder.

As she hit the floor, Bryce commanded, "Stay down there! This ends tonight! I can't take another fucking second of it. I'm losing my mind!"

Ava's tiny eyes, like dark marbles, were opened wide with terror as Abby's eyes locked onto hers. She launched herself at him again, trying to grab the baby and pry her from his grasp. He released his grip from the baby's mouth and struck Abby with a powerful backhand that sent her reeling backwards, crashing into the dresser, as the thrashing infant slipped from his one-handed grasp and fell to the floor at his feet.

Abby hurled herself on top of the baby to protect her like a football player jumping onto a fumbled ball.

"Get up!" Bryce shouted.

Abby held fast, covering the screaming baby.

"I said get up!" he screamed.

Abby shook her head no, face buried in the carpet, arms wrapped around her daughter. She felt Bryce's bare foot land with a thud in her side that knocked the wind out of her.

"I'll fucking kill you both!" he screamed as he kicked her again and again.

"Stop it! You're crazy!" Abby pleaded.

Just then, two of Bryce's men came running into the room. They were used to hearing the baby's constant crying while they spent the night guarding their boss's door, but knew that something else entirely was going on behind the closed door tonight. Expecting to find Bryce fighting off an assassin that had somehow snuck past them, they ran into the room, guns drawn, and were stunned to find him kicking his wife lying in the fetal position wrapped around the baby.

"Boss!" Donny shouted without thinking and grabbed him by the shoulders to pull him away from Abby. He was the smaller of the two men, but having surprised Bryce, he was able to tear him away.

Bryce had never heard them come into the room. He looked from one to the other, then down at Abby. She lay sobbing, gasping for air, eyes welded shut and holding fast to the hyperventilating infant in her arms.

Looking back at Donny, he said, "Clean up this fucking mess. You," he said, pointing to the other one, "bring the car out front."

Donny knelt down as Bryce left. Alone in his boss's bedroom with his beautiful wife, he had a fantasy that had crossed his mind before but never under these circumstances. He was ashamed of himself for even letting a romantic thought enter his mind right now. He leaned close and put his hand on her shoulder. "It's alright, Abby. He's gone."

It took a couple of minutes, but Abby eventually composed herself. Ava had mercifully passed out from exhaustion.

Donny left the room for a second, but returned with a warm, wet facecloth and held it out to her. "Here, sit up. Let me help you."

As he held her shoulders to help her sit up, she gasped in a little pain, but managed to right herself and sit up, leaning against the bed.

Donny sat down next to her and used the facecloth to gently clean Ava's face.

Abby quietly said, "That's OK, I'll do that." She took the facecloth from him and looked down at her daughter in her arms. She had scratches on her face from trying to tear her father's hands from her mouth with her own tiny hands. Though she was passed out, she still occasionally gasped for breath. Abby looked toward the heavens and burst into tears.

*   *   *

Safe in Robert's island estate home, Abby opened her eyes and sat up. Her heart was pounding out of her chest, and it took a moment for her to realize where she was. *Was that a dream?* As Dr. Lee's words from earlier came back to her, warm tears streamed down her face like the floodgates had opened. As realization set in, she suddenly felt warm all over and vomited into a well-placed bucket that had been placed on her lap.

"It's OK, Abby," Robert said as he rubbed her back. "It's alright. You're safe now."

Abby wiped the corner of her mouth and lay back down on her side, curled up into a ball as her tears flowed freely and soaked the pillow.

Notwithstanding the tears, she spoke in a clear, firm voice, "Put me back under. I need to know *she* is safe."

19

AVA HAD GROWN into a beautiful little girl. Abby watched her run around the playground with the rest of her kindergarten class. Something in Bryce had snapped that frightful night almost five years ago. He was never the same again.

He was distant from their daughter, choosing to often outright ignore her existence. He despised her and often pined that they should send her away and get back to the way things were. Abby hadn't slept a full night in five years, waking up two and three times to check on her, particularly if Bryce wasn't in bed. She spent her life fearing that Bryce would snap again. He was more controlling, and often went completely off the rails if Abby disobeyed him in the slightest. She suffered more than one black eye at his hand, but she kept Ava safe. She never left her side.

She knew she should leave him, but she was trapped. Bryce owned Chicago. There was nowhere she could run, and no one she could turn to for help.

As much as Bryce ignored his daughter, Abby still did her best to keep him distant from her. She never left her alone with her father. On occasions when they were all home together, she ate her meals separately with Ava, played separately with her, and watched movies separately with her. She basically acted as Ava's nanny and kept her out of Bryce's hair whenever he was around. She refused to even give Ava the opportunity to disobey him and suffer his wrath.

Except once.

Just a couple of months before Ava's fifth birthday, they had a particularly terrible version of the fight that played out on a weekly basis in their household. It always ended the same way – with Abby quietly crying and holding an icepack to her cheek, or eye, or ribs, and Bryce storming out the door.

"How dare you?" Bryce fumed. "I give you and that little bitch everything you have. You're nothing without me. A worthless coked-up stripper. Is that what you want? You want to go back to the way things used to be before you met me?" He raised his hand to strike her. It appeared that the left side of her face was the target this time, but a small voice coming from behind surprised him and made him stop.

Ava, all forty-two inches and thirty-nine pounds of her, said in the sternest voice a four-year old can muster, "Leave my mommy alone."

Bryce turned to see her. He didn't smile. He didn't see a cute little girl in pink footie pajamas trying to act like an adult. He saw a disobedient person that he owned. He saw the same person who destroyed his perfect life and his perfect wife. He seethed, "What was that?"

Abby gasped. "Ava, go back in your room. Go to bed."

"No," the little girl said defiantly. She stood her ground and looked at her father. "Stop hurting Mommy."

Her courage turned Abby's stomach and made her hate herself for putting up with Bryce and exposing her child to this for all these years.

Bryce took one step toward Ava. He clamped his large right hand around her throat and lifted her tiny frame by the neck as if she weighed nothing. "Say it again!" he spat.

God bless her, she tried. She looked him dead in the eye and spoke, but didn't get past the word, "Stop…" before he tightened his grip around her airway so hard that the words choked in her throat.

Abby jumped to her feet and pounded on Bryce with clenched fists. "Put her down!" she screamed.

He shoved her to the ground with his free hand and turned back to Ava. Her hands were wrapped around his wrist, trying to loosen his grip. He brought her nose-to-nose with him and said, "Don't ever speak to me like that again." With one hand he threw her down on the hardwood floor, in Abby's direction.

As Ava gasped, catching her breath, Abby gathered her up in her arms and ran from the room shouting, "We're leaving! That's it!"

"Like hell you are," he roared.

Abby was running down the hallway, but he effortlessly caught her and threw her into the wall, Ava still wrapped in her arms.

"Don't even think about it," he said. "Go lock yourself in the little bitch's bedroom and don't come out until I tell you to." She quickly went to run into Ava's room, but he shoved her back hard against the wall. "If you ever try to leave me, Abby, I will end you. But I'll kill her first and make you watch. Got it?"

Abby clenched her eyes shut and nodded, willing him to let her go. When he did, she ran with Ava into the bedroom and slammed the door. Locking it behind her, she leaned back against it, clutching her terrified toddler to her chest as she slid down to the floor. "I won't let him hurt you, baby. Never, never! I'm so sorry."

Watching Ava run around the playground now, months later, a tear still came to her eye thinking about that night. She couldn't escape him. How long before he lost it again? For the first time, she gave serious thought to his suggestion of sending Ava off to boarding school. If Abby couldn't save herself, at least she could save her daughter.

*   *   *

Abby sighed as she put her coffee cup down on the counter. "I just don't know how to do it, Donny."

Ava was watching cartoons in the den while Abby sat at the kitchen table with Donny for a late-afternoon coffee. He was different than the other men Bryce kept on his payroll. He didn't have that soulless killer look in his eyes. Ever since that night five years ago when he pulled Bryce away from Abby on their bedroom floor, he had made it a point to stay in close contact with Abby, though this was not widely known in his circle.

He never stopped by for an overt personal visit unless his boss was out of town, but he often checked in with her on the phone. He also made excuses to stop by for one reason or another a couple times a week, though usually with the cover of needing to speak with Bryce about something. Of course, Abby knew he was just trying to keep his eye on things and make sure she was OK.

"It's boarding school, Abby. Parents do it all the time. You guys have the money, and you have to get her out of here. I know it's tough, but it's the best thing for her. You know that."

"I know." And then Abby laughed. "I'm a lost cause, but at least I can give her a fighting chance, right?"

Donny shook his head. "Don't say that about yourself. You need to get out of here, too. You both do. Bryce is a lunatic."

"Watch it," Abby said. "That's my husband you're talking about." Abby chuckled, but Donny didn't see the humor.

"I'm serious." He put his hand on her shoulder, "You know I'm here for you, right?"

She shook her head. "You're a great guy, Donny. You're not like the rest. What are you sticking around for me for?"

"We're gonna get you out of here, I swear. Both of you are gonna start over."

"How?" Abby was frustrated. "How does that happen? He'll never let me go unless I'm dead. He can't."

"You've got resources – use them."

"Don't insult me. What resources? I have nothing. Absolutely nothing. I don't even have a fucking credit card in my own name that he doesn't know about. I don't know how, but he completely trashed my credit. I've got nothing." Abby stared at Donny with blank eyes, *If only you knew what I know, Donny, you would understand why he'll never let me go.* Tears rolled down her cheeks at the thought.

"Hey," he said quietly, "you've got your brains, and you've got me. We'll figure it out. We'll get you outta here."

Abby smiled and rested her hand on his shoulder. "I'm sorry. I know you didn't mean to insult me. You're a good man. Too good to be in this business. You know he'd kill you if he knew you were here now. Can you imagine what he would do to you if you helped me and Ava leave him? You'd be a dead man. We'd all be dead. We can't hide from him."

Donny thought about that. He had something to say, but wasn't sure how to say it. Abby could read his face, though. "Oh, just spit it out already so I can tell you it won't work, and we can move on."

"OK, hear me out. You can't go on the run with a kid, I get it. But…"

"But nothing! I'm not taking off and leaving Ava behind, no way."

"No, that's not what I'm saying. I'm saying you both go in separate directions. Send her off somewhere. Somewhere he doesn't know about. I dunno. Tell him she went right when she really went left, but don't tell him the truth. He'll be so happy she's gone, he won't care where she is. Once you know she's safe, you hit the bricks. I can set you up; you can disappear, Abby."

She stared into his dark eyes. "You want me send my child off somewhere to fend for herself without me? Are you a lunatic?"

"There's gotta be someone, Abby. Someone you trust. Someplace you can send her far away from here."

"Without me? How long am I supposed to live like that? Without my baby?"

"Just until you can join her."

"Until I can join her? How do I do that? Oh, I know. I'll use fake ID's that you get me, and money you've got stuffed under the mattress to get me there. Only problem is that Bryce knows everybody you know! You get me a fake ID, and he'll know about it before it hits your hand. Then we're both dead. Damn, all three of us. I can't take that chance." She shook her head. "I know it, I just know it. He hates her. He's hated her since the minute he found out about her, and someday he's going to kill her." Her eyes welled up at the thought.

"He hates her, but do you really think if she left he would give a shit where she went?"

Abby shook her head no. "But what do I do? Live without her?"

"Think about it. Ask yourself what you want more. Do you want to be with her, here, in this life? Or do you want to send her off into the world with half a chance to have a decent shot at a good life? Think about it. You know the right answer."

She shook her head no, but in her heart, she knew the right thing to do. "You'd better get out of here before someone sees your car out front." She stood and gave him a friendly kiss on the cheek before he said goodbye to Ava and walked out the door.

Abby stood at the window watching him get into his car. She had no idea how he ever got mixed up with Bryce. But then, anyone who knew her a few short years ago would say the same thing about her. Everyone has their demons, and right now, Abby was living with hers.

ESCAPE
Past Sins

*   *   *

Who writes letters anymore? *No one,* Abby thought. But she had no choice. After her heart-to-heart with Donny, she decided to reach out to her estranged sister. Bryce had no idea she existed. Abby and her sister had stopped speaking years before she met Bryce, and she never spoke about her family at all. Her sister was the only person Abby could think of that she would trust with Ava.

Donny tracked down an address and a phone number for the sister in New York. Abby had no idea why she was there. He also got Abby a disposable phone. They didn't want her sister's number showing up on her phone bills, or Donny's for that matter. If it was going to work, Bryce had to remain unaware she existed. The problem was that in an age when everyone had caller ID, people wouldn't answer calls from numbers they didn't know. She had hoped to at least hear her sister's voice, but it was just a generic greeting with no option to leave a message.

So, she decided to write a letter. It was brief. They hadn't spoken in eight years, since their falling out after their Mom and Dad passed away. Abby made no effort to document her life story since that time. She gave the basics, though. She was a mother, her daughter was in grave danger and needed a place to go. Would she be willing to take her in?

Don't do it for me, Abby wrote. *Ava is a smart and beautiful little girl that deserves a chance to lead a life better than I can ever give her. Please, do it for her.* She left no return address – only the number to the disposable phone.

Days went by, which turned into weeks, and Abby hadn't heard a thing. Her sister had likely written her off long ago and trashed the letter as soon as she realized who it was from. Finally, more than a month later, she received a voicemail on the throwaway phone. It was a very simple – "We need to talk" – followed by a phone number.

Abby called her back, and they spoke for hours. Her sister had worried about her for years. She was sorry that she had never returned Abby's calls after their fight. She was so angry at her, and truth be told, she was a little lost herself. She went off to find herself and moved all over the country before settling down. By the time she had her head on straight and tried to track down Abby a year later, all she ever came up with were dead ends. She had long feared Abby was dead.

Abby wondered why she didn't call back right away this time, if what she said was true. "Why did it take so long to hear from you if you were so worried about me?"

"Your letter went to an old address, and it took quite awhile to find its way to my new home. I'm not even in the country anymore. We're in Saint-Colbert, a suburb north of Montreal."

"Canada?" Abby was taken aback for a moment and briefly had second thoughts about sending Ava away. *We won't even be in the same country?*

"About your letter... of course we'll take Ava, but what about you?"

"I'll be fine. I've got a plan." She lied; she had no

plan. "I just need to make sure she's safe first."

"Abby, this whole thing is crazy. It sounds like the plot of a movie. What's the problem with just going to the police and pressing charges against this guy?"

Abby laughed. Not a light chuckle, but a hardy laugh, "Sarah, Bryce *owns* the police. If he did kill us, he's got a dozen officers on payroll that would help bury the bodies. I've got to get Ava out of here. This is perfect. He doesn't know you exist, *and* you're out of the country. We've just got to figure out how to get her to you."

Abby called Donny with the good news. It was great news as far as he was concerned. Bryce had no presence or connections that he knew of in Canada. It wasn't his turf. They could move Ava there, change her name, and let her start over. "I still think you both should go. He would never find you."

"Oh, that's where you're wrong, Donny. He absolutely would. He would find me. He would never stop looking until he did."

20

ABBY DISCOVERED that moving Ava out of the country was not a fast process. It could have been, though.

She had worried about how they would obtain a fake passport for Ava. However, a little research revealed that she only needed proof of citizenship to cross the border, as she was under sixteen years old. The Canadian birth certificate was the easiest thing in the world to forge. When it was time, Donny did it himself, in an hour, at his home.

The airline ticket was simple enough, too. They used cash to buy a prepaid debit card, then used the card to buy the ticket. The purchase was made at a public computer in the library. Not that Bryce would ever attempt to find out where his daughter was, but if he did, there would be no trace of any kind; no paper or electronic trail to follow. Again, it was done over the course of an afternoon.

It could have been a fast process, but it wasn't.

Abby agonized for weeks over the decision. She had dedicated the past several years of her life to her little Ava, teaching her to walk and talk. Reading stories before bedtime; snuggling on the couch with a bowl of popcorn to watch movies. Hospital stays, runny noses, and all the things that mothers do.

In addition to the usual parenting responsibilities, she had devoted herself to protecting her angel from the demon that lived in their home.

The thought of no longer having her little girl under her own roof was overwhelming for Abby. Letting a child go was more than most parents could bear, and for someone like Abby, it was nearly an impossible request. Donny's words continued to play back through her mind, though, and he was right. Keeping Ava here, in this life with her, was a selfish act. Ava could start a new life, a better life, than Abby could ever provide.

After steeling herself, she called Donny on her prepaid phone. "How fast can we get this done? I need it quick, like ripping off a Band-Aid."

He knew precisely what she was talking about, and absolutely knew they had to move quickly before she had a chance to change her mind again. "If you're ready – within twenty-four hours, maybe faster."

Abby was holding her breath, eyes closed. This was a moment that was about to change her life, and Ava's, forever.

"Abby?"

She breathed. "Do it."

"Call your sister."

She clicked off the call and immediately dialed Sarah before she had a chance to think anymore. "It's happening," she said.

"Oh, thank God! When?"

"Tomorrow. I'll call you with the details."

Abby remained completely detached from the decision. She tapped into a reserve she did not know she possessed. She had to be strong. She needed Ava to remember her as a strong woman who protected her, so she would grow up to be the same. She also could not let Ava know that she was upset. After all, the entire plan hinged on getting this little girl onto an airplane on her own. The airline would have an escort to see that she made it from A to B, but she had to see this as a fun adventure. If she begged and screamed for mommy, Abby was not sure she could follow through.

She couldn't remember much of the final goodbye.

She knew that she was strong and didn't cry.

Neither did Ava.

She remembered she lied. Abby told the little girl that she was going to visit her auntie, and that they would see each other soon.

"How soon, Mommy?"

"Before you know it, sweetie." Abby smiled and kissed

her on the head, praying for the strength to let her go without a scene.

Abby remembered the little navy blue dress with lace around the collar, sleeves, and skirt. It was Ava's favorite dress, and she had picked it out to wear on the flight. It was a very special occasion, and she wanted to look her best.

She remembered the tight hug and the lump in her throat as she squeezed her little girl one last time.

She remembered her bright pink backpack and matching pink beret as she walked away, hand in hand with the very friendly female flight attendant who couldn't have been any older than Abby.

She remembered how their eyes met one last time as Ava smiled and waved before turning the corner and walking down the jet way to board the plane.

She remembered that she barely made it to the nearest trashcan before vomiting. When she had nothing left in her stomach, the tears came. Donny put his arm around her in a hopeless attempt to console the inconsolable.

*   *   *

Abby's eyes opened in her dimly lit room at Robert's estate. Dr. Lee was sitting next to her looking over a computer display. "How are you doing?" he asked.

She didn't answer. She just closed her eyes again and shook her head no.

Robert was sitting next to her, asleep.

She wasn't waking from a dream – she was slowly realizing that her life was, in fact, a nightmare.

The last year of her life, now *that* was a dream. The perfect life she had created with Eric was the dream. *No wonder I told myself not to have my memory restored.* Abby silently wondered if it was too late to change her mind.

Abby didn't feel right. She reached down and placed her hands over her stomach, realizing how hungry she was. *How long have I been out?*

As if hearing her thoughts Dr. Lee answered, "It's been about twelve hours. You should eat something."

Robert's eyes fluttered open, "What's that now?" He looked at the doctor, and then saw that Abby was awake and leaned over the side of the bed. "How are you?"

She shrugged her shoulders. "Is that everything? How come I don't remember how I got here?"

"We're not done yet," Dr. Lee said. "What's the last thing you remember?"

"Ava… she…" Abby broke down sobbing as it all came rushing back again. Robert brought her close, and she buried her face in his chest.

"Let's take a break, Abby. Eric is here. Do you want to see him?"

She didn't know why, but she shook her head. "No,

I'm not ready. Can we just keep going?" Her hands were still on her stomach.

"You should really eat something," Dr. Lee said.

"You're probably right. I'm not feeling well at all."

"That's normal."

Robert had a couple slices of toast and a glass of orange juice brought to the room. Abby ate, but still felt empty because the emptiness wasn't in her stomach – it was in her heart. Until this past year, it was an emptiness that she had walked around with for quite some time.

* * *

Bryce stared into Abby's eyes across the small two-person table that they occupied toward the back of the quaint Italian restaurant. "Isn't this great?"

Abby smiled back and sipped her wine. "Thank you, it is." She leaned across the table and kissed him, but felt nothing. Ava had been gone for two months, and Abby was hollow inside. She had told Bryce at the time that she understood their lives were better without her, and she had sent her to live with her parents in California. Not that he ever cared, asked, or met them, but her parents *were* in California. They just were not alive. She simply hoped he never would be concerned enough to follow up.

She was miserable. Having spent the first several weeks crying herself to sleep, she finally decided to remove all traces of Ava from their home. She boxed up her clothes, toys, and anything else that belonged to her little

231

girl. She couldn't ship it. That would leave a paper trail leading right to her. She couldn't bring herself to throw it out either, so she stored everything in the large storage closet they were assigned in the basement.

Sometimes she would go down there when he wasn't around, pull out Ava's clothes, and bury her face in them to remember her smell.

Abby was a small woman. When she was at 125 pounds, she had a great, healthy figure. At 115, she was skinny, and her ribs poked through. As she sat there poking her salad with a fork, she was barely one hundred. If she cared enough to step on a scale in the morning without clothes on, she would have weighed in at ninety-eight that day. She looked sick. Even at the height of her drug problems she was never so skinny. Her chest had all but disappeared, her cheeks were concave, and the constant dark circles around her eyes only accentuated their sunken look.

But she belonged fully to Bryce, and he didn't seem to notice what bad shape she was in. He reached across the table and held her hand. "This is the life." He smiled.

Later that night, when they got home, he had his way with her. In the morning, she got up an hour before him to make his breakfast and lay out his clothes. She then spent the day taking care of the house and doing his errands. This went on day after day. For the first few weeks, she had tortured herself by calling her sister to talk to Ava. She was always in worse shape afterwards. Finally her sister said that the calls made Ava very upset, too, so they stopped.

Abby instead spent all of her time on Bryce, and the house, making sure everything was perfect. When she found herself with free time, she would sit and cry for a while. Sometimes Bryce would stop in during the afternoon; sometimes he wouldn't. He would call to tell her what time to have dinner ready, if that's what he was expecting when he got home.

She lived her days to serve him. To be an obedient wife who had no other purpose in life than to see that he was taken care of. *He doesn't want a wife,* she thought. *He wants a mother.* This is how her life went on for the months after Ava left.

She rarely saw Donny. She couldn't see him without thinking of Ava, and finally she asked him to stop coming around. He understood and obliged for a while, but after a few weeks, he began calling on the phone. Abby said that was all right at first, but after she stopped speaking to Ava on the phone, she wanted to stop speaking to Donny, too.

He respected that. "I'll do anything to make this easier on you. If you change your mind, you can always reach out to me. You know that, right?"

"I do, Donny, and I will. I just need some time, OK?"

That was the last time they spoke for a couple of months. The next time they did, Abby was walking back from the grocery store on the corner of their block when Donny drove by. She looked up when she heard the screeching of his tires as his car came to a stop in the middle of the road. He jumped out of the running car, without even pulling it to the side of the road, and ran

233

over to her.

"Abby?"

She smiled uncomfortably. "Donny, hi."

He did nothing to disguise the horrified look on his face. "Oh, my God, Abby. Are you sick? What's wrong?"

She laughed it off. "I'm fine." She looked down at her baggy clothes, a tank top and light sweatshirt that she would have amply filled out a few months ago. "I guess I've lost a little weight, but, you know, I haven't been myself."

As he looked into her eyes, he noticed that their usual amber glow had faded to a sad gray, and he fought back the tears that started to well up in his own eyes. "You can't live like this."

She shook her head, unwilling to admit anything was wrong. "I'm fine, Donny. I've got to go make dinner. Bryce will be home in an hour."

He wouldn't let go of her shoulders, "What can I do?"

Her own eyes filled with tears. "Nothing, Donny. Nothing."

"Well, you can't go on like this. Look at you!"

"Yeah, look at me!" she yelled. "Look at me! This is not what I want for Ava, but you said it yourself – she's better off out there, away from this life." Abby shook her head, "I just wish I could forget about her, you know?

Forget that she's out there. Forget she even exists. Forget that everything exists. Vegas, Bryce, Ava, all of it. I'd give anything to start over again, but I can't. Now get out of my way. I've got to get dinner ready before he gets home."

Donny had nothing to say. He simply watched her walk away down the street.

Despite the career path he had chosen, or more appropriately, had been chosen for him by his father, he wasn't a career criminal. He had even gone to college for a year to study film and television. That hadn't worked out for him, but his old roommate had a pretty good gig working for one of the big networks out in L.A. What Abby had just said sparked an idea for Donny. It was a long shot, and frankly, he had no hope that it would ever work out. But if there was a chance that Abby could move on and be happy, he was willing to take it.

He took out his phone and punched up the number, which immediately went to voicemail. "Hey, Seth, it's Donny. Listen, I've got to talk to you about something. Give me a ring when you have a second. It's important."

As Abby walked back to her building, she turned and saw Donny talking on the phone as he got back into his car. She didn't know it, but he was making a phone call that was going to change her life in ways she never could have imagined.

21

"OF COURSE I've heard of it," Abby said as she walked into the kitchen. She had missed Donny's visits, and when he had showed up out of the blue, she couldn't turn him away. "Who hasn't? Why?"

"How would you like to be on it?" Donny asked, sitting at the counter.

Abby laughed. "*Trial Island?* You're serious? I wouldn't last a day."

He wasn't laughing. "You said you want to forget everything that's happened in the past ten years, right? They can do that, Abby. It's part of the deal."

"Yes, I know it's part of the deal. It's part of the deal for those lunatics they get on the show."

"You could be one of those lunatics, Abby."

"Now you're just talking crazy. You've seen the people on that show, right? They're in great shape. In case you haven't noticed, I've been better. Besides, there have got to be thousands of people trying to get on. I'm the last one they'd take."

"I can't guarantee you'll get on the show, but I can get you a shot."

"Anyone can get a shot, Donny. I've watched the audition tapes on cable. They say they get them by the thousands, and we only see what, the top one hundred? Trust me, I'm not in the top one hundred. Even if I was, I'd wind up dead."

"Listen, I've got a friend that's the assistant to one of the producers. He owes me. If we make a tape, he says he can get you in the top fifty for women. What happens from there is up to you."

Abby froze. "Seriously?"

"Think about it. You'll get away from here, this life, and you'll forget everything."

She shook it off. "Look at me." She held up the sweater that hung off her shoulders not as a fashion statement, but to demonstrate that she was only a fraction of her former self. "Thanks for trying to help, but it's useless."

"Let's just make a video, Abby. You've got pictures of what you used to look like, right? We can use those, and you just talk. Tell them why they should pick you"

She looked at the ceiling, silent for a long while, before she looked across the room at him with tears in her eyes. "Why, Donny? Why would they pick me?"

*   *   *

"Okay, go ahead," Donny's voice said off camera.

"Hi." Abby smiled and waved. "My name is Abby, and I would really like to be on your show." She sighed. "I've seen a million of these things, and I know I'm supposed to tell you how much I love the outdoors, and what a survivalist I am, but I'm not. I am a housewife to a sack of shit husband who has ruined my life."

"Abby," Donny's voice said.

She looked off-camera. "What? You said to be honest." She turned back to the camera. "I'm not going to tell you what he does for a living, what he has done to me, or what he makes me do. I don't need some do-gooder intern watching this thinking they have to do something and sending the police to my door. That's more trouble than I can bear to deal with right now."

Abby was quiet for a moment while she picked at her fingernails, trying to find the words to explain what was going on in her head. "I used to be a good girl. I grew up with two beautiful parents and a dog, in a perfect suburban neighborhood. They're all dead now." She sniffed and dabbed the edge of her eye with the sleeve of her sweater.

"That's about when things started going wrong, I guess. I haven't made a good decision since then. I… I stripped for a while, among other things I shouldn't admit to on tape. I was lost…"

*   *   *

Robert found his way to his room after Dr. Lee assured him that Abby was *peacefully* sleeping and the procedure was over. There were no more memories to unlock. It may have been the middle of the night, but it was done. He recalled the many long heart-to-heart conversations he'd had with Abby during the months of her training and preparation. He could not believe the horror stories he had heard, and was so thankful that he had picked her to take part in the show.

He remembered the first time he saw her audition video. It was so different from the others. For the seven minutes they were allowed, most spent the entire time showing how tough they were. Video after video showed hard bodies running, sweating, and working out. They would ultimately end with the entrant saying a line or two about how physically tough they were.

Abby's was different. She spent seven minutes looking into the camera and just talking. She was so open and honest. Above all else, she was vulnerable. It broke Robert's heart every time he watched the video of that sad, sick girl. The Abby in that video was so different from the woman who was resting in the room a few doors down the hallway. But different only physically – she was still the same person on the inside. She had just been locked up for the past year. Now that she was unlocked, how would she react?

Robert sat on the edge of the bed and pulled up her audition video on the media center. He shook his head seeing how thin she was, her sweater hanging off her like she was a little child wearing her father's clothes.

"… I was lost," she said. "Stripping didn't pay the bills. I had no bills. Stripping kept me in a free room with a half dozen other girls in a motel just off the Strip where I slept on a thin sheet that covered a mattress stained with every bodily fluid you can think of. I didn't care, though. Stripping paid for drugs. When Bryce – my husband – when he found me, I was at rock bottom. At least that's what I thought rock bottom was at the time.

"Long story short, I cleaned up, got knocked up, and he's spent the time since then knocking me around. He hates our daughter. Hate is a strong word, but it's probably an understatement. How can you hate a beautiful little girl? I can't leave him, though. It's not because I don't want to, but I can't. I sent her away to protect her, but I can't live without her. I need to forget. I need to forget she's out there. I need to forget I created this beautiful child and gave her life, because I'm dead inside without her.

"So, I'm hoping we can help each other." She held up a picture of her in a bikini last year. It was folded in half to hide Ava, who was also in the photo. "This is me." The camera closed in on the picture of a healthy and curvy Abby. Long, brown, loose curls framed her pretty face. Her cheeks were red, either from a little too much sun or from laughing so much – it was hard to tell. It would be impossible for any man not to notice the way she filled out her bathing suit in all the right spots.

Abby dropped the photo, stood up and backed away from the camera. She took off her sweater and let it fall to the floor. She stood there in a bra that hung over her flat chest, the dim light from the side casting deep shadows where her ribs stretched at the skin. "In the interest of full disclosure, this is me, too." She sat down and pulled her sweater up to cover herself a bit.

"Your show is all about survival. Well, I'm a real survivor. The life I've led has killed plenty of others, but I'm still standing. I've already fought for my life. At this point, I just want it back."

Robert clicked off the screen and shook his head. The first time he had seen that, he demanded that she be brought in on the show. Every other producer tried to talk him out of it, but the show was his and he had the final say. He saw something in her. She was a survivor, just like she said. Of course, that video never saw the light of day. They shot a new one once they brought her in. One they could show on television and was in line with what the viewers expected.

He walked over to his dresser and took out the photo that she had held up in the video. She had given it to him before she left for her stay on *Trial Island*. He unfolded it to see a photo of a beautiful Abby and her adorable little Ava smiling at the camera from another life.

"Well, Abby, you've finally gotten your life back, and soon, you'll get Ava back, too."

*   *   *

"Does Eric know?" Abby asked, sitting at the small table by her bed, eating a hearty breakfast that Robert had brought to her.

"Does he know what?"

"I don't know... everything?"

Abby knew everything now that she had her memories back. She also knew that Robert did not know everything. He did know that Bryce was hell-bent on ending her life and that Abby was terrified of him. He had seen why she was terrified when Bryce tried to kidnap and murder her on this very property last year, but he didn't know the whole truth. He didn't know that Bryce had murdered his boss's son and ascended to power in his place, and that he would do anything to keep Abby quiet about it. Abby was happy that she hadn't burdened him with that, and wondered if she would even share that secret with Eric.

"No, Eric doesn't know anything he didn't before. I haven't told him a thing. He was disappointed that you didn't want to see him last night, but I explained what a traumatic thing you were going through, and he understood. Can I tell him that you'll see him today?"

Abby thought about it. "Yes. I mean of course I want to see him. I'm just scared, that's all."

"What of?"

"That I'm not the girl he thought I was."

242

"But you are, Abby. You are exactly who he thinks you are. The Abby he knows and loves is sitting right here in front of me. You've just got a little extra baggage now."

"A little?"

"Alright, a *lot* of extra baggage now. But he loves you for who you are, and who you are has not changed, has it?"

"How do you think he'll take it when he finds out about my past?"

"Well, I'm sure he'll feel horribly for you that you had such a trying life. I'm not sure what else you expect."

"I have a child, Robert!"

He nodded his head. "Is that what you're worried about? That he won't like the fact that you have Ava?"

"No, no. I mean, I have a child, and I need to find her. I need to hold her, and kiss her, and tell her she doesn't have to be scared anymore. I have a child and I need to get to her. Is she still with my sister in Canada?"

Robert smiled. "Yes, she is, and she's doing quite well. I spoke with Sarah last night. They will be ready for your return. Once you get back on your feet, psychologically speaking, we'll get you over to the big island, where you can be on an international flight in no time."

"You know I don't like to waste time, Robert, and I've wasted more than enough."

"Can you give me a day? Just a day. Rest, spend some time walking around the island and get your head clear. Is that fair?"

Abby gave him a good, long stare. She didn't like the thought of sitting around for a day, but the ache behind her eyes told her that she should probably listen to him. "One day, Robert, that's it."

"Good. You didn't have a choice anyway. There's only one international flight out, and it's every other day. I'll see to it that you're booked on the flight to the Chicago hub for tomorrow night. You'll land late-morning, and then it's a short hop to Montreal. One of my men has already lined everything up." Robert smiled and held out his hands as though to say, *'Aren't I amazing?'*

"You're the best," she said with a smile.

Robert stood to leave. "JJ will escort you, to make sure you get there safely."

Abby furrowed her brow. "Robert, I don't need an escort. I'll be fine."

"I just want to make sure you get where you're going, Abby, that's all."

She stood up. "I appreciate that, but I do not need an escort. I made it off your booby-trapped island. I can make it from A to B on a plane."

Robert smiled as a father would to his know-it-all daughter. "Whatever you say, Abby. I'm sure you'll be fine."

There was a knock on the door before it eased open a few inches. It was Eric. "Can I come in?"

Robert looked at Abby. "You need to rest and keep your head about you, OK?" He walked over to the door and opened it all the way, gesturing for Eric to enter as he took his leave and shut the door behind him.

Abby was awash with emotions upon seeing him. She was so excited to have her life back that she wanted to open the floodgates and gush out all the information, but she worried how he would take it.

"Hi," Eric said. "Um... are you OK?"

Abby nodded, and then ran and jumped on him, wrapping her arms and legs around him and squeezing him tightly.

He stroked her hair. "It's a hell of a thing getting your memory back, huh?"

She pulled away and smiled, wiping a few tears from her eyes. "Yes! Oh, my goodness, yes. I have so much to tell you." She stared into his blue eyes from just inches away. She could feel his love and knew that she had nothing to be afraid of. And yet, she was. "It's not all good, though. I hope... I hope you don't think less of me."

He was flattered beyond belief that this beautiful woman cared so much about his opinion of her. "It's alright. I know your life has gotten infinitely more complicated in the last twenty-four hours. But I'm here for you, and we'll get through it together. Right?"

She nodded her head, wrapped her arms around him, and whispered in his ear, "I have a daughter."

He pulled away in surprise. His dimples came out as a broad smile swept across his face. "What?"

She was smiling, tears running down her cheeks. "A little girl, Ava. She's with my sister."

"That's great Abby! That's unbelievable. I mean… I have so many questions, but wow!"

"I know," she laughed a little. "I'm shocked, too!"

"Well, where is she? We have to go."

Abby looked at him. He was so sure of himself and his life, and so willing to go along with hers. She never considered herself a religious girl, but looking into his eyes, she felt truly blessed. "It's complicated Eric. I woke up a week ago living in paradise, and now I'm kind of thrust back into reality. You too, you know? Granted, Bryce is gone, so reality is much better now than it was when I left it, but still… are you sure you're ready for this?"

"Are you kidding? I'm in this for the long haul. Listen, this past year, all the talk about our future, our hopes, our dreams, what our lives will be like… that wasn't just lip service. I meant every word of it. I knew someday you would get your memory back, and that there were some incredible things locked up in there. Of course I'm ready for this!"

Abby kissed him. "Alright, then. Well, she's in Canada, and I kind of want to go get her right now."

"Then let's catch the next plane!"

Abby smiled. "Hold on! Robert says we've got a day to kill before the next flight to Chicago."

Eric saw a thought flash across her mind. He knew there was something going on behind the scenes, and wondered what it was. He didn't even have to ask – he just tilted his head and raised his eyebrow.

"What?" she asked.

"I know you Abby, and there's something going on in there."

"Robert said something to me. He said 'Bryce may be dead, but I don't know what kind of history you have with his people. I don't want to alarm you, but I want to encourage you to be practical'." Abby was silent a moment. "Do you think there's someone else waiting out there for me?"

Eric mulled that over. "I don't know. You've got your memory back now. Is there anyone you can think of that has it in for you?"

She shook her head. "No, but he had a lot of connections. I mean, just look at the last time we were here. He *owned* half those so-called security guards that were protecting me from him."

In her head, Abby was trying to work out if Bryce

would ever tell anyone else his secret. She didn't think so. There was no benefit to it. But she still couldn't shake the feeling that even from the grave he would be out to get her and keep her as quiet as his corpse.

Eric put his arm around her. "We'll be fine as long as we stick together, right?"

Abby thought about that as she looked at their reflection in the mirror over the dresser. "Well, we certainly do look good together, that's true enough." She smiled, then was struck with a thought. "Do you think we're more likely to be recognized if we're together?"

"I hadn't thought of that." Eric examined them in the mirror, paying attention to Abby's hair, weight and overall frame. "You look really different from when you were on the show, but I don't."

"That's what I was thinking." She was fairly confident that she wouldn't be picked out as whom she was, but Eric was pretty much still Eric, with shorter hair. "I probably wouldn't get recognized on my own, but if people see us together, they'll recognize us in a second."

They thought in silence for a moment, before Eric spoke. "What if we don't travel together?"

"What? No way. I want to be together."

"No, I mean, we can travel together, but not…" he made air quotes, "…together."

Abby didn't look convinced.

Past Sins

"Think about it. We disappeared together. If someone is waiting and searching for you, they're really searching for us. So, when are we going to get recognized and have the story blow up? Probably either walking through an airport or sitting on the plane. If we're separate though, maybe no one will recognize us. Does that make sense?"

Abby agreed reluctantly.

"So, who can we trust?" Eric wondered.

"Robert. That's about it. After what happened last time, I wouldn't trust anyone else to know the plan."

"There's a little problem. He had mentioned to me earlier that the travel arrangements were already made. He had assumed I would be with you, so we're already booked on the flight together."

Abby bit her lip while she thought, "That's right, he did say that his guy had already taken care of the arrangements."

"So let's really make it legit, have him cancel my seat and I'll just get another ticket at the airport. He can tell his guy that we had a fight or something, that way there's really no one that knows we'll be traveling together."

"That's a good idea Eric, but, what then?" Abby wondered. "We can't live the rest of our lives like that. We get to Canada, we get Ava, and where do we go from there?"

Eric smiled. "Wherever we are, we'll be fine as long as

we're together. I just happen to know a great villa on a beach not too far from here, and it's available."

"You think we can go back there?"

"Why not?"

"JJ said there are others out here looking for us. Even if it's not Bryce's people, when the media finds us, everyone is going to know about it. Bryce's people don't even have to be looking for us. They'll know where we are."

"That's true, but how did it go down when JJ got to the island? How did he find us?"

Abby thought about it a moment.

Eric continued, "He didn't find us. Jay, Ben, the rest of the locals, they hid us and protected us. JJ is a pro, and he still wouldn't have found us if we didn't have Ben lead him to us."

Abby smiled at the mention of Ben. He was such a sweet kid, and she hated the thought that she wouldn't see him again. She certainly didn't need to be talked into going back to the island. It was paradise on earth, a perfect place to raise her daughter with the man she loved, and a terrific out-of-the-way place. Coupled with the fact that there were likely cold-blooded killers out there looking for her, she couldn't wait to get back if she knew that they couldn't be found. Suddenly, she looked up, her eyes wide.

"What?" Eric asked. She was excited. That much he

could tell.

Abby walked back and forth, working out the plan in her head before she turned to Eric and spoke. "OK, follow me here. We know there are investigators all over these islands looking for us, right?"

Eric nodded his head, curious to see where her mind was going.

"But, once we get to Canada, what if we make sure people know we're there?"

Eric was trying to catch up, "But I thought we didn't want to be found?"

"No, we don't want them to find us here. So, let's get found in Canada. Make sure the world knows that's where we are. Once the story is out there, we're free to disappear back to our villa on the beach where no one will look for us anymore."

Eric kissed her quickly. "That's genius!"

"I thought so, too," she chuckled.

*   *   *

Greg was away from the main house, making a phone call. He could hardly wait to share the good news with his boss.

"You were right, Mr. Haydenson. Robert already had me book her on a flight. She'll be landing in Chicago at 6:55 on Thursday morning. She's on a connecting flight to

Montreal, though. Is that going to be a problem?"

Bryce thought about it. *What is she doing in Montreal?* He counted on her returning to Chicago. He knew from his own travel experience back and forth that Chicago was her only option for an international flight to the States. He figured she would be going to California from there, but Canada?

When she disappeared a year ago, he suspected she had gone to California to be with Ava and her parents. His men tracked down an address for them; only to find out that they didn't live there anymore and, in fact, that her parents dead. He also found out that Abby had a sister, though they were never able to track her down. From what they could tell, she had moved around a bunch after her parents passed away before falling off the map.

He had no idea where Ava was, but had assumed Abby was with her. He and his men were still searching when Abby turned up on national television and put the matter to rest. Up to that point, they had still been combing southern California. Now she's going to Canada? No matter. The original plan was to grab her in Chicago before she went anywhere else, and that was still the plan.

"No, no problem." Bryce said. "You said *she* is going to Montreal. Is she going alone?"

"Yes, as far as I know sir. He said she had some kind of fight with Eric, and he's staying behind."

Bryce thought about that. It certainly made things easier. He would quickly place a man on the plane and have a couple of others in the terminal to help take care of things. Without Eric, he could reduce the number of men in the terminal. In his mind, the fewer moving parts the better. Less people meant less that could go wrong.

Greg interrupted his thoughts. "You sure you don't just want me to grab her, Mr. Haydenson? I can take care of it."

"No. I've got a guy on the main island. He'll be on the flight with her. Everything is taken care of. Call me if anything changes."

"Yes, sir."

"And, Greg, you've done good. I'm sorry about tossing you over the side of the boat, but you've proved yourself. When you get back here, I've got a nice position lined up for you. You'll get your own crew; be your own man. How does that sound?

Greg was taken back. "That sounds great, sir. Thank you."

"Thank *you,* Greg. You earned it, not me. You made a bad situation work for you. That kind of foresight is going to get you places."

"Thank you, sir."

After they disconnected their call, Bryce was left alone with his thoughts. Abby was coming back. His boss, Mr. Rosso, was gaining in years, but was still all-powerful in their world. Bryce had tried to murder Abby, and he couldn't imagine that she didn't hold a grudge for that.

She was the only person in the world who could truly ruin him. He didn't know whether she planned to reveal what she knew, but it would be easy enough to do. Every news outlet in America would drop everything to get an interview with her. If she were to reveal what he had done, that would be the end of him. *Despite that she thinks I'm dead, would she still do that out of spite?* There was no way Bryce could wait to find out. His mind was made up – Abby had to die and the sooner the better.

*   *   *

JJ looked up from his sandwich when Robert walked into the kitchen. "So what's going on?"

Robert looked back and forth from JJ to his brother, Ace. "She's going to find Ava. You've checked it out. Everything is still good there, right?"

"Absolutely. I'll book the flights, and we'll be on our way. I'll get her there, then head home myself." JJ smiled. The thought of sleeping in his bed back in Boston by the weekend was an exciting one.

Robert shook his head. "No, she doesn't want an escort. You know her. She's a headstrong girl. I'm just worried, overprotective. She will be fine, right?"

"I'm sure she will be. She's gotten along just fine without having anyone watch over her for awhile now."

"I know." Robert was nervously tapping his foot, looking out the window toward the boatyard where Bryce had abducted Abby from right under his nose.

Ace looked at JJ, and under his breath said, "She doesn't have to know we're there."

JJ looked at his brother and thought about that for a second before nodding his head. He could tell Robert was nervous and didn't want Abby on her own yet. He put down his sandwich and stood up close to Robert, speaking in a hushed tone. "Listen, me and Ace, we've got to get back to the States anyway, and there's only one flight out of big island, right?"

Robert nodded his head.

"So, we'll just follow her. Those jets seat what, four hundred people? She'll be in first class, and we'll sit in the back of the plane so she doesn't see us. Once she gets where she's going, we'll be off ourselves. Would that make you feel better?"

"It would. I know Bryce is long dead, but who knows? The people she used to associate with... who knows who else could be out there waiting for her? I'll have my man book the extra seats."

"No, I'll take care of it myself. That way we don't get any wires crossed."

Robert clapped him on the shoulder. "You're a good man, JJ."

Captain Frank poked his head in and looked around at the men.

After thinking about the situation yesterday, Robert had a proposal for Frank and convinced him to spend the night in one of the guest villas so they could talk about it. Robert thought it was a pretty good plan. Frank needed money, and needed a change. Robert needed his silence, but also wanted to keep an eye on him. He would offer him a job working for the production company. He could courier supplies around in his plane and make the occasional run to the big island if they needed to pick someone up. In exchange, he would be paid very well and given room and board in a guesthouse. After hearing about Frank's situation, and having him stay the night, Robert doubted he would say no.

"Frank," Robert said, "how did you find the accommodations?"

Frank smiled. "First class, sir. Really, you've got a beautiful place here."

"Thank you, Frank. I was actually going to come find you in a little while so we could chat, but let's talk now."

Frank swallowed. "Actually, sir…"

"Frank, please call me Robert."

He smiled. "OK, Robert. I was actually hoping to chat with Ace for a minute, if that's alright."

"No problem. You and I will catch up a little later. I've got some work to do. Come find me in my office, alright?"

"Yes, sir… err, Robert."

Captain Frank nodded his head toward the door and

Ace followed him out. Ace had been the one to threaten Frank's life back on the island before they took off. Frank knew that he was not a man to trifle with. Now that they were on the same side, it seemed to Frank that while he didn't know much about Ace, he had a better feel for him than his brother. He had to get something off his chest, but it seemed ridiculous, and he didn't know who else to tell.

"What's up, Frank?"

The pilot looked around to make sure no one was nearby. "I remember what you said, back on the island, about taking care of Abby. Obviously, you're some sort of bodyguard, so I figured I should tell you about something."

Ace leaned in, suddenly interested. "What's that?"

"Yesterday, after we landed. I had lunch with one of Robert's security guys. Greg, I think his name was. It's just... he seemed a little odd."

"Odd? How?"

"He had a million questions about Abby. Wondered where she had been hiding, if I knew what her plans were now that she was back, stuff like that. I didn't know the answers to any of it, but I was thinking that as one of Robert's guys he should have already known, don't you think?"

Ace shook his head. "No, Robert is playing Abby very close to the vest. I can't tell you what's going on, but let's just say that she's not ready to put herself in the public eye again. She definitely doesn't want her story out there. Have you heard why they're looking for her?"

"Well, I know she was married to some mob guy that got killed a few months ago. That's what the investigator said they wanted to interview her about."

"That's part of it. It's not a stretch to think that there are some rather unscrupulous people out there who would like to know where she is. That's why she's hiding."

Captain Frank nodded. "That makes sense. This guy, Greg, he just rubbed me the wrong way." He reached into his pocket. "This morning I saw him snooping around my plane. I went down to check it out after he left, and I found this." He pulled a device out of his pocket. It was a small plastic cylinder, no larger than a quarter, and about half an inch thick. On top was a small button inset. "I think it's some kind of magnet. It was stuck under the tail end of the plane. I pressed the button a few times, but it didn't do anything. What do you think it is? And why would he put it there?"

Ace took the device from him and looked it over. "Did you tell him anything, when you were talking?"

"No. What could I tell him? All I know is Abby found me in a bar, and I gave her a ride. I have no idea where she came from or where she's going."

"Good. Let me know if he approaches you again. I'll keep an eye on him, too."

"Sure thing," Frank said. He pointed to the device Ace was holding. "What about that?"

Ace smiled. "I put it there. Back on the island before you took off. It's a tracking device."

Frank shook his head. "You didn't trust me. Makes sense."

Ace put his arm around Frank's shoulder, "You seem like an OK guy, and like you said, you don't know much of anything anyway. I don't think we need this anymore." He used his thumb to click the button on the device. He clicked it three times, paused, clicked it twice, paused again, then clicked it four times and hurled it off in the distance toward the empty beach as hard as he could. Halfway through its flight, the device exploded into a small fireball, and any trace of it disappeared.

"Holy shit!" Frank screamed, as Robert and JJ came running out of the house at the sound of the explosion.

Ace was laughing. "I told you I would kill you if you crossed me. You think I was kidding?"

"What was that?" JJ shouted.

"He found the tracking device I stuck on his plane, so I was just getting rid of it."

JJ shook his head as he and Robert went back into the house, literally bumping into Robert's security detail that was hustling out the door as they were trying to go back in.

"It's fine," JJ told them. "Just my brother being an

asshole."

As Frank's pulse returned to normal, he smiled at Ace. "I sure am glad we're on the same team."

22

SOMEWHERE OVER the Rocky Mountains, a brief bout of turbulence shook Abby awake. She sat up, startled, and it took a moment to remember where she was, who she was, and what she was doing.

Unconsciously, her right hand reached down to her thigh, only to find it empty. She had left her knife back on the island with Robert for safekeeping. She wanted to travel quickly and light and really didn't have much in the way of possessions to speak of. She had a small carry-on with just a few items, and knew full well that a hunting knife capable of gutting a wild boar would never make it through security in her carryon, and she wasn't about to check a bag solely to bring it with her. The knife was a safety blanket. She wanted to believe that she was out of the woods now and no longer needed it, but she knew that might not be the entire truth and didn't want to get used to the idea.

She did allow herself a smile at the thought that she

was no longer running through trees from the bad guys, or having to look over her shoulder waiting for the wrong person to show up. Robert had forewarned her that although she had been blissfully unaware, she remained a pretty big news story. While at the moment she did not want to be found, once they were in Canada and the timing was right, she certainly hoped Robert was right and the whole world would take notice of where they were.

Abby had been confident that she wasn't particularly recognizable. Since the show had ended she had put on about ten pounds; the public would remember her being smaller. She had also straightened her long, loose brunette curls, dyed them blonde and chopped them just below her shoulders. To round out her incognito look, she wore dark-framed glasses to distract from her signature light amber eyes, and a baseball cap with her ponytail pulled through the back.

Sighing, she looked at the GPS map on the seatback in front of her. They were cruising at just under forty thousand feet, going five hundred and fifty-eight miles per hour, and about to pass north of Denver, Colorado. The map indicated they were about nine hundred miles from Chicago. She raised the shade on the window to see nothing but blackness outside. The sun wouldn't be up for a couple more hours.

Doing some quick math in her head, she figured they would land in just under two hours. After her layover, she would take a two-hour flight to Montreal, connect with Eric, and then catch a cab to her sister's home about forty minutes north of the city.

She smiled at that thought. She would be reunited with her little Ava by that afternoon.

It was tough sitting alone in first class, knowing that Eric was fifty feet behind her in coach. *What will our new life be like?* She wondered.

She had spent a great deal of time over the past fourteen or so hours on the aircraft, processing exactly where her life stood. She was a single mom, rich now, but separated from her daughter for a year. Aside from Eric and Robert, she didn't have a friend in the world. Thinking back on the past ten years, she'd really had no friends to speak of in a very long time.

She thought about the girls that she had lived with in that shitty motel behind the strip club. Calling them friends would have been a stretch. They were in the same hellish predicament together, but none of them were in any condition to maintain what a normal person would call friendship. *Most of them are probably dead by now.* Abby shook off that thought and decided not to think about the fact that she could have very easily been one of them.

Looking back on it, it had certainly been Bryce's intention to keep her distant from anyone, never letting her make any human connections without him present, forcing her to rely on him and only him. She hated herself for allowing that to happen.

Abby thought back to the night she met Rick, her pot-distributer boyfriend, at her friend's house all those years ago. It was such a small moment. Had she stayed home that night, or had he not shown up, where would her life be now?

A name suddenly popped into her head – *Donny*. She felt a twinge of guilt for having forgotten him. Without his friendship, she wouldn't be sitting where she was today. He was the one who took care of smuggling Ava out of the country. He was the one who used his connections to get Abby a shot at *Trial Island*. He was the one who sat with her in the conference room with the network attorneys and signed away all of Bryce's rights with a fake ID and a cheap ballpoint pen.

Without him I'd be either crazy or dead. She remembered when they went their separate ways after leaving that conference room. They had held each other tight, and Donny made no effort to mask his affection for Abby, a woman he had loved at arm's length for years and would never see again except on the television screen.

He stood by the door as Abby was taken by the producers off into the world of *Trial Island*. She would be isolated from everything for months during training before being dropped off on the island. *Donny… I wonder where he wound up?* He promised he wasn't going back to Chicago. Nothing was traceable as far as getting Ava out of the country, but with Abby having disappeared, Bryce was going to go nuts, and he would almost certainly find out about Donny's involvement.

His vague plan had been to move to some obscure town in Montana and start an honest life, with a completely fake identity, of course. Bryce owned Chicago, and Donny knew he could never go back. As she daydreamed about what his life might be like now, Abby wondered if she would ever see him again.

*   *   *

Connor Jackson was in the business of doing messy work for bad people as long as the money was right. In another life, he had been an undercover police officer, infiltrating the organized crime scene in the Midwest. That was nearly a decade ago. The problem he ran into was that once he was undercover, he didn't want to get out. The money was easy, and much more plentiful than the pittance of a paycheck he received bi-weekly for putting his life on the line.

He had gone through some dark times and had his share of blood on his hands. He wasn't in the killing business anymore. He was mainly in the collection business. As a young man, during a more honest life, his broad shoulders and quick hands earned him respect on the amateur boxing circuit. These days, he used his fists to deliver messages when he had to. The men he worked for had money owed to them, and Connor saw to it that they got paid.

He had spent the past few months on an extended vacation at the request of his employer, mostly relaxing and waiting for a phone call. That call came yesterday. Today, he was not a collection man. Today, he was a delivery man.

It was a massive aircraft, with seating for over four hundred passengers, yet it was still a very full flight. He had purchased his airline ticket at the last minute, and was happy to pay the exorbitant cost for extra legroom at the very front of business class. He wasn't paying, anyway – his employer was. From his vantage point on the left-side aisle of the plane, he could keep the occasional eye on the blonde-haired package sitting in first class – the package he was to deliver in just a few short hours. Abby occupied a seat not twenty feet from Connor.

He hadn't seen her in awhile, as the flight attendants were constantly pulling the curtain closed to separate the classes. However, he wasn't worried. She wasn't going anywhere while they were forty thousand feet up, and he knew from his employer that she wasn't planning to leave the airport once they were on the ground. She had a couple-hour layover before catching a flight to Montreal. Connor would grab her during this time and escort her to a waiting vehicle where Bryce would be anticipating their reunion.

With the restroom right near his seat in use, he decided to venture into the first class cabin to use their restrooms, and maybe even give Abby a friendly smile and a hello just for fun. He needed to stretch his legs anyway, as fourteen hours on a plane had him awfully cramped up.

Walking through the curtain and into first class, he was immediately stopped by a flight attendant. "Excuse me, sir, can I help you?" Her words came out with a smile plastered across her face, but she was anything but happy to see him there. Despite his large frame and big arms, the airplane, and in particular first class, was her turf and she was willing to defend it.

"No, thank you," he said. "I just need to use the men's room."

266

She somehow smiled even larger. "This is the first class cabin, sir. Please use the facilities just on the other side of the curtain in business class."

He looked over at the back of Abby's head. "It's taken."

The flight attendant gently placed her hand on his arm and turned him around. "There are several additional lavatories in the coach section, sir, I'm sure you can find one available. Thank you. Buh-bye now." If it was possible to slam a curtain closed in someone's face, she did.

And with that he found himself back on the other side. *Oh, well, it was worth a shot.* However, he did actually need to use the facilities, and the bathroom in the business section had been occupied for quite some time. He wasn't sure he wanted to go in there once it did become available anyway.

Connor walked back into the coach section where the seats were decidedly more crowded than business or first class. There were three seats on each side of the plane, and the center aisle had four. He looked past the sea of three hundred and fifty heads to the end of the aisle where there was a green indicator light telling him that the bathroom was available.

Most people walk with their heads down, not wanting to make eye contact or, heaven forbid, interact with a stranger on the flight. Not Connor. In his line of business, it was important to be aware of what and who was around you at all times. As he walked down the aisle, glancing over his fellow passengers as they stared down at their magazines or television screens, one in particular caught his eye and made him do a double take. He had never met him in person, but he had seen his face plenty of times before.

Eric.

Shit.

*   *   *

Abby watched as the bulldog of a flight attendant made her way back to the front of first class after having dismissed a passenger who wanted to use their bathroom. He had been a big man who didn't look all that friendly, but the flight attendant was a tough little women. Abby smiled at the thought that she would rather take on that tough-looking man than this little woman who ruled everything forward of the first class curtain. *Good for you*, she thought to herself.

Despite her instincts, she was looking back to see if she could spot Eric back there. She couldn't, and was a little disappointed, though not surprised. She was excited for him to meet Ava, and was sure that they would become a happy little family in no time at all.

That thought stunned her for a moment. A happy family. Abby, Ava, and Eric. *Yes*, she thought, *we will be a happy family.* She had never spoken to Eric about marriage, though they had always talked about their future lives together – they just never said the words.

Technically, she had been married the entire time that she had known Eric. Now that Bryce was gone, they could truly start a new life together. She dreamt that their future would involve a small ceremony on the white sand beach in front of their villa on their secret island. She pictured flowers in Ava's hair, and a simple ring on her finger. *Yes, a happy little family.* She allowed herself to close her eyes and dream for a bit as the plane continued toward their destination.

*   *   *

On the opposite side of the plane, in the right aisle window seat, a clean-shaven Ace nudged JJ awake. "Hey, did you see the way that guy just looked at Eric?"

JJ had his baseball cap pulled down over his face. He opened his eyes halfway and tilted his head up to look at his brother. "No… I was sleeping."

"It was weird, that's all."

"So is looking at you without a beard."

"Seriously," Ace hissed under his breath. "I don't understand why I had to shave my beautiful beard that took six months to grow out like that, and you just get to wear a baseball cap."

"I'm one of a hundred anonymous guys in a ball cap. If you didn't shave, you'd be the one guy with the crazy beard. Easy to pick out. Remember, Robert doesn't want her to know we're here."

"What about him?" Ace said, indicating Eric across

the other side.

"I don't know. He wasn't supposed to be here. I say we just lay low, make sure Abby gets to where she's supposed to go, and by the grace of God get back to Boston and our own beds by tomorrow night."

Ace was still staring across the plane at the back right side of Eric's head.

"Will you stop staring at him? He's going to see you."

"We're behind him; it's fine." Ace watched as the man came out of the bathroom and quickly walked back to business class, but not before glancing down at Eric as he walked by. "There, he did it again."

JJ sighed. "He probably recognized him from TV. Wouldn't you?"

"Well yeah. But still."

*   *   *

Connor locked the bathroom door behind him and pulled out his phone. *Shit! What is he doing here?* He was confident that he could take care of Abby, but with two of them and one of him, he needed to alter his plan. He looked down at his phone. There was no reception this high up, but he had Wi-Fi through the plane and sent a message to Bryce:

> **Eric is on the plane. I'm going to need some help on the ground. I'll be in touch.**

As he walked back to his seat, he glanced down at Eric. *Yes, it's definitely him.* He wondered why he was there, and why he wasn't sitting in first class with Abby. He also wondered why Bryce had told him that he only needed to worry about the girl and didn't bring Eric up at all.

His phone vibrated with a message from Bryce.

> **You're sure it's him? Greg said she was traveling alone. Said they had some sort of fight and he was supposed to stay behind.**

Connor thought about that. If he wasn't supposed to be here, and they weren't sitting together, then maybe she didn't even know he was there. That would certainly make things easier. The more he thought about it, the more he convinced himself that was the case. Eric had not come up front the entire flight. If they had a fight and he was supposed to stay behind, then he was probably following her, and she doesn't even know it.

If that was the case, Eric was probably planning to approach her between flights to make up. If he could neutralize him before that happened, then he could stick with the original plan. He messaged Bryce back:

> **Yes, it's definitely him. Doesn't look like she knows he's here. Have a couple guys grab him when he gets off the flight. He's at the back of the plane, so he'll be way behind us. She'll never see him.**

*　　*　　*

Eric nervously flipped through the airline magazine for at least the fifth time. He hated being so close to Abby, yet so far away. He knew that they were fine on the plane. Everyone goes through security, everyone has their assigned seats, and from what he just saw, they don't even let you walk into first class if you don't belong there. Still, they had been through so much together, and he would feel better if he had his eyes on her.

Their relationship, while wonderful, was complicated on a certain level. They had spent the past year together; however, she was a married woman. Albeit estranged from a psychotic husband who had tried to murder them both, but a married woman nonetheless. *What would my grandmother think?* He knew exactly what she would have thought. *It's time to put a ring on her finger.*

His grandmother, who had practically raised him, had been and still was a big influence on his life. She was a traditional woman, but also practical and realistic. She wouldn't have necessarily approved of their relationship, but wouldn't have voiced her objections either. Now that Abby was free, he had to do the right thing and marry her.

The thought shocked Eric. Why hadn't it crossed his mind until now? He wasn't sure. He supposed that everything had happened so quickly since they found out Bryce was dead. In light of everything, he didn't think the timing was right for such a dramatic event. Their lives had changed so much over the past ten days, and now, within a few hours, they would change even more.

He wondered, *when is the right time to ask something like that?* He relaxed and told himself that he would figure it out. He and Abby would have a long life together. For now, they would stick around Montreal for a few days to get everything in order before they revealed themselves.

They had toyed with a few different ways of doing it, but decided they would simply go out to lunch in the city and have her sister call in an anonymous tip to the local media about where they were dining. A reporter would show up, and they would just ever so briefly answer the inevitable question, "Where have you been hiding?" by saying, "Somewhere quiet and out of the way up north, so please leave us alone." After that, they would separate for their travels, disappear again, and be able to go back to their quiet life in the villa while the media turned its search for them to northern Canada.

He took solace in the knowledge that their return to heaven on earth was just a few days away, and that in just a matter of a few hours, he would be holding Abby in his arms again.

*   *   *

Abby opened her eyes. She hadn't really slept, but felt about as rested as she could. The captain had announced that they were on their final approach and would be on the ground in a matter of minutes. She had butterflies in her stomach. She was nervous to see her daughter again. She was also excited that she was that much closer to being with Eric. They had been through so much, it seemed as though she had known him all her life, not for only a year.

The thought occurred to her that although she felt that way about him, he was still a complete stranger to her daughter. She wasn't sure when would be the best time to introduce him to Ava. She'd been away from her daughter for so long, she felt she should show up alone and let Ava meet Eric later. Her sister confirmed that Ava knew of Eric, and that they had been on the show together, but didn't know that Abby had been in hiding with him for the past year.

Given that Ava had been through a great deal, and that she probably had some sort of abandonment complex, Abby decided it probably wasn't best for her to show up with Eric by her side. She figured she would go to her sister's alone, and then tomorrow or maybe the next day, add Eric to the mix.

She also knew that he would understand, and it would be all right. Before she knew it, their lives would be relatively normal again. *Well, normal for us, anyway.* She was semi-relieved at the thought of returning to normal, even if she had no idea what normal was going to be. It would be great as long as she had Ava and Eric with her.

She flipped up the shade and looked out the window at the Chicago skyline against the gray of dawn in the distance. She had mixed feelings about returning to the city, even if it was only for a short few hours.

"It will be fine," she said aloud.

23

CONNOR EXITED THE PLANE only a few minutes after Abby, though when he walked into the terminal, she was nowhere to be seen. He spotted the restrooms on the far wall and figured that, like many passengers after an excruciatingly long flight, she probably ducked in there. He decided to wait it out for a few minutes. If she didn't show up, he still wouldn't be worried – he would check the food court, and ultimately the terminal for her connecting flight to Montreal.

Scanning the area, he immediately picked out two big guys in dark sport coats sitting near the restroom, pretending to read their newspapers. Their respectable guts hung over their belts and rested on their laps. Both sported a goatee to give the casual observer some inclination as to where their chins should have ended. Judging from their greased back and somewhat curly hair, Connor rightly assumed their sizable girth was from one too many helpings of mama's spaghetti and meatballs.

He kept an eye on them, and an eye on the ladies' room exit. When she exited a few minutes later, the men noticed her, but quickly looked down at their papers. Connor watched as she stood for a moment, scanning the international terminal, before her eyes settled on the familiar orange and pink colors of a donut shop sign at the far end of the hallway. She smiled and headed that way.

Connor looked down at his phone to check the time. Abby had just over two hours before her flight to Montreal, and he doubted she would leave the terminal. He decided to stick around a few more minutes just to be sure these two goons took care of Eric. He didn't know what the plan was, but they had to be Bryce's men.

Once he was satisfied they had things in hand, he would follow Abby and grab a coffee himself. Once he saw what Abby was drinking and where she was sitting, he would drug his coffee with a potent sedative, put his identical cup down next to hers, and then take hers by accident. Given the strength of the sedative, and her petite size, just a few sips would be enough to put her down for the count for at least a couple of hours. She would sleep through the boarding of her flight and in her half-lucid state when she woke up, he would tell her that Robert had sent him and escort her from the airport to Bryce's waiting vehicle.

That plan was a bit complicated, so as a back-up, he had a syringe in his pocket. He could sit down next to her, stick her, and she would pass out within seconds before she knew what happened.

If that didn't work, he would convince her otherwise.

Anyway you cut it, she was leaving the airport in a black limousine and not a plane for Montreal.

As he stood there going over his plan and pretending to be busy on his phone, he noticed Eric walk by and head straight into the men's room. The two men looked at each other, stood up, and strode in behind him, their impressive stomachs leading the way.

Connor muttered under his breath as he walked toward the donut shop, "Way to play it close to the vest guys."

*   *   *

Ace walked down the wide corridor past the donut shop and saw Abby standing in line out of the corner of his eye. He continued walking. With his previously longish curly hair now chopped above the ears and his scraggly beard freshly shorn from his face, there was no way she would recognize him. They had only seen each other a couple of times in the first place. However, he did not want to be obviously following her.

He walked a few storefronts down, pretending to look over the selection of earplugs at a kiosk, then turned and walked back to the donut shop to stand in line a half-dozen people behind Abby.

He thought it was bizarre that Robert was so concerned about her that he had him and his brother tailing her to her destination on the other side of the world. However, Robert paid exceedingly well, so Ace had reluctantly cleaned up his hair and beard and grabbed a couple of seats on the plane for himself and JJ.

Ace heard Abby order. "Medium regular, cream, one

sugar, and a Boston Crème donut, please."

He got the sense that she had placed this order a few hundred times in the past. Ace thought it was funny how people were such creatures of habit. Abby had spent the past year of her life in isolation, as far from her regular coffee order as possible, but here she is, on terra firma back in the good old U.S. of A. for ten minutes, and she's spouting out her regular order without missing a beat.

The next thing he noticed was odd, as well. A man, two customers in front of him, also ordered, "Medium regular, cream, one sugar."

What an odd coincidence, Ace thought.

When the man took his cup and turned to hustle out of the shop and down the hall after Abby, Ace watched with intensity, trying to figure out what was happening. *That was the guy looking at Eric on the plane.* Having spent years as a private investigator and bounty hunter, he had learned to trust his gut, and right now his gut was telling him that something was not right.

The voice of the woman at the counter snapped him out of his trance a few moments later, "What'll it be, sir? Sir, can I help you?"

"Uh," he turned and watched as the man walked briskly down the corridor and out of sight around the corner. "Sorry, nothing." Ace turned and left the shop in pursuit.

"Next," the woman called.

JJ was supposed to be standing at the end of the corridor where it spilled out into the wide-open terminal, hat pulled down low. He was supposed to be there to nod in the direction that Abby went so Ace would know where to go. They had determined she would either head over toward the tables at the food court, or just to the gate for her next flight.

The only problem was that JJ was not there. Ace stopped and looked around. Not only was JJ not at his post, he was nowhere to be seen.

He scanned the crowd carefully, trying to put eyes either on his brother, Abby, or the man who had appeared to be following her. However, he found none of them. *Something must have happened,* he thought. His brother wouldn't have just left his post. *He must have noticed the guy, too.* That was the only explanation Ace could come up with.

As he continued scanning, his eye caught the back of Abby's head as she turned a corner to head down another corridor toward the gates for the Canadian airlines. Ten paces behind her the mystery man followed suit. JJ was still nowhere to be seen.

Ace hustled across the terminal as fast as he could without attracting any attention, and set off in pursuit of the woman he was tasked with protecting.

*   *   *

JJ had been waiting at the end of the corridor. His brother, Ace, had just walked up toward the donut shop to keep an eye on Abby while she waited in line for coffee, and to grab them a couple of coffees while he was at it. *Two birds, one stone. I love when that works out.*

He couldn't wait to get back home. For months they had been on boats, hopping island to island, searching for a needle in a haystack. Now that they had found the needle, he was looking forward to getting back to his own bed, going for his daily run along the Charles River, and eating a real New England breakfast.

He turned away from the corridor to face the open terminal area. Abby wouldn't recognize the back of him when she walked by. She wasn't looking for him. However, he would easily pick her out and watch where she was heading. As he looked across the terminal, someone else caught his eye – Eric. He was walking in the wrong direction with two large men, one on each side of him, and both were walking a bit too closely.

What the hell? That can't be good.

JJ looked behind him. Neither Abby nor Ace were anywhere to be seen. *They must both be in line,* he thought. He looked back toward the corridor that Eric had just disappeared down and read the sign above it out loud, "Baggage Claim and Customs."

He knew his task was to watch Abby, but it seemed at the moment that Eric might need a little watching himself.

As he trotted across the terminal and turned the corner toward Customs, he spoke a message into his phone that would be sent to Ace. "I think Eric is in trouble. Keep an eye on Abby. I'll be in touch."

Looking through the glass partition and into the customs area, JJ saw forty self-serve electronic kiosks, most of which were empty, and only a handful of customs agents. One was speaking to Eric and the two men, before making a few selections on his touchscreen and waving them through.

As JJ walked up to an empty kiosk and took out his own passport, he wondered, *What the hell is going on?*

24

WALKING THROUGH the crowded terminal, Eric couldn't believe his predicament. Having sat in the window seat on the airplane, with two sleeping passengers in the seats to his right, he hadn't used the bathroom in hours. So, after getting off the plane, he made that his first stop. He was in no rush to get to the gate for their connecting flight, as he and Abby were avoiding being seen together.

Entering the men's room, he followed the unwritten code and found a bank of three empty urinals and chose the middle one. The two men who came in after him apparently were not aware of the code, and they sidled up to the ones on either side of Eric. *They're big guys, too*, Eric had thought as each bumped into him from their respective sides.

As he finished up his business and zipped his fly, he noticed the men seemed to glance at each other from either side of him. Then the unexpected happened. The man on his right bumped into him as he stepped away to go to the sink and wash his hands, knocking Eric into the man on his left who caught him from falling.

"You OK, buddy?" the man asked.

"Yes, yes, I'm fine. Sorry about that," Eric said.

Then he felt something press into his left lower back.

"Good. I'm glad you're OK," the man said under his breath. "Now I'm going to ask you to keep your mouth shut, don't cause a scene, and come with us."

Eric was immediately confused and opened his mouth to protest, though the words caught in his throat as the cylindrical object was pushed harder into his side. *It's a gun*, Eric realized, his eyes opening wide.

"Yeah," the man said with a smile, "it's exactly what you think."

"Where are we going?" Eric whispered.

"Right out the front door."

"I figured that much," Eric whispered, "but where after that?"

"Don't worry about it, pretty boy. Let's start walking." He nudged Eric toward the door from the corner they stood in.

"We're in an airport, man. There's security everywhere. You can't do this."

"No, I definitely can."

Eric's eyes scanned the men's room for help. There was no one. There were three other men; two talking on their phones at another bank of urinals who hadn't noticed anything else around them, and the other big guy was standing by the exit waiting for them. "I'll yell for help to the first officer I see the second we walk out of here."

The man leaned in close to Eric's ear, his hot breath reeking of whatever he had gorged himself on for breakfast. "Go ahead. But I wouldn't. You're going to walk slowly, just slightly in front and to my left. You're going to stay close and walk steady. The gun will be draped under my coat and pointed at *your* back, not mine. You run, or call for help, and you'll bleed out on the ground before anyone knows what happened. I don't care about going to jail. I've been. I'm guessing you probably care about getting dead, though."

"Is this about money? I'll give you whatever I've got, but I've got a plane to catch, and it's really important. Can't we work something out?"

"We're not interested in whatever you've got in your pockets. Now, we can walk out of here together, the three of us, or you can die in a men's room. Your choice. I'll give you a three count to think about it." The man looked down at his watch, then back at Eric.

"Fine, let's go." Eric shook him off and walked ahead of them, searching for a way out as he walked through the terminal. However, they each stuck close to either side of him, nudging him from each side as they went along.

What in the world could these guys want? Eric wondered.

He figured it had to be money. They can't be Bryce's guys. No one but Robert knew he would be here. He hadn't thought about it, but if Abby was all over the news, then so was he, and he was probably more recognizable than she was right now. His hair was cut short, but otherwise, he was the same guy.

Just a couple of criminals sitting around an airport, knowing there are bound to be folks with money coming through, and in walks Eric. It was well known he had a ten million dollar pay day a year ago, and clearly didn't have any security around him. *I guess I'm an easy target for a couple of thugs.* Of course, they didn't want what was in his pockets. These guys were obviously professionals. They wanted access to his bank accounts. *Damn it*, he thought. He didn't care about the money, but he had to get to Abby. *There's got to be a way out.*

As he walked through the terminal and under the sign that read Customs, he smiled. *No way these guys are getting through customs with a gun.* As soon as he turned the corner and looked through the glass partition toward the customs area though, he got a bad feeling.

He had always imagined customs entailed long lines, hundreds of people, and security officers questioning and patting down everyone who came through. This was not the case.

Eric found himself looking at a bank of about forty electronic kiosks – almost like the self-checkout lines at the grocery store – and the handful of people that were in the area were punching at the screens making selections. Apparently it was self-serve, and the half-dozen officers milling about were just there to ask a few questions and assist travelers who couldn't figure out how to work the machines.

His escorts stopped and looked things over, then, after making eye contact with one of the officials who nodded at them, they walked directly over towards him. In his situation, Eric should have been happy to see a man in uniform, but he didn't have a good feeling about this.

The officer stopped them just short of reaching the kiosks, making a big show of it and raising his voice. "You three, come with me please." He led them toward a desk off to the side. He looked around and nodded to a couple of fellow officers and gave a slight wave of the hand that said, *No problem, we're all set.* He turned to the three travelers. "Passports, gentlemen."

Eric's escorts produced theirs and handed them to the officer as Eric just stood, a bit dumbfounded.

"Sir," the officer said impatiently, "your passport please."

Eric felt a bit of pressure on his back as he reached into his pocket and produced it, handing it to the officer.

"Thank you," the officer said.

Eric stood, mouth open, unable to believe what was transpiring. He was in such a trance that he almost didn't noticed a small stack of maybe ten one hundred dollar bills, neatly folded in half, that the officer slid from the back of one of the men's passports and down the cuff of his sleeve.

Damn. The officer had been expected these guys. The officer did some perfunctory work that took all of a minute, and then Eric was deflated as the officer handed their passports back with a smile and said, "Welcome back to the States, gentlemen. Have a nice day."

With a nudge from the right, they walked out of the other side of customs and down the long corridor toward a wall of glass doors a few hundred feet down the hall. Just outside the doors were several taxis and a large black limousine.

The man who had been doing all the talking leaned in from the right and muttered, "The big one is our ride. You've done good. Keep it up, and you might just live to tell the story." The man smiled.

Eric didn't intend to get into that car. He didn't intend to leave the airport. His mind was on overdrive looking for a way out. Then it happened. He noticed a young pretty girl, probably in her late twenties, staring at him and slowing down. Eric had a thought, *If these guys know who I am, other people would, too, right?* He smiled back at the girl and gave her a wink. She blushed ten shades of red as they passed in the corridor, and he saw her fumbling to get her phone out to take a photo.

The men escorting him didn't notice. They continued to not notice as Eric walked with his head held high, his big dimpled smile beaming ear to ear, and making eye contact with every woman he passed. Some smiled back, a few gave him a look of semi-recognition, some didn't notice at all.

Come on, he thought. They were about halfway to the exit, only one hundred feet further down the corridor. Eric decided he was going to go down fighting. He played the scene through his head. He would attack the one with the gun already drawn first. As long as he could disarm him, he figured he would be all right. Security would certainly notice a scuffle and jump in right away. Either way, he wasn't leaving this airport unless it was on a plane to Montreal with the love of his life.

He closed his eyelids and took a deep breath to steel himself. *You've been through worse; you've taken out tougher men than these clowns.* He let out a deep breath and got ready to turn and fight.

He nearly jumped out of his skin when he heard a thick New Jersey accent screech at him from no less than ten feet away.

"OH, MY GAWD! ERIC!"

He opened his eyes to see a middle-aged, busty, bleach-blonde woman running toward him, flapping her hands in the air like a top-heavy bird trying to take flight. He smiled back. *Jackpot.*

"Oh, my gawd, it's really you!" She ripped her phone from her pocket, "My name is Tammy, and oh, my gawd, I'm you're biggest fan! Can I get a picture?"

Eric had stopped, as had the men he was traveling with, who looked confused and caught off-guard. The silent one spoke up. "Sorry, miss, no time for photos."

He tried to move them along, but Eric stood firm and chuckled, "Don't be ridiculous, Mark. I always have time for a fan."

Tammy squealed and flapped her arms again. "Oh, thank you, thank you, thank you!" She handed her phone to the man Eric had dubbed "Mark." He reluctantly took it as Tammy posed for a photo with her arms wrapped around Eric.

"Oh, my gawd, where is Abby? Where have you been? What are you doing here?"

Eric smiled, willing Tammy to cause a bigger scene. "I really can't talk about it," he said very loudly, matching Tammy's tambour.

"OH, COME ON!" she screeched, "You can tell me!"

Other people were looking to see who he was. Two other young women interrupted Tammy, "Can we get a pic?"

"Of course!" Eric announced loudly.

Within two minutes, he had gathered a crowd of about a dozen women around him, all begging to have their photo taken and asking a million questions. As he took photos, his two escorts looked increasingly uncomfortable. Eric just continued to smile and engage with the ladies who surrounded him, buying time and attention.

As the crowd started to disperse, he saw one of the

women digging through her purse. She pulled out a pen and a shopping list, the back of which was blank. "Seriously," she said, "my mother is your biggest fan. She still talks about last year when you were on. It would mean the world to her if you could just write her a quick note." She held out the paper and pen hopefully.

"Sure thing," Eric said. "What's your mother's name?"

"Lorraine."

Eric smiled. "That's a pretty name." He quickly scrawled a note on the back of the shopping list and handed it back to the young woman.

"Thank you," she said, looking down to read it. She looked up after a few seconds and looked at him with an arched eyebrow. "Really?"

Eric smiled back. "Yes, tell your mom I said hi."

The girl nodded and quickly walked away as the two men took Eric by the arms and said, "We've really got to get moving now, sir." With that, they brushed off the last of the women and moved him toward the glass doors and the large black limousine on the other side.

As they closed in on the doors, only twenty feet away now, Eric glanced back over his shoulder at the girl he had signed the autograph for. She was standing with a police officer who was speaking into his radio and staring intently at Eric and his companions.

Just then, two other officers walked in through the

glass doors, one hand on their holstered guns, the other hand raised in the international sign for "stop". One of them called in a loud, authoritative voice, "Gentlemen, stop where you are and put your hands where I can see them."

Eric smiled, self-satisfied, and raised his empty hands above his head as he thought about the autograph he had signed:

These men are kidnapping me. They are armed. Please stay calm and get help. — Love, Eric

25

ACE HAD BEEN SITTING in a chair at gate C30 just a couple of rows behind Abby and to the right for the past twenty minutes. The flight wasn't boarding for awhile yet, but apparently nothing else around interested Abby, and Ace was determined to be wherever she was. He hadn't heard from JJ since his original message that he had to follow Eric, but something was definitely up, and he wasn't going to let her out of his sight. He also was trying to figure out why Abby and Eric weren't together. Was he following her, and she didn't know it?

In that time, the man from the plane had walked by twice. The third time he stopped and took up residence in a seat directly behind Abby and to her right. They were almost sitting back to back, but he was one seat over.

Ace watched as the man set his coffee down at his feet, and draped his arm over the seat next to him. He seemed to be checking its proximity to Abby. He took his arm down and rummaged through his duffel bag for a moment, occasionally looking around.

Ace didn't like it. The hair on his neck was raised. In a society conditioned not to judge or profile, Ace was an exception. He had learned long ago that one would rarely be disappointed if they did a little judging and profiling now and then. Every other animal does it. That is how they survive. It's instinct, and Ace's instinct told him that something was off about this guy. He just hadn't worked out what to do about it yet.

Abby hadn't seemed to notice the man, until he put his arm over the seatback again and, from Ace's point of view, very intentionally brushed the back of her neck. She turned and Ace heard the man apologize. Abby just smiled. The man then said something Ace couldn't hear, and the two started chatting back and forth.

After a few minutes, the man turned from Abby and very deliberately looked in both directions before turning back to her and saying, "Listen, I know we're not supposed to do this, but would you mind keeping an eye on my bag for two minutes while I run to the men's room?"

"Sure," Ace heard Abby say.

The man jumped up and walked around to Abby's side of the row of chairs, setting his bag on the chair next to her, and his coffee on the ground, next to Abby's which was also on the ground next to her feet. "I'll be right back. Promise."

"OK."

Ace watched the man walk toward the men's room, smiling. He returned two minutes later as promised, and this time sat down next to Abby, and struck up a conversation again. Ace got up and moved around to the aisle on the other side so he could have a clear view of them from the front, as opposed to looking at their backs. He wasn't too worried about Abby recognizing him, and was willing to take the chance in order to keep a better eye on what was going on.

He couldn't hear them at all from his new vantage point, but he could see what was going on much better. The man was talking to Abby, and started gesturing with his hands as if giving her directions. He pointed toward the corridor they had entered through earlier and made a looping motion with his finger.

Whatever he was saying, Abby was interested. She stood with a smile, her satchel over her shoulder, and Ace heard her say, "Can I get you anything?" over her shoulder, as she walked away. The man shook his head no, and she was off.

Ace decided not to follow Abby, and instead remained leaning against a column, watching the man out of the corner of his eye. Ace turned his head to look directly at him as he saw him bend down and switch their two coffee cups sitting on the floor.

*   *   *

As Abby walked by, she confirmed for herself beyond a doubt that it was Ace leaning up against the column on the far side of the gate. She first spotted him back at the donut shop waiting in line, and then sitting a row behind her in the terminal for the past twenty minutes or so. He looked much different without a beard and with his haircut, but the small cut she had given him on his neck when she had met him a few days before was still there and gave him away.

She wasn't sure why he was following her, but she had to assume Robert put him up to it. She was keeping an eye out for JJ, too, as she expected that it was only a matter of time before he showed up. More concerning than either of them, however, was the man who had asked her to watch his bag.

Abby couldn't figure out his angle, but something about him wasn't sitting right with her. She had said yes so he wouldn't think she was suspicious, but decided to get away from him the second he got back. She recognized him as the same guy who had tried to use the first class bathroom and was turned away by the flight attendant. Now he was striking up a conversation with her, and she couldn't help but notice the side of his coffee cup had the exact same order she put in. She was sure that he was following her, and she didn't like it one bit. She could understand Robert paying JJ and Ace to follow her, but he would never have someone she didn't know tailing her. It just didn't add up.

She went in the direction she had originally come from, hoping to find Eric. She knew that they didn't want to be seen together, but she was worried about this guy following her and wanted to give him a heads up. Standing in the wide-open area of the main terminal, she scanned the crowds, but couldn't find anyone remotely close to his description. "Where are you?" she asked out loud.

*   *   *

When Ace looked back toward the corridor and saw that Abby was nowhere in sight, he knew it was time to make a move. Ace took two steps toward the aisle where the man sat and shouted at him, "Jerry?"

The man looked up, confused.

"Jerry Davidson!" Ace trotted over to the man. "You old sonofabitch!"

The man smiled at him uncomfortably. "Sorry, you've got the wrong guy."

"Don't be ridiculous!" Ace said boisterously, holding out his hand. "Dale, Dale Harrison. You were a year ahead of me in school, in my sister Julie's class."

The confused man took Ace's hand, which Ace used to yank him into a standing position and wrap his arms around him in a bear hug, pinning the man's sizeable arms against his sides. Ace whispered into his ear, "I don't know who the fuck you are, or what's going on here, but it ends now." Ace leaned back ever so slightly to look the man in the eye. His long hair had been trimmed, his crazy beard shaved, but he had a wild look in his eyes that, combined with his vice-like strength, told the man he was not someone to be trifled with. He smiled and whispered, "Pick up the bag, we're going for a walk."

*   *   *

Connor stood still, not knowing what to think for a moment. He knew how to take care of himself, but the man who stood in front of him had a look in his eyes that was more animal than man. He quickly checked through his options and realized there was nothing he could do here in the open if he wanted to be able to wrap things up with Abby.

"Pick up the bag, we're going for a walk," the man said.

Connor bent down to pick up the bag and stood, "Where are we going?"

"Don't forget your coffee," the man said.

Connor bent down to pick up the one closest to him.

"The other one," the man said.

Connor froze for a moment before picking up the other cup as instructed. As he stood, drugged coffee in hand, he realized his cover was blown. He didn't know who this guy was, but he was obviously onto him. "I can give you money," Connor spoke under his breath. "Whatever she's paying you to watch her back, I'll double it."

"Nice try." The man laughed and threw his arm around Connor like they were old friends. "Let's walk."

*   *   *

As he walked down the corridor with his arm around the man, Ace scanned the area in front of him for options. He briefly considered just tossing this guy to the authorities, but who knew what he was really up to.

Whatever it was would tie up Ace for hours in some sort of detention area where he would have to answer questions, as well, and that would leave Abby alone and unattended with JJ still missing.

No, he thought, *I need to get rid of this guy quick.*

As they walked by the open entrance to the ladies' room Ace saw a door standing ajar out of the corner of his eye. *Custodian's closet*, he thought.

With a quick glance around to make sure there were no security officers with eyes on them, he shuffled the man off to the side and through the open door into the small custodian's closet, pulling the door shut behind him and flipping the light on. Neither saw Abby watching them from behind.

"Who are you?" Ace demanded.

The man stood silent.

As Ace opened his mouth to ask again, the man flipped open the lid to his cup and threw the lukewarm coffee into Ace's face. Ace stumbled backwards, spitting it from his mouth and wiping it from his eyes.

He lunged back at the man, giving him a hard slap across the face with his big, meaty open hand, but Ace wasn't ready for the lightening fast jab to the ribs that immediately followed, doubling him over and into the man's knee. Ace had grown up scrapping with his older brother and the other boys in the neighborhood and was no stranger to the stunned feeling of a kneecap to the forehead. He used his upward momentum and the man's off-balance position to hit him in the jaw with an uppercut that sent him reeling backwards into a rack full of toilet paper and cleaning supplies. It was the smile on the man's face that surprised Ace most of all. Apparently this guy had taken a punch or two himself.

They circled each other in the small, confined room, maybe only six or seven feet square. "So what," Ace said, "we're going to beat the crap out of each other in a tiny room? How long is that supposed to last?"

"Oh, not too long," the man smiled.

*   *   *

What the hell is going on? Abby wondered. She was standing about thirty feet from the ladies' room and had just seen Ace and the other man disappear into a utility closet. She looked around, *JJ has to be somewhere around here too.*

She didn't know what was going on behind that door, but it seemed that Ace had noticed the guy, too, and was doing something about it. Her heart beat hard and fast in her chest. She wanted to get in there and find out what was happening. Ace seemed like a capable guy, but the other man was just as big. *What if Ace needs help?* Her mind raced through her options, but every scenario resulted in her not getting on the plane and not getting to Ava.

"Damn it!" she cursed under her breath.

She looked around. Airports are filled with security,

and this one was no exception. She spotted a guard at the far end of the terminal. *If I go tell him I saw these guys go into a closet, he'll check it out, but I'm probably going to have to give a statement, too. Damn.* That option was out... *think, Abby, think...*

*   *   *

Connor expertly ducked as the wild man swung a right hook to his jaw, and he came back with a double jab to the ribs, followed by a right hook of his own that grazed the man's jaw. The man stumbled back again, and seemed to be moving a bit slower. Connor wondered if the sedative in the coffee he just threw in his face was enough to take care of the guy. *Probably not*, he thought.

Abby was a little peanut of a woman. Had she drank it, it would have done the job. But this guy was a good six-foot-three and well over two hundred pounds and had swallowed very little of it.

Connor followed up with a punch to the gut before the man could recover, knocking the wind out of him. He quickly grabbed the syringe out of his bag and flipped the cap off, turning back toward his foe.

*   *   *

Ace was feeling groggy. Whatever was in that coffee was doing its work. He was glad he had intervened before Abby got ahold of it, but worried about what he had just ingested.

As the man turned around, Ace saw he was holding a

tiny plastic syringe tipped with a shiny thin needle. As the man swung it in his direction, the adrenaline gave Ace an extra boost and he moved back, knocking the man's hand away and sending the syringe clattering to the floor and under the shelving unit.

The man dove to the floor after it, clawing under the unit, searching for the syringe. Ace jumped on his back, wrapping his arm around his neck in a chokehold, cutting off the man's oxygen supply. The man tried to stand up, but Ace was too large a weight for him to life. He tore at Ace's forearm, trying to pry it from his neck, but it was fruitless.

*   *   *

The pressure around Connor's neck increased as he tried to remove the man's forearm from his throat. He felt a lightheaded sensation and started to see faint dots of light as his oxygen supply dwindled. He knew he only had a matter of seconds left before he blacked out.

He frantically reached under the shelving unit in front of him and pawed around searching for the sedative-filled syringe, his back-up plan for Abby. He had to use it now or he would never have the chance to grab her.

His right hand settled on the small cylinder. He carefully felt it, being sure to face the needle in the proper direction, and swung his arm back toward the leg of the man clinging to his back. He felt his arm thud against the man's thigh, and depressed the plunger on the syringe as blackness closed in around him and he went limp.

301

*   *   *

Ace groaned in pain as the needle pierced his right thigh. He jumped off the man, who just lay there. Whatever was in that syringe was working fast. He was immediately lightheaded. *I have to get back to Abby,* he thought. He managed to unlock the door and stumble from the custodian's closet, forgetting where he was.

The world spun around him as he looked at his surroundings. *I'm in a bathroom? Where are all the urinals?*

He collapsed to the floor, and as his face hit the cool tile, he heard a woman scream. He saw someone through the fog that looked like Abby. He tried to speak, but he couldn't hear if the words were even coming out. Blackness crept in from the sides of his head, and the tunnel vision closed in on him as the woman disappeared.

26

ABBY HAD DECIDED to go into the ladies' room. She could hear the men fighting in the closet, and there were several other women who heard it, too. One particularly bold and heavyset brunette went to open the door of the closet only to find it locked.

"What's going on in there?" one woman asked.

Another went trotting from the bathroom. "I'm getting security."

Abby was standing by the sink with two or three other ladies, watching and waiting. The others were stunned with disbelief at the sounds of the fight, but Abby was stunned motionless at her inability to jump into the fray and help the man who had been tasked with watching her back.

Suddenly, the door to the closet burst open and a beaten and bloodied Ace stumbled from the custodian's closet and collapsed on the ladies' room floor. Abby gasped at the sight, and one of the other women screamed.

Abby knelt down next to Ace. He seemed to recognize her and tried to speak, "Get out of here," was all he managed to say before his eyes rolled back and he passed out. She ran over to the open door of the closet with another woman to see the large man lying motionless on the floor? *Did Ace kill him?*

A crowd quickly gathered as security arrived, and Abby recognized that if she was going to get on her plane and get to her daughter, she could not be involved in this. She slowly backed toward the edge of the growing crowd, and though the guilt pained her, she walked slowly toward her gate. She didn't know who the big man was that Ace had apparently taken out, but she couldn't hang around to find out. It was safe to say that the man had been following Abby for the wrong reasons, and that's all she needed to know.

Abby stood by the gate clerk's desk scanning the other passengers as they eagerly meandered around waiting to board. She didn't see anyone else of concern, but she also didn't see Eric and that, in itself, was a concern.

Abby turned as she heard the squeak of rubber on tile to see a security golf cart stopping at the gate twenty feet away, yellow lights flashing. *Is that..?* "Eric!" She stifled herself just as it came out.

He glanced at her, and she gave him a curious look that said, *Where the hell were you?*

He just smiled and silently shook his head from twenty

feet away — *I'll fill you in later.*

She motioned her head across the terminal to the ladies' room. Eric looked over and saw the crowd and security, and turned back to Abby, raising an eyebrow. *What happened?*

She mouthed, "Ace."

Both of his eyebrows shot up, and he said, "What?!"

Abby rolled her eyes and looked away.

So much for keeping a low profile, Abby thought. She saw a couple people look his way, but no one approached him. She hoped it stayed that way. They weren't quite ready to reveal themselves yet. Looking back at him, she shook her head and mouthed, "Later."

She watched over his shoulder as the security team carried the two large men away on stretchers and brought along several of the women who had been standing in the ladies' room. Abby was happy that she had the foresight to get out of there, and wasn't among those who had to give statements. Within a few minutes, there was no sign of any of the commotion that had happened.

Glancing down at her watch, Abby noticed that they would be boarding in a few minutes. She couldn't wait to be in the air again, away from this city and on her way to Ava. *Just a few more hours,* she thought.

* * *

JJ timed his arrival to the gate to cut it as close to

305

possible to boarding. He didn't want Abby and Eric to notice him. He stood at the edge of the gate area and watched as Abby, and then Eric, got onto the plane. He looked down to check his phone to see that it was just less than twenty minutes until their scheduled departure time. *Where the hell is Ace?*

Fifteen minutes later, he had made three calls to his brother, all of which went to voice mail, and none of which were returned. When the attendant made the final boarding call, he had to make a choice. "Where are you, big guy?" he asked himself as he paced the gate area. Ace was nowhere to be seen.

Damn it. He had to get on the plane. Whatever happened with Eric and those two guys was not on the up-and-up. He didn't have any friends or connections high enough to find out what had happened, but he knew someone who might. He decided to make a quick call before boarding.

"Hi, Robert… Yes, it's JJ. Listen, I'm about to get on the plane to Montreal… Yes, Abby and Eric are already on the plane. No, no, they don't know I'm here, but I'm thinking I need to talk to them. I think something is up."

"Sir," the male attendant at the ticket desk was snapping his fingers, trying to get JJ's attention. "Sir! This door is closing in thirty seconds. Are you getting on the plane?"

JJ nodded and held up a finger. "Just a second. Yes, Robert, I need to go, but I need you to look into something if you can."

*   *   *

"WHAT?"   Bryce's voice thundered through the receiver and into Greg's ear, halfway around the world.

"That's what Robert just said. I don't know what happened at the airport, but they're on the plane to Montreal."

Bryce had been getting antsy, sitting in the large black limousine for the past couple of hours outside the airport. He had expected Eric to be escorted into his car, followed by Abby shortly thereafter. Nearly two hours had passed, and he had neither – and he was unable to get in contact with either Connor or the two guys tasked with grabbing Eric.

When his phone had finally rung, he jumped out of his seat, but was entirely confused when he looked down and saw it was Greg calling from Robert's island. "How is this even possible?" Bryce was seething.

Greg spoke in a hushed tone. "I don't know, sir. I'm not there. Robert got a call a few minutes ago from one of his investigators. The same guy that found Abby and Eric. I guess he's got him following them. He said that a couple guys tried to grab Eric, so he followed them. The cops nabbed all three before they got out of the airport, but Eric was apparently released and is on the plane now. The investigator asked him to look into it and figure out what happened, so Robert has us calling our contacts in law enforcement."

"Shit." Bryce realized now why he hadn't been able to

reach his guys.

"I figured they were your guys," Greg said. "What about Abby?"

"I had someone else on her, but you don't need to know about that. He was supposed to take care of her. You said she's on the plane now? You're sure?"

"I didn't see it with my own eyes, sir, but that's what Robert said. From what I understand, his guy is good, one of the best. If he interfered with your plans for Abby, the guy didn't say anything, or at least Robert didn't share anything."

Bryce's blood was boiling. He clenched a fist and pounded the seat in front of him, yelling in frustration. *Think, think.* If they're going to Montreal, that's where the girl must be. Abby must be going to Ava. *Then that's where I'm going, too.* "Greg, I need you to do something."

"Name it, sir."

"Do you have any idea why they're going to Montreal?"

"I don't, sir, but I can ask around. One of the other guys might know something."

"Do it. Do more than ask if you have to. Finding out where they're going is more important than keeping your cover. I have to know where they're going. Understand?"

"Yes, sir."

"Call me the second you find out anything." Bryce clicked off the phone, his foot tapping furiously on the black-carpeted floor of the limousine. He didn't have any connections in Montreal. Once Abby got there, who knew where she would disappear. He had to reach Montreal before Abby, but the plane he had to get ahead of was on its way down the runway. He finally screamed in frustration, "FUCK!" He punched the seat in front of him repeating, "FUCK, FUCK, FUCK!"

His driver had been with him only a few months now. He was a boisterous guy who didn't really know when to keep his mouth shut. He rolled down the partition, "Everything OK back there, boss?"

"No, Jake. No. Everything is not OK."

"Anything I can do, boss?"

"Not unless this limo can get to Montreal faster than a plane."

Jake thought about it a second. "Sorry, boss. She can haul, but can't do that." He thought a moment. "If you need a plane, boss, we're at the right place."

"You don't say?" Bryce said sarcastically. "Turns out there's a flight to Montreal right now actually, probably pulling away from the gate as we speak. The problem is that I'm not on it, and I need to be there when it lands."

Jake looked back in the mirror, "You know, boss, my cousin works at the private terminal. He's a bartender at their fancy club over there. I used to drive his clients all the time."

"That's great, Jake."

"What I'm sayin' is, he knows all the pilots. Tells me there's always a half dozen or so sitting around with empty planes and nothin' to do. Maybe you can catch a ride over there."

Bryce's eyes lit up. "Bring me there now!"

*   *   *

Looking out the window, Abby watched the Chicago skyline grow smaller by the second. As the wing dipped and the plane veered toward the Northeast, gaining altitude over Lake Michigan, the skyline disappeared entirely.

She was getting increasingly nervous about seeing Ava. Her sister had assured her that her daughter was beyond excited to be together again, but Abby was worried. *What if she hates me? She has every right to. I chose a maniac for her father. I lied to her and abandoned her hundreds of miles from everything she knew and loved.*

The more she thought about it, the more she was convinced that it was the right decision to meet her without Eric first so they could really talk over this weighty stuff. Once they were alright, she would bring Eric into the mix. It might take a little extra time, but she wanted to make sure that things were right between her and her daughter.

*   *   *

What Bryce loved about "legitimate" businessmen, especially those successful enough to own planes, was that first and foremost they're in the business of making money. It was only a five-minute drive from the international terminal to the private terminal, but Bryce had Jake call ahead anyway. He did not have a minute to lose.

Jake spoke to his cousin, who put him in touch with Barry, a retired teacher and now pilot. Barry and his G650, or more appropriately his employer's, had come in a few hours ago on a short flight from upstate New York. Barry's employer, a Wall Street CEO, was tied up until the following morning. Essentially, this perfectly good plane had nothing to do until then, and Barry's boss was more than willing to take ten thousand dollars for a couple hours of its use to make the quick trip across the border to Montreal.

It took a little while, but after getting the necessary clearances, Barry and Bryce were rocketing down the small runway and quickly gaining altitude. Abby and Eric had a forty-minute head start. Once they reached cruising altitude, Bryce looked down at his watch and asked the male flight attendant, "How fast does this thing go?"

"Officially, six hundred and ten miles per hour, but if the wind is right. it's a little faster."

Bryce was staring at his watch and doing some quick math in his head. "Tell the pilot if he gets us there inside of two hours, there's another five grand in it for him."

The attendant smiled at Bryce. "Absolutely, sir. I'll

pass on the message. Can I get you something to drink?"

"Scotch. Whatever you've got is fine, I'm sure."

"Very good."

The attendant disappeared forward and into the cockpit. When he reappeared and gave his passenger the thumbs up a few minutes later, Bryce felt the airspeed increase as the small private jet quickly gained additional altitude.

He checked his phone and found no signal, though he wasn't surprised. He grabbed the air phone from its holder, secure on the wall. He figured he was paying enough; he could use the phone if he damn well pleased.

Bryce made a few phone calls, including one to his boss, which he didn't want to make, but he was desperate. No one had any solid connections in Montreal. It was, literally, a foreign land, and Bryce and his people had no business there.

He called the attendant over. "I'm going to need a car the moment we touch down. Literally, the minute we're on the ground, I need to get in and go. Is that possible?"

The attendant nodded. "Certainly. sir. There's an executive rental lot right in the terminal. If you'd like to give me your information, I'd be happy to arrange that for you."

Bryce smiled as he handed over one of his fake ID's and a credit card. *Damn,* he thought. *I could get used to this.*

He looked out the window, nervously tapping his foot on the floor. He still didn't know where they were going once they were on the ground. He couldn't count on just finding them by dumb luck, though if he did, he wouldn't hesitate to take them out the second he saw them. Hell, he would execute them on the tarmac if given the opportunity. If he was going to spend some time in jail, there were worse places to be than Canada.

He stared at his phone for a few minutes before he realized why. Greg was supposed to call him, but obviously couldn't while he was in the air. If Greg were calling him, he wouldn't get the message until they touched down, and he was the one getting the information Bryce needed. He used the air phone again to call Greg, "Have you found anything?"

"I might have something. One of the other guys said he heard Robert talking to Abby about getting back together with someone. He assumed it was family from the way they were talking. Does that help at all?"

Bryce took a deep breath. "Not really anything I didn't already know. You have to find out where they're going."

"Will do, sir. I'll call you the moment I have something. I know what I have to do."

27

ABBY AND ERIC were less concerned about being recognized once they were on the ground. Abby had turned on the television on the seatback of the plane, and while flipping past the news she saw Eric's face in a still shot next to a blonde in the airport.

The host, a twenty something brunette that looked good in a low-cut shirt and could read a teleprompter, was talking excitedly, "There has been an official Eric sighting in Chicago! He stopped and spoke with some fans, signed a few autographs, and then it appeared that airport police arrested him just a few minutes later. Details are few right now, but this has to beg the question, where's Abby?"

What. The. Hell? Abby couldn't believe what she was seeing at the time. When they got off the plane she walked out to the taxi stand where she had planned to meet Eric. "So, the cat's out of the bag?"

He just gave her a blank stare.

"I saw you on the news about an hour ago."

"Yeah, so…" He went on to explain what had happened. "At least you weren't with me, right?"

As they hailed a cab, she noticed a small business jet coming in for a landing in the distance. Nudging Eric, she nodded her head toward the jet, "Must be nice to travel like that, huh?"

"You should have asked your pal, Robert. I'm sure he's got a couple of those floating around. We probably could have caught a quicker ride."

"No, he's done enough for me. Besides, I kind of want to do this on my own, you know? I love Robert, but he's been pulling the strings for a while. I still can't believe he had Ace following me, but thank God he was, I guess. I feel terrible about leaving him like that back in Chicago, but I'm sure he'll be fine. Security was there, and the bad guy was unconscious, so what could I have done except screw up our plans?"

"No, you're right. You definitely did the right thing. I bet JJ was there too, so I'm sure things are being taken care of."

Abby sighed. "Robert is well-intentioned anyway."

"He just cares about you, that's all. When you have that much money, you don't have much of a reference for anything being out of your control. I'm sure the thought of you going back out into the world and getting hurt again drives him nuts."

"I guess," Abby said as they hopped into a cab.

"Traveling light today?" the cabby asked with a vague Canadian accent.

"Indeed we are."

"American?"

"Yes," Eric nodded.

"Oh, good, I can drop the bullshit accent," the cabby said as he pulled from the curb. "I'll tell you, the people around here, the locals, if you're American, they barely tip you. Another driver clued me in on that a few years back when I was pissin' about not making any tips. Name is Jack, but I started talkin' like it was Jacques, and all of a sudden the locals found their wallets. Go figure." He paused as he merged toward the exit. "So where to today?"

Abby read him an address in Saint-Colbert from a small note tucked in her satchel.

"Nice place. Colbert that is. Family?"

"Yes," Abby said. "Going to see my daughter."

Jack looked at her in the rearview mirror. "I know you're not supposed to ask a lady her age, but your daughter? There's no way you got a kid old enough to live on her own."

Abby laughed. "Well, I hope not. Thank you. She's staying with my sister. I haven't seen her in a while."

"Oh, well, that makes more sense. My son, he went to

316

stay with his grandparents up there earlier this summer. They've got a place out near the St. Lawrence River. I couldn't afford to take the time off, so I sent him on his own. I wanted him to experience nature and be able to enjoy himself, even though I couldn't be there. Didn't see the kid for a week; drove me nuts! I love that little guy. I'd do anything for him."

Abby chuckled. "We will do anything for our kids, that's for sure."

"How long has it been?" Jack asked.

Lost in thought looking out the window, Abby swallowed hard to keep from choking up. Her voice was a little shaky when she said, "A little more than a year."

Jack looked up in the rearview again. "No shit? Wow. Sorry to hear that, but hey, the good news is you're on your way, right?"

"Right," Abby smiled.

As he drove down the road, Jack punched the information into his GPS and announced, "I'll have you back to your little girl in thirty eight minutes flat. Sound good?"

"Sounds great!" Abby said, taking Eric's hand and squeezing it tight, her moist eyes meeting his.

Eric looked into the eyes of the woman he wanted to spend the rest of his life with. In his heart, he wanted to ask her right then and there. He could even feel the words forming in his mouth. But his head knew better. This wasn't the time, and he knew that. Today was about Abby and Ava. She had enough on her plate. He decided he would do it soon, though. After a few weeks, once they were settled back into their villa with Ava. He would pick out a ring while they were here since there wasn't much for fine jewelry on the island, and he would do it right. Something simple and understated. She would like that.

Abby saw the big smile on his face a second before Eric turned away to look out the window, watching the world pass by.

"What's going on in your head over there?" she asked.

He turned, still smiling. "What?"

"Don't *what* me. You're up to something."

"Nothing for you to worry about," he said, leaning in to kiss her. "You'll find out soon enough."

*   *   *

Greg found Robert alone in his office, on the phone.

"You still haven't heard from Ace? What do you think happened?" He paused with the phone to his ear, long enough to wave Greg in the door and listen to what was being said on the other end. "I agree JJ, something isn't right." He paused, listening, and then shuffled some papers around on his desk before finding the right one and reading from it, "Yes, that's it. Saint-Colbert, that's right. Call me once they get there. Very good." He clicked off the phone and looked up at Greg, "That's JJ, still trying to figure out what the hell happened in Chicago. His brother just vanished, and then the thing with Eric. Something is wrong." His voice trailed off as he looked down at his papers.

"So, what's in Montreal anyway?" Greg casually asked Robert.

"What's that?"

"Just curious why Abby's going to Montreal?"

"Oh, that's a long story, but thank you for making the arrangements. Not many folks know they're back. I just wanted to keep things in our small circle for now, so I appreciate that."

"No problem, sir." Greg waited for Robert to continue, but he didn't. "So, Montreal?"

"Oh, yes. Like I said, it's a long story. Have you guys turned up anything on Eric's problem at the airport? Don't you think it's strange?"

Greg shook his head. "No, sir, nothing yet. Didn't JJ say there were a bunch of fans around? A few of them probably just got carried away. I wouldn't worry about it."

"That's the thing, though. He said that a couple of guys grabbed Eric and were taking him from the airport, or at least it looked that way. It just doesn't feel right. Almost no one knew of their travel plans. Even if Bryce still had friends who had it in for Abby, how would they know? It just seems too coincidental."

Greg stood on the far side of the large desk, staring at

Robert and wondering if someone so smart could truly be so dumb. Robert was already asking questions; already sniffing around. It was only a matter of time before either he or someone else put everything together, so Greg decided to speed up the process.

Taking his gun from under his jacket, he pointed it at Robert's chest. "Montreal. Tell me where she's going."

Robert looked up, stunned to see the weapon pointed at him. It didn't look quite right, but after a second he realized that was because there was a silencer attached to the end of the pistol. "What the hell is this, Greg? Put that thing away."

Greg stepped closer to Robert. "I like you Robert. Do not make me ask you again. Where is Abby going in Montreal?"

As the initial shock wore off, recognition and understanding filled Robert's eyes. "It was you? Why, Greg?"

"That's not important right now. What is important is that you tell me where she is going, and you tell me fast."

Robert stood tall, "No, I'm not telling you a thing."

"Don't test me."

Robert took a step closer, closing the gap between them to just a few feet. "Are you going to shoot me? Then what? Sorry to tell you Greg, but I've faced tougher guys than you in my day." They stared hard at each other, each willing the other to make a move. Time stood still for a moment. Robert very deliberately glanced over Greg's shoulder, and as Greg cocked his head a bit to see what he was looking at, Robert swatted at the gun, catching Greg by surprise and sending it clattering to the ground.

In shock, Greg dove for the gun as Robert dove on top of him. Greg grabbed the pistol, but Robert got a hand on it, too, before he could do anything with it. They grappled with it, rolling around on the ground. Greg rolled over so he was facing up, and caught Robert in the crotch with a swift knee.

As Robert dropped, Greg jumped up and clubbed him in the back of the head with the butt of the gun, sending him crumpling to the ground. He ran to the desk and shuffled the papers around until he found the small yellow note with the words, "Saint-Colbert" at the bottom. It took him a second, as it looked slightly different from the American version, but Greg realized he was looking at an address. Saint-Colbert was the city. "Bingo." He whispered.

He heard Robert groan and try to roll over. He briefly considered putting a bullet in him, but decided not to. He was on a tiny island that this man owned. He planned to be on a boat and motoring away in the next few minutes, but still, if he got caught, he didn't need a body count in his wake.

He gave Robert a swift kick to the ribs for good measure. Once he was satisfied that Robert wasn't getting up, he quietly let himself out the door that led to the gardens and set off toward the boatyard at a sprint, dialing as he ran.

*   *   *

Bryce had just climbed into in his large, black, rented Mercedes as his phone rang. He grabbed it immediately. "Tell me you've got something, Greg."

"I do, sir. An address."

"Good work, Greg. Give it to me." Bryce rummaged through the glove box and, finding a pen, quickly scrawled the address on the back of the rental agreement. "This is outstanding, Greg. Sit tight. I'll be in touch if there's anything else."

"About that, sir," Greg said, slightly out of breath. "I had to take drastic action. I can't stay here. I'm on the run."

"Good enough. Do what you have to. Get in touch when you're in a safe place, and we'll figure out a way to get you back here."

"Thank you, sir." As the call was disconnecting, Bryce heard shouting on the other end of the line, but couldn't make out what he was saying

He tapped the screen on his dashboard and pulled up the navigation menu. His hands were shaking with anger, but he sung and giggled as he punched in the address. "You're dead. Every one of you. You're all FUCKING dead!"

*   *   *

In his haste to leave the scene and sprint toward the boatyard, Greg neglected to close the door behind him. He had also not seen Captain Frank having lunch on the patio twenty feet to his right.

Frank watched for a moment as Greg, the odd security guard who had asked him so many questions about Abby, sprinted across the lawn. An odd flash of light caught his eye. It took him a second to realize it was the sun glinting off of the handgun in Greg's fist.

"Shit! Robert!"

Frank jumped up and ran into Robert's office to find him sprawled out on the floor.

"Robert!" He called, but got no answer. He leaned over him to look at him, and saw his chest rise and fall. He was unconscious, but breathing. He moaned a bit as Frank lightly tapped his face, but he was completely out of it. Frank looked out the door and across the lawn to see Greg hopping into a boat, talking on the phone. Frank muttered under his breath, "You son of a bitch."

He took off out the door. His middle-aged legs weren't used to running, or exercise of any kind, but Robert was kind enough to offer Frank a chance at a new start in life, and he wasn't about to let that scumbag get away with whatever he was up to.

Fortunately, Greg's back was to the main house, and he was preoccupied with whomever he was talking to on the phone. He never saw Frank ambling across the lawn toward him. The pilot jumped down into the boat just as

Greg was disconnecting the call. "Hey, asshole!" he shouted.

Greg whirled around in shock, his spinning head perfectly positioning his jaw for a collision with Frank's fist. Frank had been in more than his share of bar fights and knew how to throw a punch when he was drunk off his ass. He was shocked to see how much easier it was to hit a target while sober. His fist smashed into Greg's jaw, snapping his head to the side and laying him out on the deck of the boat as the gun went rattling to the floor.

Greg came back low, landing a solid fist into Frank's ribs, knocking the wind out of him, and teaching him that it also hurts a hell of a lot more to get hit while sober. Frank doubled over on top of Greg and repeatedly smashed his elbow into Greg's back, to little use. Greg expertly wrapped his arms around Frank's mid-section and tackled him to the deck of the boat.

It was obvious that Greg had formal training, but Frank had a lifetime of "on the job" training, and he knew how to improvise. He in turn wrapped his arms around Greg's head and started thrashing about like a maniac. Greg quickly went from having the upper hand and control of the situation, to struggling and trying to back up out of Frank's grasp.

Frank let go, sending Greg tumbling backwards, and smacking his head on the side of the boat. Captain Frank quickly scrambled to pick up the gun and held it on Greg as he slowly staggered to his feet.

"Don't shoot, don't shoot. I can explain," Greg

begged.

Frank looked over Greg's shoulder to see Robert standing in the doorway, his two other security guards running across the lawn toward the boatyard. He chuckled at Greg, "I'm sure they'll love to hear this."

*   *   *

Jack's cab crawled along the highway with Abby and Eric in the back. The thirty-eight minute trip that Jack had promised, so far, had turned into nearly an hour and thirty-eight minutes.

"I'm so sorry," Jack said. "I know you're excited to get to your kid, but…" he threw up his hands at the traffic in front of him, the veins on his forehead much more pronounced than when the ride had started.

"Don't blow a gasket," Abby said, teasing him. "It's been long enough. We'll get there when we get there. It's not your fault."

"Thanks," Jack said.

Abby turned to Eric and said more quietly, "Like I said, she knows about you. My sister Sarah didn't let her watch the show. It was too violent, but she's seen your picture and knows that you're my friend. I just think it would be best for me to meet with her alone. She's got to have some hang-ups about me. Once we work through those, then you can be in the picture."

"It's up to you – you're the mom. You just tell me what to do, and I'll do it." He spoke louder, toward the front of the cab. "Jack, you know any good hotels around where we're going?"

"Plenty," Jack said. "And you're far enough away from the tourist spots that you'll find a room without a problem."

Jack looked down at the dash and noticed the temperature gauge looked a little higher than usual. *Probably from sitting in traffic the past hour*, he figured. He assumed that once they got moving, it would settle back down. Looking ahead and seeing five wrecked cars pulled off the side of the road a few hundred yards up, he was hopeful that they would get moving soon.

Eric noticed where Jack was looking. "So that's the hold up?"

Jack called over his shoulder, "No one up here knows how to drive. From here it's less than twenty minutes, so just sit back, I'll get you there." Jack smiled as he depressed the accelerator and his cab picked up speed as they finally passed by the scene of the accident.

However, that smile only lasted for about half a mile before the temperature gauge climbed into the red, "Shit."

"What's that?" Abby asked.

As the engine gave up, Jack coasted to the side of the road. "Engine overheated. I'll take a look."

Abby traded glances with Eric.

28

JJ SPENT THE better part of the last hour and a half – since he last spoke with Robert – sitting in traffic in his rental car. Therefore, he was not the least bit pleased when traffic began to slow again less than a mile after he got past the accident. Fortunately, it wasn't backing up yet.

Looking ahead, traffic seemed slower in the right lane, so he moved to the far left and breathed a sigh of relief as things picked up. He saw a cab with its hood up and the driver scratching his head in the right-hand breakdown lane. Apparently this was the first time anyone had seen such a sight, as people were making a point to slow down to take notice. There was nothing JJ could do but accept that it would be slow going for the next few minutes.

He was not at all comfortable with the fact that he had lost Abby and Eric at the airport. They were somewhere in front of him, heading toward her sister's house in Saint-Colbert, and he was bound and determined to get there as soon as he could to ensure that there were no more issues.

He checked his phone again. Still nothing from Ace. *What the hell happened?* he wondered. If something had gone drastically wrong, Ace would have called, if he could. It was the last part of that statement that made JJ uncomfortable – *if he could*. JJ told himself that he would turn up, and there was nothing to worry about. Ace could take care of himself.

As he set the phone down on the passenger's seat, it rang again. The moment he said "Hello," a panicked Robert was off and running at the mouth.

"JJ, thank God. Wherever you are, stop. Abby and Eric cannot go to her sister's house. Something bigger is going on here."

JJ sat at attention, "Robert, I don't know where they are."

"You lost them?"

"It's a big airport. They were first off the plane, way before me. I couldn't find them at the rental companies, so I just grabbed a car myself. I'm heading to the address now. I assume they're somewhere in front of me. Probably not too far in front either. What's going on?"

"One of my security men might have had something to do with what happened at the airport. He's the one who arranged their travel. He was one of the only people who could have told someone they would be there. I'm certain he had something to do with what happened to Eric."

"What makes you so sure?"

"Right after I got off the phone with you, he assaulted

me, grabbed Abby's sister's address, and took off running. We caught him, but he talked to someone on the phone first. JJ, if he gave information to those men who tried to grab Eric, he's probably passed along the address in Saint-Colbert, as well. We can't let Abby and Eric get there without knowing they could be walking into a trap."

"Well, that's a little tough, Robert. I have no idea what they're driving, and no way to get ahold of them. I'll get there as fast as I can." As JJ passed by the stranded cab, he glanced at the obviously frustrated driver. He picked up speed, quickly putting the cab and the traffic in his rearview. "Traffic is clear now. I should be there real soon. That's the best I can do."

"Damn it! Why didn't I give that girl a phone?" Robert said to himself. The thought had never even occurred to him when she was leaving the island. He let out a long sigh.

JJ interrupted with a pressing concern of his own. "Not to change the subject, but any word on Ace, yet?"

"No, but we'll let you know the moment we hear something."

"Whoa!"

"What happened?" Robert asked.

"Some Mercedes a few cars back just went nuts and swerved across a couple lanes and almost caused another accident. Everyone is beeping their horns. I'll tell you, Robert, these Canadians aren't impressing me as drivers."

329

"Just stay safe and find them, OK?"

"I'll call you when I get there." JJ disconnected the call and pressed on the accelerator. He figured Abby and Eric couldn't be too far ahead. If he couldn't stop them, maybe he could at least pass them and beat them there.

*   *   *

Bryce was going out of his mind. He had been sitting in stop-and-go traffic for the better part of the last hour and a half and was ready to explode. Finally traffic cleared and he punched his foot down on the gas, bringing the five hundred German engineered horses under the hood to life.

His excitement lasted all of half a minute before traffic slowed again for some unknown reason. "At least it's moving a little this time," he said aloud to no one but himself. He moved over to the far left, where traffic seemed to be moving a little more than the other lanes. He glanced down at the navigation screen on the dashboard to see that he had about twenty minutes left on his trip.

As he moved past a disabled taxi on the side of the road, he picked up speed, finally reaching thirty miles per hour, and put some distance between himself and the traffic. Just a few moments later, something caught his eye in the rear view mirror. He looked back to see a woman standing next to the cab. She was petite. Then a man walked up next to her and they joined the cab driver looking under the hood.

Suddenly it struck him. "Holy shit!"

Bryce slammed on the brakes and jerked the wheel to the right, swerving his black Mercedes across several lanes. Car horns all around him erupted in unison, but he just yelled at them. He drove forward, staring in the rearview at the people a few hundred feet behind him on the highway and getting more distant, "You've got to be kidding me!"

He looked ahead to see a sign that marked an exit ramp coming up in half a kilometer. He hit the map view on the GPS and figured he would get off the highway and double back. Abby and Eric were standing helpless next to a cab on the side of the road. He chuckled to himself as he thought about how shocked they would be when he pulled up behind them.

*   *   *

JJ looked down at his ringing phone, and immediately punched it on when he saw who was calling. "Bro, are you OK?"

"I'm fine." Ace sounded stressed, and exhausted.

"What happened?"

"I'll tell you in a minute. Where are you?"

JJ looked at the dash. "The GPS says I'm on the 40, heading north, about thirty minutes outside of Montreal."

"Do you have eyes on Abby?"

"Negative, but I'm doing my best. I just talked to Robert a few minutes ago. Something is going down. One of his security guys is in on it. He thinks they're walking into a trap."

"That's probably not too far from the truth," Ace said. He recounted what happened at the airport. "I just got out of holding. I had to call Pete back in Boston to get me in touch with one of his friends out here to spring me."

"Pete's the best attorney there is," JJ said.

"How long was the flight up?"

"Just over two hours, I think."

"I'll be on the next plane," Ace said.

JJ thought about that for a minute. "Things are moving pretty quick here. Sit tight. There might be some loose ends in Chicago when I wrap up here."

"Good idea. I'll have my phone on me, so keep me in the loop. I'm going to check into one of the airport hotels and order room service. Airport prison food sucks worse than regular prison food."

As they disconnected the call, JJ thought about what he had said. Things were indeed moving quickly. He would feel a lot better if he knew exactly where Abby was, but for now, he depressed the accelerator, pushing the speed limit, and continued on his way.

*   *   *

Bryce got a little lost on side streets as the GPS chirped over and over, "Recalculating... Recalculating..." but he was finally back on track. The cars from the accident had finally been cleared and traffic was moving. It had taken fifteen minutes, but he was back and approaching his target. His heart pounded with anticipation when he saw the bright yellow cab with its hood raised a quarter mile up ahead.

Putting on his directional, he eased into the breakdown lane and rolled to a stop a respectable distance behind the cab. The driver was the only one standing outside. He figured Abby and Eric must have gotten back inside. He reached down and checked that he had a full clip in his gun, and one in the chamber. He smiled as he screwed on the silencer and slid it into his pants pocket as he flicked off the safety.

He checked around, making sure no one else had stopped, then drove up closer behind the cab. It was perfect. He stopped right behind them and would get out as a good Samaritan. He didn't feel badly that he was going to kill the driver, too. Poor guy was just in the wrong place at the wrong time. It was rush hour at dusk, and people were in a hurry, so it was likely no one would notice him.

He decided he would shoot Abby and Eric inside the car. No one driving by would see or hear it. He would stand on the right side of the vehicle, open the rear passenger-side door, and shoot them. When the driver came around to see what was happening, he'd shoot the driver at close range, and either sit him next to the car or in the front passenger's seat.

Bryce was disappointed that he would not be able to prolong and enjoy Abby's death more, but this would have to do. A job done is a job done. He smirked at the thought that maybe he would take a memento from her with him. *Hell, she's small enough – maybe I'll just carry her over to my car and take her with me.* He sneered at the evil thoughts of what he would do to her.

He took a deep breath and stepped out of the car. His loafers crunched the sand and gravel as he walked the twenty feet or so to the cab. The driver was still at the front of the car on the other side of the hood. He couldn't see Bryce coming, nor could he hear him over the sounds of traffic racing by.

He stopped next to the car, just behind the rear passenger-side door so he wouldn't be seen by either of his victims. His heart raced and butterflies flew through his stomach. He had killed before, but he never wanted it this badly. He took a deep breath to calm his hands, shaking from the adrenaline. In one smooth motion, he slipped the gun from his pocket, threw open the door, and shoved the gun into the cab as he yelled, "Surprised to see me, bitch?"

29

WHAT THE HELL? Bryce couldn't believe his eyes. The cab was empty. He jumped out and looked around. There was no one. He whipped around, looking back toward the woods off the side of the highway, gun at his side. "Where is that little bitch?"

The cab driver peeked around the hood of the cab and saw Bryce standing, crouched down looking in the car, "Hey buddy, can I help you?"

Bryce was startled by the cab driver coming around the corner of the car. However not as much as the driver was startled by the sight of this man with a gun and a crazed look in his eyes.

"Whoa, buddy," the driver said, holding up his hands. "I ain't got no money."

"Where are the passengers, your passengers, a man and a woman? Where did they go?"

"My engine is shot, so another cab pulled over and he gave them a lift. Maybe five minutes ago."

"SHIT! Shit, shit, shit!" Bryce was pacing and

cursing, paying little attention to the driver, who was reaching down to his belt to pull out a can of pepper spray. As Bryce turned toward him, the driver's hand flew up to spray Bryce in the face. He never stood a chance.

Bryce put two bullets in his chest and was back in his car before the driver hit the ground. No one saw a thing, or at least no one stopped. The only thing the commuters noticed was Bryce tearing out into traffic and nearly causing another accident. He floored the large sedan and sped down the freeway, scanning the traffic for another taxi where he hoped to find his prey. Yet a full ten minutes later he was still a ball of rage. He had seen two other cabs, neither of which had the passengers he was looking for.

The GPS chirped up, snapping him back to reality, "Exit on right in one and one half kilometers." He looked down. Five minutes to his destination. He hadn't found them, but he knew where they were going.

He jerked the wheel to the right as he raced down the onramp, dreaming of killing them – Abby, Eric, Ava, and anyone else he found. His gut wrenched as he hoped there would be more. Children, dogs, anything that breathed. He intended to kill them all.

*   *   *

JJ had rolled by Abby's sister's house fifteen minutes ago. He was sure Abby and Eric weren't there yet. He never did find them along the way. There was a beautiful little girl with long brown loosely curled hair tied back in a ponytail, sitting in the window and watching the street with a serious look on her face. It was a look that he was well familiar with, and there was no mistaking it; she looked just like a little Abby, the mother she hadn't seen in over a year.

Somehow he beat them, though he wasn't sure how. As far as he could tell, there was nothing untoward going on at the house. Occasionally a woman, a little older than Abby, would come to the window and talk to the little girl, then she would disappear back into the house.

JJ knew he had to talk to Abby and Eric, but he also didn't want to ruin the reunion. He parked a few houses down with his rental car pointed at Abby's sister's house. It was a well-kept upper middle class neighborhood, and the modest sized houses all sat on nicely landscaped properties. The street was only about a quarter mile long and straight as an arrow. In his rear view he could see the intersection behind him, and anyone who might approach from that direction. Out the front window he could anyone coming from that direction. Abby was going to the house exactly halfway down the street.

He figured from here he could keep an eye on things. If anything suspicious came up, he would intervene and ruin the reunion. Otherwise, he would let them settle in and knock on the door a little while later.

From his conversation with Ace, it seemed that the threat was nullified for the time being. However, JJ remembered that Robert said his security man had swiped the sister's address, so someone else could come along any minute. He unbuckled his seatbelt and sat up on high alert, wishing he had his pistol that was sitting in his nightstand drawer just outside of Boston.

A few minutes later, at the far end of the street, a taxi approached and eased to a stop against the curb on the opposite side of the street from Abby's destination.

*   *   *

Abby and Eric sat in the back seat of the cab holding hands.

"Are you nervous?"

She smiled. "A little, yeah."

"It's going to be fine," he assured her. "You're going to be fine."

"How about you? Will you be OK?"

Eric chuckled a bit. "Don't worry about me. Go, be a mom."

"How can I get in touch with you later? Where will you be?"

He thought a second. "I don't know. Do you still have that paper with your sister's number?"

She nodded.

"You don't need it anymore, so just give it to me. When do you want me to call?"

She rummaged through her satchel, found the small yellow note with her sister's address and phone number, and handed it to him, "Give me a couple hours?"

"No problem." He looked past her to the front door slowly being opened. "Look," he pointed.

Ava stepped out onto the front porch and stood, staring hopefully at the cab.

Abby's eyes welled up at the sight of her daughter. "Oh my God, she's so big!"

"Go," Eric said. He held her face in his hands and kissed her on the lips. "Go."

"I love you."

"I love you, too. Now go!" he said with a chuckle.

She opened the door and stood frozen for a moment, staring at her little girl. As she stepped away from the car, the driver began to pull away.

"Hold on a second," Eric said. "I want to enjoy this." He opened his own door and stepped out to lean against the back of the cab, watching their reunion and enjoying the moment from afar. He felt complete, not driftless with no job and no one to care about. He was so happy and thankful to have met Abby.

Abby had crossed the street, and from twenty feet away, she couldn't believe what a grown-up girl Ava had become. With her hair pulled back from her face, she looked like a little woman. "Hi, baby!" Abby called.

"Mommy!" Ava jumped over the three porch steps

and sprinted toward her mother.

*   *   *

Bryce came tearing around the corner at the end of the street where he saw a cab parked facing him on the left side, about halfway down. The GPS chirped, "Your destination is six hundred feet on the right."

He saw Abby and Ava running toward each other on the front lawn of a farm-style house opposite the cab. Overcome by rage, he floored the gas, and the five hundred horses under the hood roared to life.

*   *   *

JJ heard a loud engine behind him and looked in the rear view mirror to see a large black sedan jump forward and come rocketing down the road toward his position. He grabbed the door handle and jumped from the car, but he was in no way prepared to do anything that could stop what was about to happen.

*   *   *

Abby and Ava were beaming, completely consumed by the moment. They ran to each other, and Abby lifted her up in her arms in a tearful embrace. Her heart felt like it would pound right out of her chest as she clung to Ava as tightly as she could, inhaling the sweet scent of her little girl.

For all her awareness, Abby was completely oblivious to the two tons of steel careening toward her from a football field away.

Eric looked down the street when he heard the roar of an engine that seemed out of place in such a quiet suburban neighborhood. He saw the large black sedan jump as the huge engine fed its full power to the wheels and drastically increase speed. He immediately realized its trajectory. Without thinking, he took off at a full sprint toward Abby, who was standing in the middle of the lawn holding her daughter, eyes sealed shut, tears streaming down her face.

He screamed a desperate cry from ten feet away, "ABBY!"

She whipped her head toward the scream. As she did, her eye caught a glimpse of the sedan bearing down on her as it jumped the curb at the edge of the lawn. Her head continued on a swivel toward Eric, eyes wide open as he crashed into her and shoved her and Ava as hard as he could, a split second before impact.

30

ERIC SAW HIMSELF as a young boy on his grandfather's ranch, riding the tractor with his grandpa. His grandmother was waving from the house, flagging them down to come in for dinner. A moment later, he was in high school, laughing with his friends after their football game. They had lost, but went out to have the night of their lives afterward. Suddenly he got out of his old beat-up pickup truck at seven in the morning and strapped on his tool belt, ready for another day on the site.

Then there was Abby, standing a hundred yards away on the beach, slipping back into her clothes. He knew she was special the first time he spoke to her, and he never wanted his life to be the same again.

Time stood still on the lawn as he watched Abby fly through the air, eyes closed, gripping Ava tight. The front passenger corner of the car clipped her leg as she spun, landing on her back and cushioning Ava's fall.

She wasn't unscathed, but she was safe, and the little girl was safe.

Eric felt pure bliss.

*   *   *

Abby sailed backwards and screamed in pain as the front corner of the car clipped her left leg. As she fell backwards, she watched in horror as the front of the sedan smashed into Eric's leg. His thighbone and hip were shattered on impact. He took flight over the hood of the car, his head smashing into the windshield a split second later, launching him ten feet in the air up and over the roof.

The airbags on the car blew as it smashed into the garage, and Eric came crashing back to earth behind it a second later.

"ERIC!" Abby screamed as she tried to jump up, only to collapse back to the ground screaming in agony, her leg broken in two places.

Ava was screaming hysterically, unable to form words.

The door on the black sedan swung open and Bryce stumbled from the vehicle covered in white powder from the airbags. The car was totaled, but the driver was alive and still standing.

Looking behind the vehicle, he saw Eric lying motionless on the ground twenty feet behind the car, and Abby just to the side, rolling around. He smiled to know that she had survived and approached her, gun in hand. "You thought I wouldn't find you?" he shouted as he approached.

Abby momentarily forgot about the searing pain in her

leg as she laid eyes on Bryce. "You piece of shit!"

He laughed. "So I've heard."

He walked right by her, continuing to Eric. She struggled through the pain and managed to get herself upright on one leg. "Leave him alone, you son of a bitch. You're here for me. Take me."

Standing directly over Eric, he sneered, "Isn't that sweet?" Without looking down he put two bullets in his chest.

Abby screamed, "NO!" She lunged forward, only to have her leg collapse out from under her and send her tumbling to the ground.

Bryce laughed, and then noticed Ava standing just a few feet behind Abby, absolutely frozen in terror. "Well, hello, dear," Bryce said sweetly as he raised his gun and took aim at the child.

Abby struggled to her knees and grabbed Ava close, "Don't you dare, Bryce! This is your daughter," she shouted.

"Isn't she the reason we're here in the first place?"

From her kneeling position, Abby put Ava behind her, using her own body as a shield. She stared past the barrel of the gun and into his cold eyes. "We both know why you want me dead, and it has nothing to do with her. You'll have to kill me first."

"So be it," he said. Just as he squeezed off two shots,

JJ came flying from the right and tackled Bryce at a full sprint, sending the two men tumbling to the ground.

Abby looked down at her chest and watched as blood trickled from a hole just above her right breast. She looked toward Eric, ten feet away, his chest slowly rose and fell. She waited for it to rise and fall again, but it didn't. "No," she said quietly.

Dragging herself on her hands and knees, she collapsed beside Eric. Taking his hand in hers, they locked eyes. His hand was limp and blood trickled from the corner of his mouth. "Eric," she whispered as the tears began to flow, "please…"

She felt him faintly squeeze her hand for just a fleeting moment as his eyes went vacant.

He was gone.

It sounded worlds away, but she heard her sister screaming, "Someone stop him!"

Blackness began to creep in from the edges of her vision as she slowly faded away. Lying on her back, she saw Ava appear over her.

"Mommy!" She couldn't say anything else. The terrified look on her face said it all.

"It's OK, baby," Abby whispered with a smile.

Her world faded to black.

Epilogue

HER EYES FLUTTERED OPEN, and she squinted in the harsh fluorescent light. There was a beeping sound to her left, and the faint smell of antiseptic in the air. Realization set in – *I'm in a hospital.*

"Auntie Sarah, she's awake!"

Abby's sister, Sarah came into view. Ava was smiling ear to ear. Sarah was smiling, too, despite the tracks of her recent tears.

"I told you she'd be OK." Ava smiled and leaned in to hug her mother.

Abby gasped as Ava accidently pressed against her gunshot wound.

"I'm sorry, I'm sorry!"

Abby gritted her teeth and smiled at her little girl. "It's OK."

Sarah spoke up, "Ava, honey, can you go tell the doctors that Mommy's awake?"

"Yes!" she squealed, running from the room.

Sarah sat down on the edge of the bed. "How are you feeling?"

"About as bad as you look," Abby quipped, then smiled. "How's Eric?"

Sarah's eyes welled up and spilled over. She shook her head. "I'm sorry, Abby. I'm so sorry."

Abby stared blankly for a moment, trying to process what Sarah was saying. When realization set in, her own eyes gushed as she stared up to the ceiling, unable to breathe, unable to feel. She moaned and wept like a child, "NO!" Sobs wracked her body, causing excruciating pain to her wound, but she could not stop.

Robert came running into the room, smiling ear to ear, "Abby!" As she looked to him through her puffy tear-soaked eyes, their eyes connected and his smile faded. "I'm so sorry, dear."

He came close and put his arms around her. She weakly held onto him as she shook with pain and sorrow.

She closed her eyes and allowed herself to be swallowed by the emotion. Sobs shook her body as the image of Eric being hit by the car played over in her mind. The man she loved had made the ultimate sacrifice and given his life to save hers. Finally, after what seemed like an hour, Abby managed to get control of herself and calm her sobbing, if only to keep from upsetting her daughter who wanted today to be a happy day.

She opened her eyes. "Just, please, please tell me they

have the death penalty in Canada."

She watched as Robert and Sarah exchanged a look.

"What?" Abby asked.

With a slight quiver in his voice, Robert said, "He got away."

Abby's eyes opened wide, "He WHAT?"

Sarah recounted the story, "A man tackled him as he shot you."

"JJ," Robert interjected.

Sarah continued. "The police say that's probably why you only got hit with one of the bullets."

Abby stared at Robert, "Tell me this isn't true."

"It all happened so fast," Sarah said. "They scuffled; Bryce lost the gun. The man – JJ, I guess – JJ went to grab it, and Bryce kicked him right in the side of the head. He went down. At this point, there were sirens screaming everywhere around us. He looked back at me. I was standing by you, holding Ava. He saw you on the ground, soaked with blood. Then he smiled and just took off. I screamed for someone to stop him, but he had grabbed his gun and stole the taxi you came in. He was gone before the police even got there."

"They can't find him?" Abby was beside herself.

"They found the cab this morning, a few hours south in a little fishing village on Lake Ontario."

"This morning?" Abby asked. "How long was I out?"

"Nearly twenty-four hours," Sarah said.

Abby sighed, "Well, they found the car. They'll find him soon enough, right?"

Robert spoke. "They think he crossed the lake to the U.S. border."

"So, that's it? He's gone?"

"They're chasing a ghost," Robert said. "Until he turned up in your sister's front lawn, the world thought he was dead. The police have nothing to go on."

Abby sat in shock and stared at the wall. Bryce had taken everything from her and was walking out a free man.

Robert picked up the newspaper from her bedside table. "There is one silver lining, Abby, that you should know about."

He handed her the paper where she read the headline

Trial Island **Mystery Couple Found Dead**

She looked at Robert. "What's this?"

"You're dead, Abby. At least the world thinks you are." He leaned in to whisper, "I have a little bit of power and influence, and this is the story that's going out. It was already out there that you were married to Bryce. So, the story is that a mob hit man killed you and Eric. The world thinks you're dead. More importantly, as far as Bryce is concerned, he killed you."

349

"So what's the silver lining?" Abby said through her teeth, wondering if the searing pain she felt was the bullet wound or her white-hot rage boiling up inside of her.

"You're free, Abby. It's done. It's over. He killed you. You don't have to worry about him anymore. We'll get you back on your feet, and you can live out the rest of your life with your lovely daughter and be safe."

Abby's eyes stared through Robert like daggers. "So let me get this straight. Two weeks ago, JJ found me on my island and gave me the news that Bryce was dead. For the first time in months I thought I was finally safe. Yet, I'm lying here in a hospital bed nearly having been killed, Eric *was* killed – and you're telling me that now I'm safe because *Bryce* thinks that *I'm* dead?"

"Precisely," said Robert, nodding his head somberly.

A sinful glare came over Abby's face. "Then he'll never see me coming."

ESCAPE
Past Sins

Author's note

Thank you for reading my book! I would love to hear from you. You can email me from my website, www.Antocci.com, or follow me on Facebook and introduce yourself. I personally respond to everyone. You will also find news there about my other books and what I'm working on next!

I certainly hope you have as much fun reading my books as I have writing them. If you enjoy my writing, please tell a friend – or better yet tell the world by writing a quick review on the Amazon page. Even a few short sentences are helpful.

As an independently published author, I don't have a marketing department behind me. I have you, the reader. Thanks for spreading the word and telling a friend!

All the best - Dave

Made in the USA
Lexington, KY
08 July 2019